FORECAST

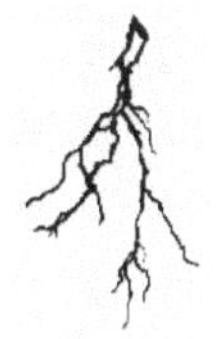

AARON RYAN

Award-winning Author of the bestselling
"Dissonance" Sci-Fi Alien Invasion Saga

**HE CAN SEE INTO THE FUTURE, BUT IT'S
NOT ALWAYS SUNSHINE AND RAINBOWS.
SOMETIMES, IT'S TERROR AND MURDER.**

Published in 2024, Edition 1.

Paperback ISBN # 9798990661189 · Hardcover ISBN # 9798990661172
eBook ISBN # 9798990661165

Edited by Denouement Editing. Published independently.

Cover art man by Asaf Rozanes · Cover art background by Trivuj
Rear cover art image by Gerd Altmann through Pixabay

This is a work of fiction. Any similarities to persons living or dead, or actual events is purely coincidental.

For Sweeps, Bren & AJ:
my true loves.

You are all the rain and
all the sunshine of my world.

CHAPTERS

"Consider the little mouse how sagacious an animal it is which never entrusts his life to one hole only."

- Plautus

"You must be the change you wish to see in the world."

- Mahatma Gandhi

"I am not what happened to me. I am what I choose to become."

- C.G. Jung

Note on A.I.

We live in an age of AI. Every day, more and more services spring up promising revolutionary and innovative results using artificial intelligence. The authoring industry is not immune to this.

I want every one of my readers to know that not once did I employ, nor will I *ever* employ, the use of AI to sculpt any part of any of my stories. Those who know me know that I am staunchly and adamantly opposed to such cheats.

I'm very proud to be a verified human. The ability to create is a gift that I was endowed by my Creator, and I will never forfeit that nor set it aside to propagate something synthetic and imitative.

Everything you've read by me in this novel, and in my other works, is 100% entirely created by me, the genuine article. I'm a verified human, and always will be.

To my fellow authors, I urge you to preserve the sacred gift of human creation and never stoop to such lows. Always cherish this gift you've been given. If you encounter writer's block, take a break. Don't cop out. Don't take the road more traveled by. Don't cheat. Toe the line for all of us, and keep creation – *true* unadulterated creation – alive.

Long live humanity.

Sincerely,

Aaron Ryan,
Verified Human

PART ONE

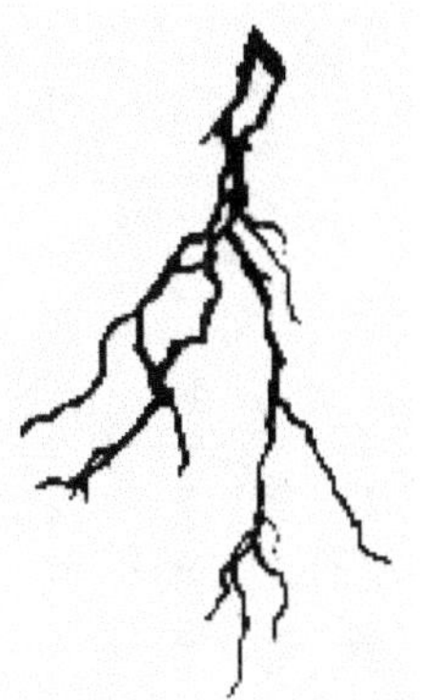

23 Days To Go

August 19th, 2001 • Manhattan, NY

It was utterly confusing, and utterly terrifying. I just stood there, wondering what all of it meant this time.

A blinding flash had lit up my mind with white once more; my body hummed and buzzed, and I couldn't move until it was all over: the same paralysis always set in and took over until the vision abated, and then I'd come to and find people awkwardly staring at me. But why was this happening?

I was still reeling, trying to catch my breath, panting hard. The sweat trickled down my temple. I clutched the pole in the subway car to steady myself, and once again everyone was staring at me awkwardly like I was a homeless drunk. Some shifted uncomfortably away from me and gawked from afar, murmuring to other passersby.

A kind, elderly woman leaned in toward me and asked "Sir? Sir, are you alright? Do you need to sit down?" She motioned to her own seat, willing to let me take it.

I shook my head. "I'm fine, thank you," I said to her, and she smiled. She reminded me of my sweet Nona, gone long before her time. If only I could have done the thing then, and staved off her death for a few more years, maybe. Who knows? It was like chaos theory or the butterfly effect, only I couldn't alter time. What the hell was happening to me?

The first one: that poor girl. I still can't shake that guilt. I could have done something. No, I *should* have done something. And the second one, at the bank: all those innocent people just…gone. I should have helped there too. I got the visions. And then when I saw the perpetrators in both situations afterward on the news, and knew that they were the same people I had seen around Jersey and New York in my mind's eye. I was racked with shame. *Racked.* That was so hard to get through.

But…this was the starkest one yet, and now I knew beyond the shadow of a doubt that this was a powerfully massive threat. How I could possibly intervene, I wasn't certain. I was just one man. I wasn't sure I could help at all, frankly, but I had to at least try.

The first two I initially chalked up to coincidences… but then each came true. I looked around. Who had triggered it this time? I didn't recognize any of the few people whose faces I dared connect with. None of them were in my vision. It had to have been someone who just got on the subway, close to me, as before. But who? People were crammed in here like sardines, and you just don't look at people.

I swallowed hard, knowing full well that I had to find a way to stop this latest one from happening. Something about planes this time. Airplanes. Large commercial airliners. A hijacking? Just snippets of images. Fights high in the sky. Dark-skinned men. A language I didn't recognize, but something from the middle East, arguably. And then…black.

The headaches were too much, the bloody noses were getting thicker, and now I was starting to pass out from exhaustion. The last time, someone stole my wallet and I wound up at the hospital, questioned by the police. I clutched the handkerchief in my pocket, readying it for the inevitable nosebleed. A woman saw me perspiring and made a face, putting some distance between us.

Everyone should technically have known who I was. I was a weatherman, for goodness' sake. I guess I looked different in real life without the green-screen weather map behind me. Now, here, they all pretended I was just some intoxicated buffoon. Maybe the sweat and the strained look made me fairly unrecognizable.

I searched around me again, anxiously, still not seeing the face that had come with that flash, doubting myself the whole time.

I'm Roland Bishop, and I know where I am, I repeated in my mind. I had to tell myself that over and over just to center myself…and to bring me back to the present.

The subway began to move once more, and I held on, headed for the PATH Station.

It had literally only been two weeks since the hospital released me. "Lightning never strikes twice," they said, but that didn't curb the tension or make things any easier. Since the strike, the air was so thick around me I could chew it, and the buzzing in my ears wouldn't dissipate or disperse.

In the New York subway system, you don't really look at people for too long. That just freaks them out and makes them tense. Penny – Dr. Penelope Eggers, that is – believed me at least, and she told me not to stare. That would just make people uneasy, and I might lose the tail. But she cautioned me to be extra careful and not go being any kind of Lone Ranger vigilante.

The roar of noise rushed over us as we made our way into downtown Manhattan. There, I knew, rising somewhere above me in vast fingers pointing triumphantly into the sky, stood the Twin Towers, the World Trade Center.

I'd never been up in them. I'd heard about the Windows on the World Restaurant and all the big businesses in there, but it was a bit imposing, and I wasn't a fan of heights, really. Down on the ground I could gaze up at them with my feet still attached here to the earth, and I was still *me* down here. I was safe.

But I'm losing me to these damned visions. I sighed. *I'm Roland Bishop, and I know where I am. I'm Roland Bishop, and I know where I am. I'm Roland Bishop, and I know where I am.*

Nope. Still confused and blurry. I probably looked like some stupefied idiotic vagrant staggering around in here, aimless and bereft of home *and* purpose. All I knew was I had to find that face before it was too late again.

More white flashes, and somewhere in the mix the hazy, barely distinguishable number *twenty-three* materialized mistily, being driven off by a wind as little bits of it splayed clumsily around. It wasn't clear what it meant.

The Kawasaki PA5 stormed over the rails, and then started to slow. People jockeyed for position to get to the doors first. I never understood why people did that. *So you're five seconds later than if you had just stayed where you were in line…big deal. Why such urgency? You don't even know what urgency is. What* I'm *doing is urgent,* I thought, disapprovingly. My head throbbed.

The doors opened. We filtered out like cattle. People jostled all around me. Someone bumped me hard and didn't even say 'excuse me.' Another person swore at the sheer idiocy of people who push and shove others out of their way. I let both go. They weren't my mark. I needed to find the face I had seen.

A good twenty or thirty of us were walking across the concrete platform to the stairs. I could feel something warm trickling out of my nose. My skin began to tingle and my head started to swim. They were close, whomever they were. Abruptly, the flashes resumed, without warning.

A plane streaking across the sky.

People screaming.

Rubble everywhere. Smoke. Dust. Ash.

A cockpit being intruded into.

That was all I needed. I was now certain that this particular vision was of a hijacking.

I looked around me. A young man met my eyes and then pulled away in revulsion at the blood I wiped from my nose onto my handkerchief. He put a few other people in between us and went on his way.

Suddenly, a face stood out to me in the crowd. A familiar face. The one I had seen in my vision.

There he is! That was him, from my vision!

I found the target shortly up ahead. He was walking with someone, briskly, and talking with them. The other man was looking back repeatedly.

My target had thick, puffy black hair, thin pursed lips, a solid clenched jawline, and beady eyes set under darkly outlined lashes. He looked around. I didn't know who the other man was. I didn't even know who my mark was. I just knew he was going to do something awful.

My head was buzzing. The mark turned to look almost right at me. Dr. Penny said not to confront people, and I wasn't going to. She cautioned me to just follow them at a distance – observe and report – but no more. I was starting to feel like that might not be enough.

Sudden white flash. And just like that, I was down.

People cleared away from me, eager to get to where they were going and not be inconvenienced. The old woman finally caught up to me and asked me again if I was alright. *God bless this saint,* I thought. The good Samaritan insisted that I should get to a doctor as I struggled to my feet and braced myself against the wall.

I shook my head and told her once more that I was fine. The buzzing lessened. He was getting away. I don't know why, but I was getting a name this time. The flashes of

airplanes seared through my brain once more. I felt heat.
Heat and wind.

I felt like I was going to pass out.

"Sir?" the old woman asked me again.

"M-Mohammed," I muttered. She tilted her head,
confused. "Mohammed," I repeated. "Mohammed
something. And…something about airplanes. I think there's
going to be a hijacking."

That's all I remembered saying before I turned to look
at my target again, and then the white faded to black. As my
head fell to the floor and my body crumpled beneath me, I
thought I caught a brief glimpse.

The man was of Egyptian descent, at the top of the
stairs now, and the other man was with him. They were both
staring back at me, and then rounding a corner.

The buzzing was gone. And so was my target.

And then, so was I. My Nokia 3310 fell out of my
pocket and clattered to the ground, right before my head
smacked into the concrete.

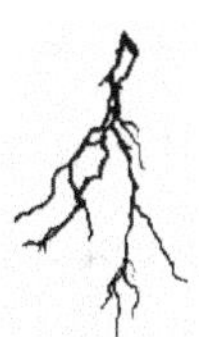

"Mr. Bishop?" said a voice. Smelling salts were
snapped under my nose, and I awoke with a start. "Mr.
Bishop, are you alright?"

My vision swam for a moment and then coalesced
into clarity, gathering in focus. I looked around. *Oh great,
another ambulance.* I felt *so* drained after this latest
episode. That was some stark imagery.

I turned to the paramedic. "There's a man, uh, a m-man I saw down in the subway. I think he's planning a hijacking. Yes, I'm fine," I said.

I enlarged my eyes to see better around me.

The paramedic looked at me sidelong and then turned his attention to his partner. "A hijacking? What makes you say that, sir?" I'm sure he thought I was crazy. New York City paramedics must hear every story in the book thrown their way every single day. I was surprised that he didn't roll his eyes. But the night was young.

"I-I can't explain it," I said. "But I get these visions. I'm not crazy," I said, looking at both of them and putting my hands up. "Seriously. Check JCMC. They'll have a record of me being there two weeks ago. *Roland Bishop?*" I pointed at myself. "No? I was the guy struck by lightning at Millenium Park," I said sheepishly. "They said I was on the news. On my own station. News 12. I'm the weatherman there. *Keep your sunny disposition?*" I asked, desperately flaunting my tagline in the vain hopes they'd recognize it.

A look of zero recognition passed over their faces, and my paramedic looked at the other one again. Apparently, my signature forecast sign-off meant nothing to them. "You bonked your head pretty hard, Mr. Bishop. You don't remember passing out at PATH Station?"

"No, I *do* remember it. I'm not crazy. I'm just-I'm," I faltered. "I've been seeing visions since the lightning strike, and two of them have come true. I think- I'm pretty sure I just had another one. No. I mean, I *had* another one, for sure. Mohammed is his name, I think. You gotta check that name. You mean you don't recognize me?"

They chuckled. "You want us to check for a guy named Mohammed. In New York City." He turned to the other paramedic and exchanged a knowing glance of exasperation. "Take a number, pal. Anyway, we gotta take you to NYP, Mr. Bishop. That's your first stop. Your nosebleed has stopped but you gotta get that head x-ray'd. After that, you can get yourself to the police station and make any kind of report you like, but your first stop is radiology."

I started to protest, but he gently pushed me down on the stretcher. "Just lie back, sir. We're almost there."

I sighed and shook my head. I truly believed my mark was about to commit a hijacking – or *something* to do with airplanes – and yet these yahoos were insisting that it was *me* who needed the x-rays. This latest one was so real, so vivid, and this time I even had a name! Why doesn't anybody ever take prescience seriously? Why is the human race always so cavalier about what's to come?

I rode the rest of the way to New York Presbyterian in frustrated silence.

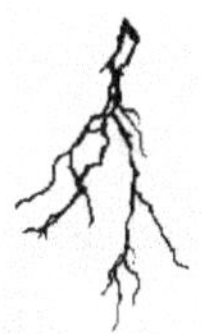

At long last, the doctor returned.

I had been in the x-ray machine for nearly an hour, and another fifteen minutes after that awaiting my doctor's return. Information is power, but I felt powerless from the moment he started speaking.

"Hello again, Mr. Bishop!" he chirped. "The good news is that I don't find anything wrong with your head. No cracks, lesions, tumors, abnormalities, or anything overly concerning. You do have a mild intracranial hematoma, but it's not cause for alarm."

"In English?" I asked, sitting up. I love it when they talk medical speak and we have no idea what they're even saying but they expect us to follow along obligatorily.

"A hematoma is usually a bit of blood pooling outside of your vessels. An injury can cause it, and I know you mentioned that you collapsed. If you hit the ground just right, you might break a blood vessel. Here, let me see," he said, coming over to me and feeling behind my head. "Right about here, is this tender?"

I winced. "Ow! Yes," I complained, irritated.

"Uh-huh. Yeah, that's this right here," he said, referring me to a darker spot on the x-ray, but fairly small still. "That must have been where your head decided to merge with the floor at PATH. You blacked out? Fell to the ground?"

"Yes," I answered, "right after I saw the man who had shown up in my vision."

The doctor tilted his head at me. "Vision? Explain."

I heaved a sigh and rolled my eyes. "That's what I was trying to do with the paramedics. They weren't listening. You wouldn't believe me or listen either if I went into it. Nobody believes me except for my psychiatrist."

He said nothing. Just looked at me and raised his eyebrows, motioning to me as if wondering why I wasn't just continuing.

I sighed again. A willing audience? Could it be? "Well," I began, "I was at JCMC two weeks ago. I'm the weatherman who got struck by lightning at Millenium Park. *Keep your sunny disposition?*" I tried again.

Still no recognition from him either. Either there are a lot more lighting-struck weathermen than I was previously aware of, or no one ever watches the weather. The novelty of my condition didn't appear to be all that exciting.

"Whatever. Since that time, I've been seeing visions. Visions of people who are about to commit some kind of crime or atrocity, and then they do, and I see them on the news. I get these…flashes… of the person's face, a kind of…montage, I guess…of what it is they're about to do, and then I get a nosebleed and pass out. Really convenient, huh? Started happening after the lightning strike. Seems like it happens when they're in close proximity."

"No kidding?" he asked, with surprisingly genuine interest. "Lightning has to exit the body. Maybe it left some residual effect in you somehow."

"Look, Doctor, uh…?"

"Walker. Dr. Walker," he replied with a smile.

"Look, Dr. Walker, I'm not kidding. It's happened three times now. Well…two times where it's come true, and I just had another episode in the subway."

"Have you talked to your psychiatrist about this latest episode?" he asked, coming over and lightly examining the back of my head again, and then peering in my ear with an otoscope while I winced.

"Yes. Dr. Penny. Well, no, actually. The others, yes. But not this latest one. Ow," I said, as he poked the inner lining of my ear.

"And what does she say?"

"Nothing. She listens. That's what I pay her to do."

"Yeah, I know how that is." He pulled away from me and crossed his arms. "You have some mild swelling in your ear canal and some general wax buildup, but nothing substantial. When do you see her again?"

"Tomorrow, actually. We keep a pretty regular schedule."

"Are you on any pharmaceuticals right now?"

"Yeah, she prescribed some benzodiazepine."

"Makes sense. There are some rare reports of benzo causing hallucinations in some recipients. I would ask-"

"You think I'm hallucinating? I'm *not* hallucinating. Not any of it. I promise."

"I believe you. I would still ask her," he said, waving me down. "I believe you that you're seeing things *and* people. I mean, you were struck by lightning. That can have some pretty dramatic after-effects. If you *are* seeing things, your mind might be making imaginary forecasts based on concrete current events or people, and it can be hard to connect the dots between the two empirically. She could feasibly help you connect those dots."

I took a deep breath. "Okay." He sounded like he was potentially a believer, but not to the extent that would have really made me feel truly heard. But it was fine; I always felt like Dr. Penny heard me, and I'd see her tomorrow anyway.

"Alright," Dr. Walker said. "You got any Ibuprofen at home?"

"I think so."

"Not much needed. It's not a big bump. Just to reduce the inflammation. Of course, an ice pack is as good as anything and then you're not messing with your blood. With those nosebleeds you said you're getting, you don't want to thin out your blood."

I nodded.

"I'll have the nurse come back in and give you your summary and then why don't you come back in a few days for a follow-up, sound good? Pretty sure I have a fairly light day on the 23rd."

"Sounds good," I said, but it didn't sound good.

What did all of this mean, and why me?

It was so confusing, and so terrifying.

22 Days To Go

August 20th, 2001 • Jersey City

I would see Dr. Penny soon.

I was home, and I had ten minutes until I had to leave for my appointment with her. She was always nice to see, but her cancellation policy sucked, and she was punctual with a capital P. But what practicing doctor wasn't these days? You did *not* want to be late for your appointment with her. Nonetheless, she was a sweet sexagenarian with a direct assessment of you. She would stare at me for the longest time over her cup of tea, burning lasers through me with those eyes of hers, until I squirmed.

Pretty sure she took great pleasure in making her clients squirm.

I made sure to feed Winston the cat with his little can of Nine Lives that Jenette usually sets on the countertop. He takes his time with it.

I took my bike and rode to 22 Woodward Street. It was only a ten minute bike ride away, and the station was picking up all medical expenses for right now. Thank God for News 12. I was actually eager to get back to my desk, and Jones would just get on my nerves anytime I tuned in and saw him. He was a decent meteorologist, sure, but he couldn't fill my shoes. I'd been with News 12 for almost two years now. I knew what I was doing, and they were eager to have me back. I was thankful for the monthlong leave they had extended for rest and recuperation. Lightning strikes aren't a tiny deal. You need time to recuperate from them.

I arrived at Dr. Penny's only slightly winded, lugging my bike up onto her porch, chaining it to the pickets, then ringing her bell. I was early. I swept my hair back and took a deep breath. Looking at my watch, it was 8:57am. I didn't like it when she waited. So, she made me wait. Because I didn't like it. Like I said, she was punctual with a capital P.

Precisely at 9am, I heard footsteps, and here came Dr. Penny down the stairs. She unlocked the door.

"Roland! Right. Good to see you. Are you ready? Come on in," she greeted cheerily, in her thick British brogue. I nodded. She had emigrated here, so she had said, in 1994, with her husband. He was a- I couldn't remember. Something about accounting, or numbers or something. Two left brains under one roof. Her thick British accent was complimented with offers of hot tea and a biscuit or two with honey each time. I appreciated it. At least that way I wasn't paying only for the counseling; I could actually get some groceries out of it too.

"Nice ride today," I said as I huffed past her into the downstairs great room, which served as her unofficial home clinic. She was licensed, and that was nice. She had it in a little gold frame up on the wall. Masters Degree, Psychology, and LMHC, Seattle Argosy Institute, 1998. Apparently, she had a practice over in the UK and had some international education credits that transferred to continuing education over here.

"Oh, good!" she bubbled. "Always nice to have good weather for a bike ride. But you know all about good weather, right?"

"I sure do," I chuckled, and just then I noticed a large red mark on her left arm that she quickly covered up, pulling her sleeve down. "Ouch, what was that, a burn? You okay, Dr. Penny?" If I didn't know any better, I'd say it resembled a big red triangle.

"Oh, yes, it's nothing. I was cooking something for dinner last night and scalded myself on the oven. Not to worry. I've got some Mineral Ice and Alocane on it. Hurt like the dickens! Don't you fret about me though, I'm fine. We're here to talk about *you*," she said, waving me away while sitting down in her chair and pulling up her mug to stare over it at me.

I stifled a chuckle, but couldn't help feeling sorry for her. That burn looked painful. "Well, alright," I said, sweeping my hair back and plopping down in a big cozy yellow Barcalounger. "I've had a few more."

"Visions. Mm-hmm."

"One was profoundly clear. Like some middle-Eastern men. Terrorists, I think. And a vision of airplanes. I couldn't shake the word *hijack* out of my head. There were two of them."

"Fascinating!" she exclaimed, tilting her head at me. Something in the way she said it made it sound like more than clinical interest. More along the lines of genuine tantalizing intrigue. "When was this one?"

"Just yesterday. On the subway in Manhattan."

"Why were you in Manhattan?"

I laughed. "Well, that's the funny thing, doc, I just can't remember anymore. I was just on the train, and then," I stammered, "it-it was only the train, and the man, and the vision."

"Nosebleed?"

"Oh yeah."

"And did you collapse again?"

"Yep."

"Hmm." She stared at me over her coffee. "And you say it basically zaps the rest of your memory, for a time at least? So you had no recollection of why you were there in Manhattan?"

"Yep."

"That is truly fascinating." She took a long time to speak again. "How intense would you say this vision was compared to the one of the girl, or the bank robbery?"

I thought to myself. "I don't know. About the same. Except," I held up a finger for her to wait, "this one felt more pronounced, and definitely longer. The visions seemed longer and more pronounced. More…clarity," I finished.

"I see. As opposed to the kidnapping victim, that was just a quick few flashes, and the bank robbery, that was a much longer series of flashes."

"Yes. Correct."

"But each time you could see them clearly, as if they were standing right before you, and their images were 'seared into your brain,' as you put it. So much so that you instantly recognized them on the news."

"Yeah, I mean, that's it. I don't know when this guy from yesterday will be on the news, or when it might happen, I have no idea. But it was just as tangible, and he was right there. And then I saw him in person at PATH. Only this time I actually got a name that I couldn't shake, Dr. Penny. An actual *name*. Mohammed."

She raised her eyebrows and lowered her mug, tilting her head at me in incredulity. "You received a *name* of the perpetrator this time?"

I nodded.

"Mohammed. Hmm. No last name?"

I shook my head. "I wish."

"How *very* interesting, Roland. This sounds like your precognition is experiencing somewhat of an evolution. If you're now able to assimilate an *identity* into your precognition, that could be very helpful for the authorities. Now, I know what you're going to-"

I rolled my eyes. "I've already tried, Doc. They just chalk me up to some weird anomaly. They didn't listen to me before; they won't again. They're just all caught up in their hegemony of incredulity and standoffishness. They won't ever open their minds to me. You know that."

"Indeed I do know that they didn't listen to you *before*, Roland," she said, waving me down. "However, someone's endorsement of you - or lack thereof - has very little to do with your trajectory. You must understand that. You are on a trajectory here that you must follow to its end, obediently."

I stared at her, grasping her words and the implications that they held for me.

"At any rate," she continued, "you went *after* those other two incidences. Goodness, Roland, if I was a beat cop or a desk jockey and had to field all those countless reports from some of the whack jobs on the streets of New York City, I would be quite skeptical as well."

"Is that the clinical term? 'Whack jobs'?"

"Stay focused."

"Sorry." I cleared my throat. "But I contacted the police, like you asked. All they did was look at me crazily, take a few notes, and stuff it into some file somewhere at the bottom of a cabinet. I'm just a 'whack job' to them. And they all know that I'm on the air and wonder why I'm resorting to parlor tricks and crystal ball crap."

"Well that's nice, I should think. At least someone recognized you, yes?"

I rolled my eyes. "Yes, I suppose that part was nice," I said, and then the tension grew palpable between us. I let out a giggle, and so did she. "Fine. Yes, that was nice. It's nice to be recognized, for crying out loud. I get struck by lightning, and no one knows I'm the guy who predicts lightning, Dr. Penny. It's ridiculous."

"Well, it is quite serious, Roland. This is not unprecedented, what you're describing. Whether it's

Nostradamus with his numerous predictions, or Mark Twain predicting his own death, or Ferdinand Foch predicting World War II, all of them predicted the future with some measure of accuracy. I'm confident that in each case they were also, like you, shown visions for what would take place, and by whose hand it would take place. It's not unreasonable to assume this is the case with you."

"Yeah, but, these guys weren't struck by lightning. They just had a natural gift."

She held up a hand. "But therein lies your saving grace and spares you from being an anomaly, Roland. They were given that gift, certainly, at some point. You were also given a gift, supernaturally, vis a vis the lightning strike which you suffered."

"You think that was a *gift*?" I asked her, sneering. "Doc, I get *nosebleeds*. I pass out in strange places. I've had my wallet stolen already. Cops think I'm a nut job. People lean away from me when I start bleeding. This is *not* a gift."

Dr. Penny said nothing.

So, neither did I, just looking at her. The ticks of her grandfather clock were maddeningly loud.

Finally, she looked out the window, took her mug and put it on the table to the side of her chair. "Roland, I want to tell you something."

I said nothing.

"In life, we all have two dials. A pain dial, and a willingness dial. Most of our lives we have no control over our pain dial. It turns itself. Sometimes, it will be cranked up to ten," -here she mimed turning a dial up with her right hand," -and sometimes it will be at zero," she said, as she mimed turning the dial the other way back to zero. "What we *do* have control over is our *willingness* dial. If one were to live their entire life with their willingness dial set at level zero, they would be quite miserable. Not even fluffy newborn kittens or winning the lottery could extract a smile from them. Their willingness to deal with anything painful is nonexistent, so they've shut themselves off from the rest of life. Therefore, they resist the truth of the matter, and it's what Wesley said to Buttercup in *The Princess Bride*."

My therapist is going to counsel me with movie quotes. Awesome.

She waited for me, presumably to see if I knew the line of movie tripe she was going to feed me. I just sat there, trying to make her squirm this time.

"He said, 'life *is* pain, highness. Anyone who says differently is selling something.' When you start turning up your willingness dial, the pain becomes more bearable. The anguish of the suffering decreases as your willingness to deal with it increases. The intensity with which you resist being *willing* to deal with pain? *That* is in fact what is causing you pain. Might I suggest that you crank up your willingness dial in order to be able to deal with the suffering that is transpiring all around you? I think then you'll find that the intensity and specter of all that discomfort and pain diminishes once you see the greater good that can potentially come of this."

I was watching her intently. "And just what is the greater good? That's what I'm having trouble seeing."

"No you're not. You see it, and you know it. That's why you came to me. You wanted to help those people. You saw what happened to them before it had happened to them, and the guilt that you feel compelled you to come here and deal with it. Even now you've turned up your willingness dial to at least level two, because your newest vision compels you to act, and to intervene. For that, I commend you. But I urge you to take it higher. I think you've been chosen to help save lives, plain as a pikestaff."

"Is that a British expression?"

"Indeed," she said, retrieving her mug and drinking deeply. "I save the good ones for my most challenging clients." She smiled faintly, peering at me.

Granted, this was only my third session with her, but she was intuitive, definitely. Sometimes the light would reflect from outside, through the windows, glancing off her spectacles and dazzling me with a glint. I think she arranged all of her furniture that way, specifically to that end.

I heaved a big sigh and exhaled noisily.

"What do I do about Mohammed?"

She clenched her lip and thought for a moment. "Well, the last thing I would suggest in good conscience would be to tail *anyone* you suspect as a malefactor. You could be placing yourself in considerable danger. Let me make a call to a detective I've spoken with and see if she would be amenable to receiving your reports and treating you with a bit more respect and dignity. That might help you even crank it up to willingness level three," she said, and a faint smile spread across her lips.

"Level twenty-two would be nicer."

"Yes," she agreed. "I'll make the call and let you know. Detective Byers, Roxanne Byers. Until then, you have a few more weeks until you have to return to work, Roland. Use them to your advantage. A lightning strike is no laughing matter in any respect. Take care of your health, make sure that you're being safe, and that you're being good to yourself in all of this, yes?"

I nodded. "Is this where you tell me to lay in a hot bath and play some Kenny G?"

"I am allowed to smack my clients solidly in the head at least once per session, you know."

"Noted."

"Now, tell me about Mrs. Bishop. What's new with her?"

Big sigh. "Nothing, really. We still aren't speaking."

I thought back to my last conversation with my wife, right as she was leaving. After all, that's what had made me head to the park for some fresh air, and that's when the lightning struck, right in the middle of the day, on a relatively cloudless afternoon.

Jenette and I were having problems, for sure, but the fact that she hadn't come to the hospital to check on me, hadn't called or emailed to wish me well, and hadn't made any attempts to reconcile, was very concerning. I'm sure she wasn't watching News 12 daily to see where I was, but she had to have heard that I wasn't there, and had to have at least asked why.

Maybe not. Maybe we truly were finished.

"Well, there's certainly no harm in reaching out to her. After all, the first person to apologize…wins."

"Is that a fact?"

"Mm-hmm, yes it is. I've always maintained that humility is the doorway to harmony. It's the hardest door to go through, however; those who go there must enter on their knees. It's a painful entry to that which we desire most: the other side, where usually lie all of our hopes and dreams. If Jenette is indeed a part of that, choose humility, Roland. I'd suggest the same thing for this new gift of yours."

My eyes narrowed at her. "Meaning?"

She squinted back. "Meaning, accept this new gift. With humility. It might be just the fresh start and good reset that you need."

I squinted harder.

After all of the small talk and lesser details about my life, I had written a check to Dr. Penny, and we were once again back out on her porch. A blue sedan pulled up on the street as I was readying my bike and helmet. *Might be her next client,* I thought. *Prepare to be squinted at, buddy.*

"Do keep me posted if you have another episode, Roland," Dr. Penny said. "And do keep your cellphone handy. Those blackouts once cost you your wallet. It would be a shame if they ever cost you more. Promise me you'll take care of yourself out there."

"I promise. I will. Whoa…*ow!*" I exclaimed, as I doubled over in pain. A thick shock passed through my gut and a blinding flash seared through my head.

"What is it? Oh dear! Roland?" Dr. Penny put her hand on my shoulder.

"Here, here, let me, dear," said a voice. I looked over.

An older man in an outdated fedora and a tweed coat was huffing up the walk to the porch, wearing round spectacles. Dr. Penny backed off. "What is it? Young man, are you quite alright?"

I looked over at him. A flash jolted behind my eyes, and I recoiled and steadied myself. I could feel the hot fluid in my nose preparing its downward march as my head pounded. "Oh, man, yeah, just headrush I think," I stammered, looking at the two of them, and I started to sweat as well. My legs buckled momentarily. "I just need to sit down for a moment." I did so, and fetched my water bottle from the cylinder holder on the bike stem.

"Dear, this is my client Roland, he was just leaving," Dr. Penny said to the man. She looked to be on edge at my instability. Hell, her client was sitting here with a bloody nose and weak knees on her front porch, about to vomit, right in front of her husband. "Roland, will you be alright?"

I looked up at her strangely for a moment, and then back to the man. This was not her client, but her *husband*. I had never met him before.

"Yes, I think so, I'm sorry. I-" I started, and had to shake my head and clear my vision, reaching for my handkerchief to wipe my nose, "I- it's just-just aftershocks of the strike. I was hit by lightning a few weeks ago, Mr. Eggers. Sorry, I'll be just fine."

Without warning, another flash of white shot through my mind and clouded my vision momentarily. I looked up at Dr. Penny and then back down at her left arm. Her sleeve had ridden up when she had steadied me, and I could see the red mark again. She quickly covered it. I winced and looked back at her face incredulously, then back at Mr.

Eggers. Then back at her arm. Her face. She looked at me sidelong for a moment.

I swear that I saw her eyes flash to Mr. Eggers almost imperceptibly, and then back to meet mine. There was something there. She knew that I knew, and she was terrible at hiding it.

Dr. Penny was tense, and I could see it. She was nervous, and I perceived it. She was afraid of him, and I knew it, *plain as a pikestaff*, as she put it.

"I'm-" I started, and then my eyes went wide, and I had to take a deep breath. "I'm sorry, I'll be just fine. I get them all the time. Not to worry, Mr. Eggers. I'll see myself out. Thanks."

"Well, that does sound rather nasty. If I were you, I'd head to the emergency room straightaway," Mr. Eggers insisted. "A serious predicament, to be sure. Well, come along, Penny, let's go inside. Good day to you, Roland," he said, quickly tipping his hat and heading into the house.

As he put distance between us, the buzzing in my ears decreased, and the colors around me swam less. I could see clearly again.

Emergency Room. That's practically where I had just come from. I caught my breath and waved him away. Dr. Penny watched me. I looked at her, and inhaled a deep, labored wheeze. She watched me curiously. I looked down at her arm, and then gave her a faint clenched lip smile of understanding. I wanted her to know that I sympathized. I had no idea if she knew what I was thinking.

Without a word, I hoisted my bike up in my arms and took it off her porch, staggering up the walkway to the street, setting it down and wheeling it into position. I flung my leg over to the other side and donned my helmet.

Just before I pedaled out of there, I cast one slow look back. Dr. Penny was standing on the porch, studying me, her arm covered, but she was holding it as if it was needing some fresh Alocane, or perhaps a coating of the freedom of truth.

I summoned up a weak smile of understanding her way, but it's really hard to smile at someone properly when your brow is furrowed, especially when it's furrowed because you knew how she got that mark, and you knew her husband would someday kill her, and you knew exactly how he would do it.

I shook my head at her, and all I could do was mime a willingness dial being dialed back to zero, hoping she would catch my drift.

I called her a few times from home. There was no answer. "C'mon, Doc, pick up." I was getting edgy and nervous. It didn't help that Jones was on News 12 giving the forecast for tomorrow, and he was just so damned formal and unattainable. Made me sick to watch it.

My gut had already been roiling since seeing that vision with Dr. Penny. Could I have been mistaken? Was it just a fluke, some figment of my own imagination that I was now lumping in with 'the gift?' That mark on her arm was a burn for sure. Was it an iron? I didn't know. It looked like one. But I *knew* Mr. Eggers did it. And I *knew* what he would do next.

Someone picked up. "Hello? Dr. Penny?" I asked. The line disconnected almost immediately. I did the only thing I could, and redialed. I went straight to voice mail. *That's it,* I thought, *I'm going back there.*

I tore through the house as a panic zipped through my bones. I had to get there. I wondered how long Mr. Eggers had been hurting her. I wondered how much of this she had dialed up her willingness to accommodate over the years. I just couldn't accept that someone so keen could be with someone so mean.

When did it start?

What lies or excuses had she told herself to make it okay?

What inescapable threats had she silently borne to smooth things over and sleep with the enemy?

All of these thoughts raced through my head – which still throbbed – as I got closer to their house.

I saw the lights from three blocks away. The facing houses were awash with flashes of blue and red, and the looky-loos were out in full force, scattered across the adjoining sidewalks in curiosity. There were several squad cars, and an ambulance. A fire truck was parked a little further up the street.

I had tried to call a few more times on the way, hoping I'd have enough breath between pedals, and then resigned myself to just pedal and stop trying to call. *There wouldn't be an answer anyway,* I thought. Almost lost my balance and crashed as I tried to call, swerving nearly into a garbage can on the sidewalk.

A crowd of onlookers was gathered. There was a dense throng outside her house. No one could advance beyond the police tape.

A body was being wheeled out.

I'm too late. Oh no. I'm too late!

A lump formed in my throat as I saw the white-sheet-draped silhouette on the gurney, being loaded into the medical examiner's car. I shook my head and looked down. *I'm too late. Dr. Penny had been killed! I could have prevented this one too! I failed!* That refrain bounced and thundered throughout the caverns of my shame and guilt.

And then I saw the perpetrator. Standing there, on the porch, ushered out of the house. I recognized the face. It was a face I had seen before. Police were escorting them out in handcuffs.

To my amazement and dismay, it was Dr. Penny. My head tilted in confusion. And then I realized it, as the cold truth hit me plain as a pikestaff.

She wasn't murdered. She *had* murdered.

She had turned it around and had killed Mr. Eggers.

What?? I could only hope then and there that it was self-defense. She had to know that I knew. Beyond that, this was the quickest turnaround from vision to death yet. The others had been a few days apart, each. This was only hours.

No. Dr. Penny was not dead. She had killed her own husband. She had cranked her own willingness dial back down to zero, and had refused to endure any more suffering at the hands of her now-deceased oppressor. All the very opposite of what she had just counseled me. But the very counsel she had given me would have imperiled herself, doubtless. She was no longer willing to receive his abuse. She had returned to zero and had burned the bed.

I watched her in shock. I had literally just sat across from her a few hours earlier, receiving instruction and wisdom from her. All of that instruction and wisdom had crumpled and imploded within her, and she had killed him.

She turned, as if sensing me out in the crowd. Or looking for me? Hoping that I would be there?

Our eyes met. I looked at her, and she at me. She was far away, being led into a squad car as she walked, but I swear she smiled, faintly, in understanding and full recognition of the gravity of these developments.

Deep in my heart, a dim, radiating awareness was growing that I may have actually saved her life. But had I? Maybe she was extra vigilant tonight and saw his attack coming? Maybe her counsel to me was actually meant for herself? Perhaps she was more prepared for his attack, and had her own fair dose of bleak prescience: her own 'gift' as she had called it, and had used it to save herself from her husband.

I would find out soon, I figured, because I knew what I would be doing tomorrow.

I would be seeing Dr. Penny soon.

21 Days To Go

August 21st, 2001 • Jersey City

There was no escaping the truth.

I was at the Jersey City Jail, and was waiting to see her. She had used her one phone call on me, and the Caller ID was not a surprise at all.

I knew instantly who it was.

That was last night, late. She must have been interrogated for hours beforehand, alone in a small room with the whole good-cop-bad-cop routine performed on her. I told her I'd be in as soon as I could the next day.

I rode there and checked in, got fingerprinted, and the Visitations Officer actually recognized me. *Finally.* Always a nice touch. Nice to be missed. *Right, Jenette?*

Now, I was just waiting to see Dr. Penny. Ridiculously long wait. It had been twenty-one minutes so far. At long last, they led her in. We were in a small bank of chairs set between dividers, and there was thick glass between each one. I grabbed the intercom phone on the wall and held it up to my ear as she approached.

Granted, I had only seen her three times in the two weeks since the lightning, but each time, she had a decorum to her; a classiness. One that could easily make you look up to her and respect her. One that made you admire her for her collective wisdom and her air of confidence.

But now, Dr. Penny was reduced to a shell of her former self. Her hair was flattened, her glasses were missing and replaced with cheap readers, she was without makeup, and her shoulders were somewhat hunched. The chirpy intellectual wisdom-giver had been replaced by an alleged killer, and her eyes were downward.

Wordlessly she approached me, and sat down. She slowly lifted the intercom to her ear. It was some time before she looked up, but I think that was more out of a realization that we were on a time limit as opposed to a desire to meet another human's eyes.

"Hi, Dr. Penny."

She looked at me, confused, and didn't reply.

"Are you okay?" I started, and tried to make light of it, looking around. "Quite a change of pace from yesterday afternoon, I bet," I fumbled. "Are they taking care of you?"

She slowly nodded.

Awkward pause. "I'm knackered," she said, quietly. "Very tired. Didn't sleep well at all, you know."

"Can I…do anything for you?" The very question seemed so antithetical to our relationship thus far. She was the one helping me, not vice versa.

She seemed too wrapped up in guilt to answer.

"Look, Dr. Penny, you called me. I want to help. And," -here I looked around the room briefly- "I saw it," I said, clenching my teeth and squinting at her.

She looked at me.

"Yeah. I saw it. *I know.* I know about your arm. I know that he was planning on denting your skull in last night with the iron. I saw the whole thing."

She flinched. "The iron?" Her head tilted.

"That's what I saw."

"The iron," she said, and this time it wasn't a question. "He-he never got that f-far," she stammered, mumbling quietly. "But the iron, oh my goodness," she finished.

"What about the iron?"

She seemed to be searching in her memory, then she did a double-take and finally sighed, looking at me. "He gave me this," she said, holding up her red-marked arm. "With the iron. He," she stammered, and managed a weak smile, "he said I never ironed his shirts well enough. So he wanted to show me how to do it properly. This is how he showed me."

She paused again, taking a deep breath.

"But apparently I still hadn't mastered it," she finished, and then clenched her lips into painful acceptance.

"So, he was going to kill you with it."

She slowly nodded again, then inhaled and exhaled a deep, labored, acquiescing sigh. "Our marriage had been crumbling for some time. He could be so cruel. He beat me fairly regularly, you know."

All of this slowly tumbled out of her as if we had done a role reversal. I now had the tea in her front room, and was squinting at her over my cup.

"He deprived me of food and beat me if I spent his money without his approval. I-I was *never* quite good enough," she faltered, and her head dropped. And just then, a solitary tear trickled out of her eye and graced her left cheek. I wanted to use some of whatever this power was that I had to be able to reach through and cleanse her face of it. She began to cry, clearly, covering her head in her hands. Her cheeks and eyes flushed red.

"You know, they teach psychiatrists everything there is to know about pulling people out, but nothing whatsoever about letting people in. I just…I just couldn't let anyone else in to the truth of how I really was inside. This… this… *masquerade*," she ended, sobbing into her hands.

I took a deep, intense breath. "Dr. Penny," I breathed slowly through the intercom, "I'm so sorry. I'm *utterly* sorry. You *are* quite good enough. You didn't deserve this. I-I've only known you a short time now, but you've helped me crank up my willingness dial. But," -here I knocked on the screen to make sure I had her attention, and she looked up at me slowly- "sounds like you had your pain dial at 10 for a long while. But, see? You had your willingness dial up there too. To my eyes it looks like you finally cranked down that willingness dial, and because of that, your pain dial is down now as well. I'd call that a fresh start."

She stopped, and looked at me, remembering. Dr. Penny smiled faintly, receiving her own wise counsel back to her as she regarded me. "And a good reset," she echoed slowly, flat and monotonous, eventually managing a feeble grin.

We looked at each other for a moment and just savored the connection of empathy.

"Thank you, Mr. Bishop," she finally breathed faintly, and then looked around sheepishly as if reluctant to say my name too loudly. Whether that was out of caution to keep me from being a witness at her trial or something else, I don't know. They already had a record of me visiting her. She had to know that. But then again, I was pretty sure she was unacquainted with the judicial system. Pretty sure this was her first incarceration for murder. "You've certainly kept 'your sunny disposition.'"

"You're welcome," I said back to her, smiling enough for the both of us. "I'm just sorry about all this. I-I wish I had seen something sooner."

"How could you have?" she defended me. "You'd never been near him before. Isn't," she stuttered, "isn't that how you get your premonitions, you have to be near the eventual offender?"

"Well, yeah, I guess you're right. Only with you, he wasn't 'eventual.' Sounds like you've been living under this cloud for a long time, Dr. Penny."

She nodded, quietly, taking a slow, deep breath.

"I just wish, I don't know, maybe we could have had more sessions, or more at different hours or something, so that I could have been around to, I don't know, *run interference* or something like that. I don't know," I ended in a whimper, running my hand through my hair with a labored groan. "And it's really, *really* odd that I only saw his offense, and not-" I stopped short and looked at her.

"Not…mine," she acknowledged. "Hmm. Yes, that is odd. Maybe his sin was greater. Or, maybe mine was just."

"Well, I'm no judge of sin or justice."

"Neither am I. But it seems you're good at detecting it." She looked at me inquisitively. "Have you had any more of them since my husband?"

I looked back up at her. "No. Not since him. But I knew. I guess I knew as soon as I saw the mark on your arm. You didn't do a very good job hiding it."

"No, I suppose I didn't."

"Do you have an attorney yet?"

She nodded briskly. "Public defender. At least for now. We have a family attorney, but I couldn't reach him last night. But yes, I have someone I was able to talk to instead. She supposes a good case can be made for battered wife syndrome. I hate that term," she muttered, shaking her head.

"Yeah, I know what you mean. I do too. But," I tried to reassure her, "if the shoe fits…right?"

She summoned up another meager smile that I could see right through. "Right." Dr. Penny tried to shield her eyes with her left hand, and I saw her burn mark with increased clarity up close this time, wincing as I saw it.

I looked at her. "How long?"

She met my eyes.

"How long has it been?"

Her left arm dropped, and she raised her eyes to the ceiling. They were glistening. Evidently the years piled up on her answer far heavier than I knew.

"Nine years," she said stoically.

My heart sank. He had been beating her for nine years. Three thousand two hundred eighty five days of living in fear, trapped in abuse. How many times had she promised herself in the dark to take action, to flee, to deliver herself from him, to call for help, only to finally react and murder him? Being a weatherman was what I did. I understood living under dark clouds all too well.

"How did you do it?" I flinched, incredulous that I asked her that; it had just slipped out.

Her quick reply surprised me. Apparently, she was ready for a confessional. "Sledgehammer," was what she said, and that was all she said. My mouth dropped. "He was sleeping. I had brought it up from the garage last night and hidden it in the bedroom."

My eyes widened, and I think she actually chuckled. It wasn't a sinister chuckle, however; instead, it was the chuckle of someone who was actually now free to laugh, liberated from the shackles of abuse. Released from the threat of constant control and violence. It surprised me.

"Wow, that'll do it. You either wake up with one helluva headache, or…" -here I paused and my eyebrows went up- "you just…don't wake up."

"Well, Mr. Eggers chose Door Number Two, I'm afraid. Door Number One would require *taking* some painkillers. Door Number Two required someone *being* a painkiller. I chose to kill my pain."

I nodded. "Thus, the good reset."

"Thus, the good reset," she said, and she smiled again, and as she did so it seemed many lines of care were smoothed from her aging face.

Dr. Penny and I bantered a bit more, and she dared to ask me questions about my own situation while marinating in the gravity of her own. I indulged her and shared about my symptoms, about Jenette, about News 12, about my last real flash prior to Mr. Eggers. About Mohammed, and the airplanes.

"Well, it looks as though I'm not going anywhere," she finished, "and I do genuinely care about your predicament and would like to know what comes of it. If it wouldn't be too much trouble, I'd love to be kept abreast of any new developments. The session are now, hmm, *free,*" she ended.

I smiled, grateful, but it was unnecessary. I shook my head. "Let's not call it free. Let's call it an I.O.U."

She nodded, understanding. "I apparently know something about owing somebody."

Her husband.

I grimaced.

"Well, with my debt," I said, "nobody gets hurt; you just get a check later. Assuming of course that you take checks written by anomalies."

"Your money is good here. And yes, well, we shall see. It might be better, Roland, for you to write your checks to my attorney. I'll provide his information later. I don't suppose I'll be going anywhere soon, so for now, our sessions will have to be conducted just like this."

"Fine by me. I'll come as often as I can. I promise."

"Thank you, Roland. You really are a kind soul. Jenette truly doesn't know what she's missing."

I grimaced again. *Jenette.* Still no call, no inquiry as to my well-being, nothing. It's practically as if she had been waiting for this escape hatch all along, and jumped through readily, never looking back.

"Thank you, Doc," I replied, shrugging. "We'll see what happens there. Time will tell. I've got a few more weeks to recover and then get back to work, and I'll try to work on that side of things in the meanwhile as well. Who knows? Maybe she'll get struck with lightning too. Heck, maybe she'll finally wake up to how immeasurably awesome I truly am."

"Immeasurably awesome *and* immeasurably humble," Dr. Penny corrected me.

"Emphasis on the latter," I said. "Anyway, I'll let you know. I promise."

"Just, if she does get struck by lightning, don't have her stand next to me please. She might know when I plan to commit my next atrocity." She giggled, but then stifled it, realizing it was in poor taste. I felt for her; she was obviously trying to make herself feel better about her predicament, and her new surroundings.

Her smile faded, and she regarded me carefully and somberly. "This is where I'll stay, isn't it? This is where Dr. Penelope Eggers goes to die. In here, or in some prison somewhere, wherever they'll deposit me." She sighed and nodded to herself. "Well. I suppose it's some consolation to know that I ended up here and not in the grave. That would have been most unjust."

I just stared at her. "Dr. Penny-" I began, but she held her hand up. Dr. Penny arched her back, looked up at the ceiling and sighed, meeting my eyes again.

"It's quite alright. I'm free from that pain. Now I must undergo another. But my willingness dial is back up to ten now. So we shall see how I fare as society's scourge. In the meantime, you should really go have that chat with Detective Roxanne. Although," -here she paused, her eyes dropping- "I'm not too sure she'll feel too fondly about me anymore, given what I've done." She shrugged.

"I want you to know something," I said to her.

She looked back up at me, curiously.

"Society's endorsement of you - or lack thereof - has very little to do with your trajectory."

Dr. Penny's face slowly awakened in recognition, and then the faintest smile emerged. "Thank you, Roland."

I nodded, and clenched my lip. I felt so bad for her, and for her plight.

We would see how she fared, indeed.

The truth was that she had killed her husband, and she would be cast as a murderer. We'd both have to see how her defense worked out. For now though, the truth, like her jail, were fortified and irrefutable.

There truly would be no escaping either.

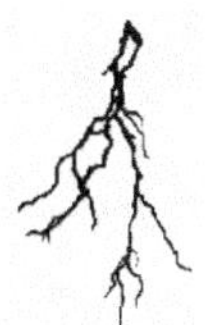

20 Days To Go

August 22nd, 2001 • Jersey City

The rest of yesterday was pretty tame.

I came home, straightened up the house, made a few calls to friends and family, and started writing a letter to Jenette, not that I would send it. Maybe right now it was just for therapy. What did I want to say to her?

I fell asleep pondering that very question.

The next morning I awoke. I checked my phone. A missed call from Jenette! *Damn*…I had had it on vibrate. She hadn't left a message. I dialed her back immediately, waiting, silently urging her to pick up. I didn't really know what to say, and I didn't really know if she wanted to hear it. I just knew she was on my mind.

No answer. Why was I not surprised? I had been filled with hope for a moment, eagerly anticipating potentially rekindling our relationship, only to plop down on the loveseat in our living room, the unanswered call in my hands. *Loveseat*, I thought. *Ridiculous name.*

Jenette and I had met in Seattle, fallen in love and got married there in 1998. It was bliss. For a while, at least. I got a really good opportunity to come to the Big Apple for News 12, and I had to take it. I wasn't getting anywhere with KOMO-4, KING-5, or KIRO-7 in Seattle, even though I'd interned there and submitted plenty of demos. Meteorology isn't rocket science; it's just studying the signs and watching the patterns. Part of the time it's cheating and repeating. Everyone knows that. You hear what someone else is predicting, compare it to what you know of previous weather patterns, watch the winds, and you just go with it. Consensus wins. If you're wrong, you're wrong, no one really wants your head. You just call it a freak storm and try it again. But I rarely did that. I knew what I was doing, and I had developed an excellent track record.

Apparently, however, Seattle didn't seem to think I knew what I was doing. So, I widened my search and found a willing station on the other side of the country. But that of course meant one thing.

Uprooting.

Jenette wasn't super interested in moving here, but she loved me, and I loved her, and she promised to follow me. With that promise, we moved to Jersey in early 2000. With the passage of time, however, it became clear that she was unhappy, and just missed our hometown. Twenty months of unhappiness. Did I miss Seattle too? Sure. I just didn't have the same emotional pangs that she did, and never felt like returning. I kept in touch with my folks, and she with hers as well as her friends, but the long-distance friendships wore on her. On top of that, she just wasn't making the connections here that she had hoped for. I felt truly bad for her, as she always had been so great at connecting with people, but for one reason or another, now she felt trapped. Uprooted. Bored. *Alone.*

It was just a matter of time, really. In the spring of 2001, after only one year in New Jersey, our arguments really heated up, and she made it clear in no uncertain terms that she wanted to move back home. By that time, however, I'd become the face of weather for News 12. It's not like I could just quit. Sure, now I would have a video resume to show the three top stations in Seattle what I could do, but I'd be taking my chances with that. With me. With us. She just didn't understand that.

So, on the evening of Saturday, August 4th, we had our blowup fight, and she stormed out. She was going to stay with her one New York friend, Amanda, 'until I came to my senses.' *Yeah, well, good luck waiting for* that *to happen!* I yelled, and then realized painfully that I had insulted myself. She shook her head, and drove off in our car. Thankfully, I still had the bike.

I kicked a few rocks in our tiny backyard for a half hour, and then headed down to Millenium Park.

The lightning struck at 5:30pm, out of nowhere. I had literally just set foot in the park, and my left foot had only just touched the first blades of grass when that thunder hit.

There was only one cloud in the sky, and it was directly overhead. The lightning came down before I could even look up. All I remember is being tense, paralyzed, and everything became white. The only way I can describe it is like a dense, molten, churning and blazing fiery core at my body's epicenter. And from there emanated this nonstop pulse of pure throbbing agony, as if I was being consumed by fire from the inside.

Then…peace.

That was a little over two weeks ago, and neither one of us had made any inroads toward repairing our relationship. I had called her number, and left her many messages, but there was no answer. I had tried her friend Amanda, but she never answered my calls. I couldn't help but feel like they were sitting there ignoring their phones.

Really hard to believe that my wife and I were at such an impasse, but *que sera sera.* I wasn't terrified that it wouldn't work out. As far as I knew, she still loved me. I knew I still loved her. I think.

That night, I finished with my letter *and* with thinking back to the incident. I wouldn't even know how to get it to her, because I didn't know where Amanda lived. I just shook my head in frustration knowing that this was going on *two weeks* now, with no semblance of restoration on the horizon.

I was just about to head out for some crisp clean nighttime air after cleaning the house, when it happened.

Flashes. Heat. Tremors that almost leveled me. The trickle came out of my nose almost instantaneously.

Then…the shouting.

The neighbors, Jake and Renita, were shouting at each other, and it happened so abruptly that it shook me out of my reveries. They had done this before, but something was heated over there tonight, and I wasn't sure what it was. I tried to listen through the stabbing fog, and my eyes rolled back in my head for a moment. Their baby was screaming. I couldn't remember how old he was…nine months? Ten?

Nosebleed. Both nostrils. Throbbing pounding in my head like a piledriver to my soul. I fell to the ground, and as I did so, I reached out my hand to try to steady myself against the wall. A current of energy shot through me, emanating from the other side of it.

Jake. I saw him. Swinging something over his head…what was it?

A receipt flew through the air. For a moment it hovered there in the air, floating. I almost felt I could reach out and touch it. It had the Jersey City Home Depot name at the top. I could faintly make it out, but that was it, for sure.

Something flashed in the night…a reflection of moonlight glinted off metal, and I heard a scream. The glint rose and fell, rose and fell, and guttural cries sounded out at each fall. A jet of crimson shot up toward Jake as the knife repeatedly fell. His expression was twisted into a contortion of rage and vitriol.

Jake was killing Renita and the baby.

I knew right away that what I was seeing hadn't happened yet, but I also knew right away that it would.

A door slammed as I was about to lose consciousness and collapse to the floor. My hand slipped and I dropped.

Doors slamming. More yelling.

Baby still crying, helplessly, in the middle of it. Something heavy falling with a thud.

Footsteps running down the walkway outside our apartments, angrily. The door opened and Renita shouted out something to him…muted…confused.

I fell elbow-first into the floor and lay there like a dead thing.

I came to forty-five minutes later, lying in a shallow puddle of my own blood and sweat. My face was tinted red, but my nose had stopped bleeding at some point. The pounding in my head remained, however.

Everything was buzzing.

I staggered up and grabbed a handkerchief, putting it to my nose. My bleeding had stopped, thankfully, but my nose was plugged with dried blood and blotted masses. I wiped them out gently, took a deep breath, put my hands to my temples, and stumbled out the front door, turning to face the neighbors' door.

I couldn't hear anything.

I gave the door a soft knock, and whispered Renita's name, saying it was her neighbor. Must have been Jake that had stormed out.

In a moment, I was right. *Renita.* She opened the door in a hurry, and her eyes were red and inflamed. She had obviously been quiet-crying into a pillow.

"Hey. Oh. What happened to your nose?" she asked, pointing.

"Huh? Oh this, n-nothing, I, uh, fell."

Her damp pillow was behind her on the couch, next to a baby boy. He was crawling toward me, about to fall off the couch. Joe-Joe was his name, I think. He was clad only in a diaper.

I had barely ever talked to them except when we'd needed butter or relish or some sundry crap like that. They had mostly kept to themselves.

I guess we had too, since we had never once had them over for dinner.

"Uh…your baby, uh…," I said, pointing and motioning behind Renita.

"Huh? Oh, crap. Joe-Joe, no!" she said, running back and fetching him to safety, putting him on the floor.

"Hey…I'm-I'm sorry, I just…," I trailed off. "Uh," -here I paused, assessing whether or not I should be intruding- "are you okay?"

"So you heard all that?" And then she laughed grimly to herself, folding her arms against her chest. "Duh. How could you not?"

"How could I not?" I said, sheepishly, with an understanding smile. "Just wanted to make sure you two were alright."

She shook her head. "I'm sure he'll be back in a minute. He was just going to the store. We're fine. If, ya know, *fine* means *my world is falling apart.* That kind of fine. Yeah."

The store. "St-store, did you say? Home Depot?"

"Yeah, why? How did you know?"

A panic tore through me. He could pull back in at any minute. "Oh my Go- okay, Renita, I know you're not gonna understand this, I don't expect you to, but I just need you to-" -here I looked wildly around, behind her into her apartment, and back into the parking lot- "I just need you to get stuff for Joe-Joe and stay with me. Please. I'll explain later. *Please?*" I was begging now.

She stared at me, her face askew with confusion, her eyebrows thrust downward. It must have been the way I said 'please,' because she eyed me curiously with her mouth agape. The words gradually slipped out of her. "Uh, sure, okay, gimme a minute," was all she whispered, retreating back into her apartment to get her things.

"Okay. Good. Okay," I said nervously, fidgeting. He could return any minute. "Please hurry."

She flashed a look back at me as she fetched a diaper bag, her keys, purse, a few toys, and finally, Joe-Joe.

In three minutes, they were in my apartment, and we closed and locked the door behind us and headed for my bedroom, toward the back.

It was quiet. Joe-Joe was playing with an old desk phone I had that wasn't on a landline. I plugged it in for him, and he was pressing the buttons with great delight, looking up and smiling at us, delighted at each button press. His binky bobbed slightly in his mouth. Winston scurried across the carpet and occasionally tried to bat at him. He laughed.

"It's up to you, Renita, I assure you. But I'm telling you the truth. Been going on for two weeks now."

She studied me. "That is weird. What a gift, huh?"

"Gift. Yeah. I don't know about that. But I see things, and they all, well, at least I think they all, uh, usually come true. And I-I saw him hurting you. He's coming back here. I don't want him to hurt you or Joe-Joe. Please stay."

She considered it briefly, and then she took such a deep breath and held it, I figured she would pop. At length, she released it in a forcible gust, and nodded slowly. She mumbled just above the threshold of silence, "For Joe-Joe."

"No," I corrected her. "For both of you."

And with that, we called the cops. They said they'd be on their way in fifteen minutes to take a statement from Renita for domestic assault, and from me as a witness.

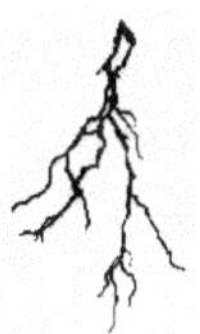

What had I gotten myself into? I wondered.
The night was getting on.

"I don't know," I said. "She won't return my calls, and I don't know what to say. Voicemail after voicemail, man," I said, shaking my head.

"And she knows what happened to you?" Renita asked. "She knows about the lightning strike? And that was like two weeks ago!"

I nodded. I had left it on her voicemail of course.

Renita shook her head. "Wow. Lame. That's not cool. I'm sorry, Roland."

I shrugged. "We'll see what happens," I said tiredly, though I wasn't filled with optimism in the slightest.

At that moment, there came a knock at my door. It was the police! I motioned for her to stay back. I didn't want for Joe-Joe, or Renita, to be surprised.

I half-closed the door behind myself and walked up to the front door.

I unlocked it, opened it and stopped short.

Jake.

"Oh, hey J- uh, Jake, right? It's Jake?" I tried to play dumb. *Crap. Pretend like you just remembered his name!* "How are you and your wife doing?"

He was sweating, and he was angry. His muscles were tensed under a light, patterned button-up shirt and jeans, and his hair was mangy, as if he'd tried to smear his stress into it one too many times.

"Have you seen her?"

"Who?"

"*Renita!* Have you *seen* my wife Renita?" he suddenly screamed at me.

I jumped a little at his volume. A lump formed in my throat. *Joe-Joe, please don't make any noise.*

"Uh, no, I-sorry, I didn't remember her name, it's been a long time since we've seen you guys."

"Yeah. But you remembered my name's Jake. Dammit! You haven't seen her at all?"

"No, sorry, Jake. Uh, is everything okay?"

"Does it *look* like-" He stopped. So did I.

Joe-Joe. A little laugh, hardly noticeable. But parents, they say, can pick out their child's laugh or cry out of a lineup. *Dammit.*

Jake looked at me with betrayal written across his face. "Move!" he said, and he thrust me aside.

"Jake, now, wait a minute. I- oof!" I exclaimed, as he punched me in the gut. I doubled over and saw stars.

Winston's hair was up. He hissed and bolted.

Jake was fast-walking back to my bedroom. I leaned against the open door of our apartment and tried to catch my breath.

Jake threw open the door to our bedroom and went straight for Renita, grabbing her by her hair and yanking her to the floor, pulling her behind him. She screamed and tried to hang on to his hands to preserve her hair. Stray wisps of it trailed on the floor behind her as Joe-Joe watched them awkwardly with widened eyes.

"Jake, please, let her go!" I yelled, but my air failed me. My head throbbed as my rage grew.

"Shut up!" he said, and he was almost to me.

Something arose in me. A force I couldn't explain sent shivers through my veins and my sinews, electrifying me for action. I shot up, and all I could see was blue. Everything was blue, and looked as though it was sizzling.

I grabbed Jake by the arm, and he winced. Smoke rose from my hand, clutching his arm. Jake cried out in pain and tried to tear himself away. His arm erupted into blue flames. I released him as he frantically waved it about, shrieking. He extinguished his flaming arm with a thin blanket on my couch, but his arm was now blackened and burned.

A hoarse cry arose in me, welling up from the depths of my soul as it grew in intensity, rising like a fire through my lungs and blazing forth out of my vocal cords in a monstrous roar. I tilted my head back in agony as my flesh seared with intensity and the blue turned to hot white.

Lightning has to exit the body.

I remembered Dr. Walker's words back at the ER. Did lightning just exit my body? Was there still some trapped inside me? If so, how?

Something flashed in the night…a reflection of moonlight glinted off metal, and I heard a scream.

Renita broke free of him, running back to take shelter and shield little Joe-Joe. Jake's knife came out of his back pocket in his hand, and he swung toward me. I heard his yelling, but it didn't sound like him.

I held up my arms over my face in defense.

Gunshots. Three of them.

Jake stumbled backward, dazed, and just stood there, slowly looking down at his own paralyzed form. The knife dropped clumsily from his hands. Red circles appeared on his chest through his thin button-up, their diameter slowly expanding outwards.

In a moment, my assailant, Renita's husband, was down on the ground next to me.

The knife was beside him, next to a crumpled-up receipt. I already knew what it said.

The police had come.

Tomorrow would not be tame.

19 Days To Go

August 23rd, 2001 • Manhattan, NY

I had no idea what it was.

It was 9:20am, and here I was, on the PATH train back in Manhattan, on the way to see Dr. Walker for my scheduled follow-up.

I stared at my hand. Not a trace of the flame, or any injury from it, remained.

What had happened? How did I do what I did? Jake's arm was smoking when he ripped it away from me. Blue flame was pouring out of me. My hand felt hot. Had some residual electricity stayed? *Impossible,* I thought.

There was simply no way. What would Dr. Walker say to that? I had to go see him again.

I thought back to when I had seen 'Mohammed' or whatever his name was, at the PATH station. Here I was in Manhattan yet again. Call me crazy, but I wanted to find him. Frankly, I wanted to see what my hand could do. Had I immobilized Jake? Electrocuted him? How the hell was that even possible?

Renita and I had given our statements to the police and they took Jake out to the emergency room on a stretcher. But he was already dead. I knew it before they pulled the sheet up over his face.

That made two dead people I'd seen in two days. *Standard for most people in New York,* I wondered.

I almost didn't care. Renita was safe. I had prevented her death. Jake was gone. I think I actually might have killed him before the police. I had to go see Dr. Penny, and before that, I needed to do a check-up with Dr. Walker.

But there was something else I had to do first.

I arrived at the PATH station and walked out. No idea where I should go, except up. So many people crowded out around me, and I felt that same stifling feeling when you're just surrounded by too many people and you crave a big open field.

In Manhattan, the only big open field you wade through is crowds.

So, I waded.

I just wanted to walk through and see if I could 'pick up' on anything. What could I pick up on? What signals could I possibly receive?

It started with sitting and closing my eyes. Just listening to the hum of the station and the bustling of my fellow humans around me.

I'm Roland Bishop, and I know where I am, I again repeated in my mind. *I'm Roland Bishop, and I know where I am*. Whereas before I used that to center myself and get a grip, re-emerging after an incident, now I was using it to focus and draw myself back in. *I'm Roland Bishop, and I know where I am*. I breathed and let time do the rest.

I could see before me, in my mind's eye, the souls of people moving throughout the station, oblivious to the needs of their fellow man, intent upon one thing only: their destination. They moved with purpose, intentionality, and speed. They projected their path ahead, and set their course, plotting the best routes through the traffic. And if someone's course converged with their own up ahead, no problem: they course-corrected with the best of them, deviating from their path and choosing an alternate route to take. They all had places to be and people to see.

Not I. For myself, I had to just sit here and *feel*. I could see them, but I just had to wait and see what happened after that.

I waited for a solid fifteen minutes, sitting there, almost statuesque with anticipation. Nothing. No signals, no flashes, no nosebleeds. Here I was practically wanting them now, when just a few days ago, even yesterday – they were still a major irritant.

What the heck had happened to my life in so short a time? I didn't have any explanations. I gathered myself up off the seat on which I was perched, and caught the bus up to East 75th St and New York Presbyterian to see Dr. Thinks-I'm-Crazy.

In the meantime, my stress was building. Somewhere out there was a middle-Eastern man named Mohammed that was going to commit a hijacking. I knew it.

Where he was, I did not know.

When he would do it, I did not know.

All I knew was that he *would*.

"No, no, I'm telling you my hand, like, spontaneously combusted! And then it literally burnt him - or something, doc. I'm not crazy here."

He had his hands up defensively. "I didn't say you were. The story just sounds a bit…extreme." He bit his lip as I rolled my eyes. "What does your psychiatrist say to this? You're still meeting with one, I presume?"

I wasn't about to tell him that she was now in jail. That would do nothing more than certify me as batshit crazy in his eyes. "I haven't told her yet," was all I mustered.

"Do the police know about your alleged burning incident?"

"It's not alleged!"

"Fine, Roland. Fine. Do they know about it?"

"Hell, I don't know. Everything happened so fast. They took our statements and all of that, but I didn't mention it. I suppose that the coroner will pull it up when they do a medical examination, but what does it matter? He's dead."

He nodded. "Well, let me have a look at those hands."

Dr. Walker came over and took my hands in his, turning them over and inspecting them. "I don't see anything from a cursory analysis, and there are no exit points on either of these, which is weirder, but they do feel unusually warm for being inside an air-conditioned building. Let me take your temperature for an overall baseline." He fetched his thermometer and stuck it in my mouth. As he slipped it under my tongue I briefly found myself hoping for the day when they would just have some kind of head scanners or something they could just point at you instead of putting some only-God-knows-where-this-has-been stick of glass under my tongue. He continued to study my hands, and then extracted the thermometer.

"97.6," he muttered blandly. "Nothing special or unorthodox about that. Let me have a look inside your eyes and ears for a sec, there, Mr. Roland."

"Bishop." I complied, letting him stare deep inside my soul, perhaps searching for some oddly giddy lightning ball dancing around in there just longing to escape out of its human incarceration.

Incarceration – that reminded me, I needed to go visit Dr. Penny. I glanced at my watch. 11:15am. Visiting hours start at noon today.

"Got somewhere you need to be?" he asked.

"Yes- well, no, just…curious," I stumbled, still not ready to let on that I was going to see my incarcerated counselor.

"Yes-well-no. Hmm. Seems that lightning may have affected some motor skills with regards to decision making," he joked.

I gave him the stink-eye. It didn't do anything.

Dr. Walker laughed and sloughed it off. "Relax. I'm just teasing, Roland. Your ears and your eyes look good, are you still taking your benzodiazepine?"

I nodded. "Yep."

"Okay. Might want to talk with your shrink – sorry, I owe my wife a quarter; I'm not supposed to call them that anymore – might want to talk to them about upping your dosage slightly. The only thing I think might really be working on you is some increased anxiety. This sounds like a byproduct of that, and if it's having physical manifestations as you say, a higher dosage working to calm you might counter that."

I shrugged and slightly shook my head. "Okay, fine."

He smiled. "By the way, speaking of shrink – there's 50 cents now – did you get a load of that woman who offed her husband a few nights ago in Jersey? Freakish. She was a psychiatrist, no less," he said, turning away from me and staring at his computer to tap in an update about my condition, presumably.

I swallowed hard. "Yeah, I heard about that."

"Just goes to show you that they don't know everything. *Physician, heal thyself!* Right?"

"Right," I tacitly agreed, wanting to get out of there as he had just subtly insulted one whom I now considered a friend.

"Anyway. I'll update your chart here. I think you're doing fine. My job is to make sure there are no lingering physical manifestations of that lightning strike, and to make sure you're working properly. Everything looks okay from my vantage point."

I almost gasped. *Physician, heal thyself*, I directed at him in my mind. "Nope! All good here, doc. No lingering physical manifestations except for electrocuting other humans. That sure sounds like I'm working properly, wouldn't you say?"

"Well, that aside," he uttered.

"Right," I sneered, looking away.

"Check in with Judy on your way out and she'll schedule you for your next follow-up. Next I have available is the 19th. Mmkay?"

"Alright, doc," I reluctantly agreed.

"How's the chow?" I asked her.

"Oh, certainly nothing to call home about. Has Roxanne Byers called you yet?"

"Who?"

"The *detective*, Roland. The detective I mentioned that I would call on your behalf."

"Oh!" I exclaimed, recognizing the name. "No, not yet. I'm sure she's busy. It's fine."

"Well, she will, I assure you. She was not happy with what I had done of course, but she's busy enough. And, as there was nothing to 'detect' in my case, that lightened her load. So, her schedule should allow a call sometime soon, I should think," said Dr. Penny.

I nodded, pressing the intercom phone up to my ear as I looked at her. Her mood and countenance had improved and lifted, respectively. She was adapting to her new surroundings, 'keeping her sunny disposition' as it were, and for that, I was glad. My brother was in prison back home in Seattle, and we hardly ever spoke. He was a changed man: prison had hardened him. But so had the murder he had committed. Maybe prison would harden Penny as it had Burt.

She was of course headed for prison; there's no way she'd get a light sentence and stay here in jail unless they won some kind of crazy battered-wife-syndrome act-of-passion case that had the jury falling over in the aisles. She would end up there. That would make *two* people in my life doing serious time. But for now, she looked lighter, and her shoulders weren't as hunched as last night. She was accepting the reality of her new predicament.

She smiled at me, lifting her eyebrows. "Anything new since yesterday?"

"You wouldn't even believe me if I told you."

Her head tilted. "Oh?"

I shook my head and let out a steam of air. "Let's just say I've had more than my fill of murders lately." At that, she flinched somewhat, her eyes widening, as if she was uncertain about the gravity of her own crime. "I-I don't mean that, Dr. Penny. I just-" I stammered, "I had another vision last night. While I was at home. I was going to go out and get some fresh air, and…"

"And what?" she said, eagerly. "Another vision of a tragedy?"

I nodded.

"My neighbors. A man and wife. Fighting. Oh, there was lots of noise, big commotion, yelling, doors slamming, and then he left. All the while I could *feel* them through the wall. I knew what he was going to do. I saw the visions."

"And what? What, Roland? Did you stop it?"

I looked at her. "I stopped it," I conceded.

Her face lit up. "Roland! This is *wonderful news!* What a development! Tell me more, did you go over there? What *precisely* happened in your vision?" I tried to start answering. "Did you find out that he was going to do it exactly as you foresaw?" I tried once again, my mouth clicking shut as she continued. "Did you tell her what you saw? And she believed you? Tell me!!"

I broke into wild uncontrollable laughter, and it felt good, I must say. "Which question do I answer first?" I jested.

"Now, stop that. I'm very eager to hear what transpired," she said, practically lifting off her seat and panting. "You did it, Roland!"

I calmed myself and took a deep breath. "Yeah, I did it." And then, I recounted for her the visions of the Home Depot receipt, the knife, his angry face, the stabbing, Joe-Joe, all of it. I told her what I said when I went over there, and walked her through Renita's surprise and acceptance. I shared with her what happened when Jake came over and burst into my apartment looking for them. How I grabbed his arm and it burst into flame. The roar from my soul.

"*Incredible.* Simply incredible. You are one daft individual, taking him on, do you know?"

I chuckled. "Yeah. But apparently he was just as shocked as I was – literally. I don't even know how I did it, Penny. Oh, sorry – *Doctor* Penny."

She clicked her tongue. "Tut-tut. Stop that. Penny is fine," she said, her chin resting on the fingers of her left hand.

"Very well then, Penny," I said, still laughing and sporting my best English accent.

"Now, now, *that* is *not* fine," she corrected me with a stern look.

"Sorry," I gulped, stifling a laugh. "Okay."

She regained her composure. "Oh, Roland," she said. "How extraordinary. Let me see your hand please. Hold it up to the window." I did so, and she examined it up and down. "How…extraordinary. What did it feel like?"

I didn't actually know the answer to that. Everything had happened so fast. "I don't know, Doc- uh, *Penny,* it just, all of it happened so fast. I just wanted to grab his arm to stop him, to defend myself, and then, it just shot out of me."

"Sounds like irrepressible emotions manifesting into physical symptoms. Much like *Firestarter.*"

"Firestarter?"

She gawked at me and leaned back. "Roland Bishop. Are you not a weatherman, and have you never seen the movie *Firestarter*?"

"I guess not."

"Amazing movie. Movies today are rubbish. Too much fluff. That one had a lot of heart. It was originally a book by Stephen King, you know. Remarkable bloke, and a cheeky author to boot."

"Cheeky, huh? Okay."

"Indeed. Anyway, the main protagonist is a little girl named Charlie. Last name, 'McGee' I think, if memory serves. She was endowed with special powers. I know that sounds a bit dodgy, but there was science that started it all. And Roland, do you know, whenever she would lose control emotionally, she could project fire onto whatever object of scorn she directed it at. Rage," -here she waved her arms about- "consumed her, and that little girl could suddenly make an entire building explode into flame. She could make people spontaneously combust, you know. All because of her emotions at play."

I stared hard at Penny. "Okay. Right. Sounds intriguing. Are you saying that I was overly emotional last night and that's how I fried Jake before the cops shot him?"

She clenched her lip and shrugged her shoulders. "It's certainly conceivable. How else do you explain it? I would look to Occam's Razor."

That one I knew, and I nodded. "All things considered, the simplest explanation tends to be the right one. So now I'm a superhero."

Now it was her turn for wild, raucous laughter. "Oh, codswallop, Roland. Your head needs to be tightened back on, my friend."

I let her simmer down while I watched her, laughing. It was surreal yet welcome, watching her. She was my senior by a few decades, but here she appeared as jovial as a child. This newfound freedom allowed her to jest, to relax, to let her hair down, and to fully be herself. It was truly refreshing to see, given her circumstance.

Here she was, facing even perhaps the death penalty for what she did – who knows? – and yet she laughed in the face of circumstance. My situation helped her do that. I brought her a fresh dose of lightness. Maybe I truly was a superhero after all.

If only Jenette could see that.

"Well," she said at last, "whatever it is, I think you're now far more gifted than I had at first suspected." And then she calmed, as if sensing some greater gravity descending upon us. "And now you must find a way to control it. That's where I slipped, Roland. I did not grasp my own power over Mr. Eggers. I used what power I had to destroy him. I'm certainly not saying that's what you did with your neighbor, Jake. Not in the slightest. But what you did is astonishing, Roland, and this is yet another gift you've been imparted."

She looked at me, trying to convince me, trying to play the part of the counselor from the other side of this glass, but I was stuck on something she said earlier. About her husband.

"What was his name, anyway?"

"Who?"

"Your husband."

She paused, perhaps reticent to in any way resurrect him through the invocation of his name. The color slightly drained from her face. Her brightness faded to gloom.

"Geoffrey."

I wasn't sure I wanted to ask the question, but I did it anyway. "Do you miss him at all?"

"Oh, bollocks," she blared. "Hell, no. Certainly, not. Do I miss what we *used* to have before the nine-year mark? Perhaps. You might say I miss the *old* Geoffrey. But I'm certainly not ready to ruminate on any of that yet, Roland," she said.

Dr. Penny lost her composure, and a tear trickled out of her eye, trying to make its downward slide. She briskly wiped it aside. The pain was definitely there. I thought of the best thing I could possibly say.

"I think somebody has permission to turn their willingness dial back up now."

Penny looked at me thoughtfully, and then crinkles began to appear at the corners of her eyes as her lips slowly spread into a smile. "Yes, I do believe you're right. I can receive again, can't I?"

"Of course you can, Penny. We can do it together."

My counselor sat there and just let me appreciate her as we thought about all that had transpired over the past few days. I'm sure this was a breath of fresh air for her, and a much-needed one.

"We can do it together. Thank you, Roland."

I smiled at her.

And then I felt something for Penny – something very maternal and binding. Something I had missed from my own mother, aloof and dictatorial, who had never let me be right and never let me fly. I had a troubled relationship with her, and my brother did as well, obviously: it had landed him in prison. After all, Burt had killed my mother, and he was never getting out. My dad had run off when I was three, so he wasn't even in the corner of my mind.

But sitting here, with Dr. Penny – now, just *Penny* – I felt kind of like I had not just a mother, but a *mom*. Headed to prison, for sure, but a new mom nonetheless.

I had the strangest clarity about all of it.

18 Days To Go

August 24th, 2001 • Jersey City, NJ

It was her.

Jenette. She was calling me back, finally.

"Hon! Good grief…where are you? How are you?" I said, snatching up my phone and speaking right away. I was lying in bed, ready to take on another day, wondering what I should do, and hoping for a call from Detective Roxanne, actually. This call, however, was so much more needed.

She stopped me. "Roland, listen, I'm sorry I haven't called. I've just needed time to think. To really think, ya know? I heard about what happened, but I only heard about it five days ago."

"The lightning strike?"

"Yeah. Amanda told me. I'm sorry. I'm glad you're okay, truthfully. She didn't want me to get all worked up, and she was just protecting me. Don't be mad at her."

"Mad? I'm- I just-," I faltered. "What? Honey, I don't care about Amanda or what she's doing or any of that. I care about *you*. Where are you, and where are *we*?"

Silence. And then a long, drawn out exhale.

"I don't know, Roland. You tell me. Where are we?"

"Jenette, you know where I am. I want you back, and I just want you to be hap-"

"No, I mean, *where are we?*"

I stopped in my tracks. "I don't understand. I thought I was answering your question." I sat up, running my hands through my messy bedhead.

"I mean, *where are we*?" She repeated. "We're still in New Jersey. I hate it here, Roland. I've told you that. I still do. I don't want to be here anymore. So, I've made a decision."

"What's your decision?" I asked in a monotone voice, growing weary with the one-sided conversation.

"I'm going back to Seattle. I- I love you, Roland. I do. But this, this upheaval, this move…I wanted it to work, okay? I did! But it hasn't. I know it's worked for you, and that's great. I'm happy for you. I am. But it hasn't for me, and I no longer want it to."

"You no longer want New Jersey to work, or you no longer want *me* to work?"

She sighed again. "You know what I mean."

"No, actually, I don't, Jenette. Why don't you tell me?" Now I was standing up, walking around in nothing but my boxers. The bright sunlight streamed through the window, and I closed the blinds as people were strolling by outside.

"I think you just said it. You called me 'Jenette.' You never call me by my name."

"What do you mean? I called you 'hon' at the beginning of the call! You haven't called me that once in our call. So, who's not wanting this relationship to work?"

"I just- ugh! This is not what I wanted for us. This is not where I wanted this conversation to go. I should just hang up. I just wanted-"

"Wanted *what?*"

Awkward pause. "I wanted to say goodbye."

And then she hung up. And, well, that was her saying goodbye. My phone-holding hand dropped to my side, and I clicked the end button.

And then I threw my little Nokia against the wall. Luckily for it, it survived. I wasn't so lucky, because I felt shattered inside, as things were shattering around me.

There was a knock at the door. Thankfully, it hadn't come while I was showering. I hated missing visitors. The doldrums of this waiting period were starting to wear upon me. I felt like I needed to get back to work, but that long, exhaustion-defeating shower felt good.

I went to the front door and opened it.

"Renita, hi!" I said, greeting her with wide eyes. "You wanna come in?"

"No, no, I can't," she said, balancing Joe-Joe on one hip. The brisk morning air filtered in behind her, and she was dressed more for fall or winter than summer. "I just wanted to pop by and ask how you were doing. I stopped by yesterday but I missed you."

"Oh, I'm fine, yeah…sorry. I went to the doctor for a follow-up for the nosebleeds and all that."

"From the lightning strike?"

"From the lightning strike." Joe-joe giggled for some reason. I looked at him and smiled.

"Well, I've got to pay a visit to the coroner today."

"Oh. Yikes," I said, grimacing. "Fun times. Do you need me to go with you?"

"No, I'm good, thanks. Just gotta do the duty and get his clothes and all that."

I nodded. Awkward.

"Anyway, doctor said you're okay? Everything okay?" she asked, biting her lip.

I gathered some air into my lungs, breathing out an uncertain *Yeah!* "Yeah, I think so. I mean, first time I've ever electrocuted somebody. I'm just glad the cops finished him off, and not me."

Insert foot in mouth, you idiot.

Her face contorted into a scrunched mess. Jake was her husband, after all.

"I-oh man- sorry, I didn't mean-"

She shook her head and closed her eyes. "No, no, it's fine. I understand," she said, tilting a shoulder as Joe-Joe tugged on some free strands of her hair under her knit hat. "Anyway, just thought I'd check in."

"No, yeah, thank you…I…appreciate it. And hey, if there's anything I can do, or if you wanna get together for some coffee or something sometime, I'm here. Here's my number." I handed her my business card with my mobile number *201-555-1818* on it.

"I'd like that," she said, and she meant it. And then she heaved a big sigh and clenched her lip. "I want to tell you thank you, Roland."

"Thank you? For what?"

"You saved my life. I believe your story. I believe what happened to you. I wanted to tell you thank you for saving Joe-Joe's and my life." She looked around awkwardly.

I just stared at her for a moment. Had I really done that? Is that what warning someone of impending doom means, that I saved their life? In this case, it most certainly did. Jake was clearly coming home to murder her.

"You're…welcome," I answered, slowly accepting the reality of it. "I just, hey, I'm happy that I could be there. Happy I was here to hear the commotion and to try to, I don't know, intervene somehow."

"Well, you did, and I'm grateful. Thank you again."

"You're welcome, Renita. You too, Joe-Joe!" Her little boy looked at me in recognition, and then smiled and turned away sheepishly, burying his face shyly against his mama's shoulder.

"Well, let me know if I can do anything for you."

"Will do. Have you heard from Jenette?"

"Uh, yeah, we, uh, spoke this morning."

"Eek. That bad, huh?"

I stopped, words failing me for a moment in the back of my throat. "Oh hell. Everything's, uh, gonna work out just fine, I think. Eventually."

Renita smiled at me.

"Well, I've gotta get going…got a full day of errands. No rest for the weary, right?" I laughed. "Be sure and keep your sunny disposition," I said, employing my tagline to try to elicit some laughter.

"Ha! Alright. Sounds good," she said, turning away with a smile. "Bye, Roland."

"Bye, Renita. Take care Joe-Joe!" Joe-Joe waved at me shyly, his head still buried in his mama's shoulder.

I closed the door behind me and sighed, leaning against it. There was a reason I was supposed to be here the day they were arguing. There was definitely a reason I needed to be here in order to avert that murder.

It was Renita.

15 Days To Go

August 27th, 2001 • Manhattan, NY

I couldn't take any more of it. I had to get out.

The weekend had passed with extreme boredom, except for cuddling with Winston here and there. I was so surprised that Jenette hadn't taken him with her; he was always more her cat. But he was a snuggle-buddy, and always nice to wake up to.

I got caught up with cleaning the apartment after Jake was killed, and I had to rearrange a few things to purge the lingering sense of tension. It was like a hovering specter in the front room: a looming presence.

I couldn't really walk around in the front room without seeing Jake's body there. It was eerie and disquieting, as if his spirit somehow lingered: a foreboding presence hovered in that room. His body was gone, but it was as if the heavy cloud of his felt rage remained.

I left Monday mid-morning at 11:15am, throwing on a light windbreaker over a T-Shirt, jeans and sneakers. I figured I could just stalk Manhattan once more on a busy weekday morning, and see what I came up with. Every superhero has an origin story, right?

So here I was, once more in the Big Apple. I didn't think I had a prayer in the world of finding that man, but I figured the PATH Station would be the best place to hang out and people-watch.

I'd done so much passage through here over the past few years; I never thought I'd be *loitering* in here one day, intentionally searching for someone, much less searching for a killer.

I knew he was a killer. Everything in me told he was going to commit a hijacking. Either he or the other man with him was. Or, maybe both of them? But I never saw the other man's face.

Jenette passed briefly through my mind, and I wondered if she was leaving today. No sense calling her. Her calling me 'Roland' and not 'hon,' us continuing to argue, her perpetual dislike for New Jersey, my throwing the phone: all of it communicated *we were through*. And the worst part of it was that I didn't feel bad about the fact that I didn't feel bad. That said much more than everything else combined.

I took the same perch that I had before, leaning against a concrete column midway through.

People ambled by, on their way to who knows where.

Young and old, business and casual, rich and poor, it didn't matter. Everyone met at PATH Station. All walks of life passed through this place, getting to where people needed to go.

Sooner or later, I would find him, I assured myself. Sooner or later I would see that familiar fa-

A shudder passed swiftly through me. A quick flinch, a brief spasm, and my head throbbed. I looked around, quickly. I had only been here for 15 minutes, but the truth slapped me coldly. *Someone else was here.*

I glanced around in all directions, frantic. I started to sniffle. The inevitable and unmistakable first sign of a nosebleed. Here it came. And then the hot flashes once more. Here they came. Suddenly I was bending over myself and clutching my stomach.

That first one felt more powerful than any other first had felt. A pang wracked my body, and this time it felt like a wave of nausea. And then I saw him.

Not the middle-Eastern man I had been looking for. No…through the halls of my mind a vision flitted of a mid-twenties man in a blue Mets baseball cap and grungy clothes. He had a grim, determined look about him.

White flashes.

Someone beating someone soundly. Pummeling them. *Flash!* Fists flying high, sailing through the air, crashing down on someone's skull, neck and back. *Flash!* A face flew out of view, too quickly for me to see who it was.

And just as quickly, the nosebleed came. Only, this time, it was thicker. I extracted my handkerchief from my pocket and held it up to my nose.

And then I saw him. There he was! Up ahead, heading up the stairs and outside. He was following someone.

My heart thudded within me. I did the only thing I could do. I followed him. I had to follow him! Despite Penny's advice to the contrary, I had to follow him. I had these abilities, and they weren't given to me for nothing.

My head swam, and I nearly collapsed, but I willed myself to stay up. To stay here.

I was at PATH Station. That's where I was. And I knew all too well who I was and what I had to do.

I'm Roland Bishop, and I know where I am, I repeated. *I'm Roland Bishop, and I know where I am.*

I followed them.

And then my phone rang suddenly. I quickly extracted it, not daring to look away and lose my target. "Hello?" I asked annoyedly. "Who is this?"

"Hi, is this Roland Bishop?" It was a woman. Whoever she was, she had a heavy giveaway Bronx accent.

"Yes it is, who is this?" I asked, panting.

"This is Detective Roxanne Byers. Your name and number were given to me by Dr. Penelope Eggers," she said, and then she paused. "Are you alright?"

"Yes, well, no, not exactly, Detective. Now's not a good time. I'm sort of in the middle of a situation."

"A situation? Are you okay?" she asked curiously.

"Did Dr. Penny tell you a bit about what I'm going through?"

"Yes, she did. A little."

"Yeah, well, it's happening again. I'm tailing somebody because I had another vision." I bumped into someone going the other way, trying desperately to keep my eyes on my target.

"Excuse me, you're *tailing* someone did you say? Are you following a perp?" she asked.

"Yes. At least I think so. I have to go now. I'll call you back in a bit, I promise."

"Wait-" she tried, and then I hung up. I couldn't be on the phone right now.

There he was, up ahead. As in my vision, there he was. Scruffy, wearing a blue baseball cap. Everyone was heading somewhere this morning: to work, to business, to see loved ones. This man was heading to a murder. But who was he pursuing? And why?

I tailed him, looking around. At one point I had to catch my breath.

We exited up the stairs and out of the building onto West Broadway heading north to Tribeca. People passed me by. I could tell they were gawking and staring. My nosebleed had stopped. The flashes, the pounding and the blood remained.

Blood. There would be blood, according to that man, I thought. And then, just as swiftly, the thought occurred to me: *not if I can help it.*

He was about thirty feet ahead of me, still heading north. The man was oblivious to me. We continued north, and I could feel the sun on my face washing over me as we passed Park Place and the Tribeca House. Where was he going? I glanced down at my watch. 11:51am. I quickly polished off a drop of nasal blood that had dripped upon it.

I looked back up. *Where did he go?* The man was gone! In the blink-and-you'll-miss-it moment I looked at my watch, I lost him. I frantically looked around through the sea of people out headed to lunch, or wherever they were going.

My phone rang again. I sneered and blew out a frustrated grunt and gust of air as I wrenched my phone from my pocket, my eyes dancing all around to find the mark. I quickly glanced down at the caller ID. Same one. Detective Byers again. I declined the call once more and looked back up, searching.

There he was! He had crossed the street over to the west side, heading toward Murray. His gaze was firmly fixed ahead of him at someone some distance ahead. I couldn't see who it was.

Suddenly, competing images flashed through me and I cried out in pain, clutching my temples. White flashes once more. Hot pulses shot through me. Other signals, mixed with indistinguishable noise and unintelligible signals swamped my vision. I shook my head to clear it out. Thankfully, they passed, but now I had a new problem.

The man had heard my cry – as had everyone else around me, some of whom drifted away from me or averted their path to avoid a homeless weirdo. I didn't look strange, I thought, other than the nosebleed. People are so superficial.

But now the man had glanced back at me and perhaps knew he himself had a tail, though he was tailing someone else. *But who!?*

He resumed his quick pace and hung a right onto Chambers Street. I followed him. By now I was sweating, trying to keep up with the feverish pace of the man. Who was he? Where was he going? Why was he pursuing whomever it was he was hellbent on destroying? Whomever he was tailing was faster than both of us.

I turned the corner onto Chambers, cautiously, and spotted him heading into The Frederick Hotel. For a moment, I thought I caught a glimpse of someone up ahead of him walking briskly inside. And then I noticed the subway stairs in the sidewalk and wondered why they both hadn't just taken that. Maybe neither one of them wanted to be in a crowd of people, or in close quarters. Either way, my target headed into the hotel, and I followed him at a distance.

My phone. One more time. Stupid phone. It was the Detective again. "Mr. Bishop, are you in danger? Please tell me where you are!" she requested calmly yet forcibly.

I grit my teeth. "The Frederick Hotel," I said, and then hit 'end' and walked in.

A voice stole my focus and attention and I jerked to my right.

"Welcome to the Frederick Hotel, can I help you?" asked a concierge at the counter as I walked in. She looked at me strangely as she took note of my handkerchief.

I waved her off with a brisk "no thank you, uh, I'm meeting someone here." She nodded and continued to stare.

I couldn't find them. *Think.* Elevators. Maybe the signals would persist and grow stronger once I got closer; after all, the man in the Mets hat had increased the distance between us. I ran to the elevators. I was going to have to take my chances. Two of them were already in operation, which gave me a 50/50 choice. Both were going up. The south elevator stopped at the third floor. I chose it and pressed the button repeatedly.

Slowly, eventually, it came back down. *Come on, come on, come on*, I thought, wringing my hands together. I glanced back at the female concierge and she quickly averted her eyes. I knew then she had been staring at me virtually the whole time.

The elevator dinged, and then opened. I practically hurled myself in there and pressed the *3* button. All at once a man appeared out of nowhere, wanting to get in. I stuck my hand out, palm outward, and they stopped short and squinted at me. I showed them my handkerchief. That did it. They backed off and put their hands up as if to say, *no blood for me, thanks*. The doors silently closed.

Third floor. I emerged quickly, and scanned up and down the hallway. I was right. Immediately, my head began to throb. I started heading west. No change in the throbbing. My heartbeat quickened, but that was it. I could feel the sweat starting to roll down my neck. I wiped the back of my head with the sleeve of my windbreaker. No flashes, no increased nosebleeds, no further change in my heart rate. I could stand properly.

I reversed direction and began to head east instead, toward the adjacent building.

I knew they were in there somewhere. Not because I started experiencing another nosebleed, or because of a quickened heartrate, or flashes.

The noises alerted me first. Strange, scuffling noises. Thumps. Thuds. Quick breaths. My eyes widened in alarm and I raced down the hall. A door was ajar! Room Number Fifteen, the last suite on the right, was slightly open. I crept in quietly. Immediately white flashes surged through my eyes in intense heat. The room lit up in scorching bluish-white ardor.

There they were! I could dimly make them both out.

The Mets man was on top of the other man, trying to choke him. His possessions were scattered across the floor: car keys, a license, some breath mints. The man's wavy black hair was in disarray as the Mets man pummeled him with one fist and had him in a chokehold with the other.

But why?!

My phone rang yet again, chiming loudly and vibrating against my keys. *Dammit, Detective Byers!*

The Mets man was suddenly aware of me, whipping around and glaring at me threateningly. His face sported a large red bruise. He looked in the very throes of breaking the other man's neck, whose face I couldn't see. It was turned toward the window.

Suddenly, the Mets man loosened his hold on the man's neck, and he fell to the floor, coughing, retching and gagging. The Mets man lunged at me, hurling us both back into the wall. My phone continued to ring. The man on the floor continued to cough.

Everything in me wanted to stop what he was doing. Why had he been pursuing the man on the floor? What the hell was going on?

My thoughts were cut short as I received a punch to the stomach, and then another. Then to the face. That sent me into a rage. Molten lava spilt through me. Suddenly, the words of the good doctor Penelope Eggers rang through my mind: *And now you must find a way to control it. That's where I slipped, Roland.*

Was I slipping? I didn't know. All I knew, lying there with the full weight and anger of the Mets man on top of me, being pummeled left and right, I was getting angrier and angrier. Visions of Penny murdering her husband flew through my mind. Visions of Jenette. Of Renita. Of airplanes being hijacked and passengers screaming. Hot flashes. Searing white behind my eyes.

My stomach tensed. My skin tingled. I erupted.
Firestarter.

And then, suddenly, before I knew what hit me, I was ablaze with fury. I craned my neck to look up at the man on top of me, and I caught and clutched his fist midair as he threw. I squeezed as hard as I could, and his fist burst into blue flame and splintered down to the elbow. With my right I reached up and grabbed his neck, as energy exploded through my limbs.

My vision skewed to blue. Everything around me was on fire in my mind. Bolts of energy coursed through my flesh and exited from my hand, straight into Mets man's neck, and he spasmed and choked with eyes wide. Wicked blue pops as if from erupting circuits sizzled through the air.

Smoke poured from his ears. His head fractured. And then flames. Flames. *Flames.* Bluish flames licked up and consumed him entirely, as he staggered backward and fell to the ground, crying out in agony, moaning, and rubbing his own body all over in a desperate and mad attempt to swat out the flames.

And then, he dropped and lay there, burning. A charred husk of a man, incinerated before my very eyes, went up in black smoke, rising toward the ceiling and choking both of us left in that hotel suite.

My phone continued to ring. I didn't pick it up, but suddenly I heard a different voice, crawling toward me, desperate to evade the blackened fumes swirling around us and enveloping us both as we lay there, panting, recovering.

The voice had an accent. "I don't know who you are, but I thank you with my life," it said. And then I looked over.

Horror coursed through me as my eyes met the eyes of the man who was being assailed. I recognized him.

His thick, wavy chestnut hair.

His pronounced middle-Eastern accent.

His Egyptian face.

His thin, pursed lips.

His solid, clenched jawline.

His beady eyes set under darkly outlined lashes.

I breathed out one word in horror.

"Mohammed," I said, and then screaming white hot flashes overtook my vision. My skin tensed, and my stomach churned. My nose freely bled yet again, streaming down my face. I staunched it with my handkerchief as I jerked away from him in revulsion.

Planes. So many airplanes. Commercial planes taking off for their destinations, and yet any one of them were going to be used in a hijacking. I just knew it. Tremors ran through me and my body quaked, this close to the source of those dangerous and terrifying visions.

And the number *fifteen*.

He looked at me in confusion. "What is wrong? I am thanking you for saving my life, sir," he sputtered amidst choking coughs. And then he reached out his hand to me.

Before I knew it, I was out of there, sprinting down the hall, ripping off my windbreaker and stuffing it into a garbage can, hurling myself violently into a stairwell. I raced out the back entrance and set off the door alarm, throwing myself down Chambers Street toward God knows where. I just had to get away.

That was the man! That was my target! What had so seized me that I had to flee?

I had just killed a man.

This man, Mohammed, was undoubtedly going to kill others. Yet I had just done what he was going to do.

Mohammed.

I screamed east, not knowing where to go. Before I knew it I was at City Hall Park, panting and hiding under the trees. My phone wouldn't stop ringing.

I couldn't stay in that hotel. I couldn't be near him. He was a terrorist. A freaking *terrorist!* And I had just saved his life! I had just enabled him to continue in his atrocity!

Penny would have a thing or two to say about this. So would the detective, and perhaps many others.

I couldn't take any more of it. I had to get out.

14 Days To Go

August 28th, 2001 • Jersey City, NJ

There had been too much in this day for me.

It was the dead of night when I returned home. I checked the clock. 12:14am.

I couldn't stay here, that much was certain. I didn't know if they had any cameras in that hotel or in the periphery, but it was a foregone conclusion that they did. Somewhere, at least. I just tried to stay in crowds and make myself less conspicuous.

Thoughts screamed through my head. One stood out from the rest.

I was now a fugitive! I had just killed a man. Out of this new uncontrollable power, this freaking 'gift,' as Penny called it!

And what was that number *fifteen* from yesterday? What was that? Now, for some strange reason, I was seeing, dimly in my mind, the number *fourteen*. Fifteen, and then fourteen? Was it some kind of code? Was it one minus the other? One plus the other? What did it all mean? I had no idea.

I was panting, and reeked of body odor. My body was tired, tired, *tired.* Sweat adhered my clothes to me, and I was chilled from the night air and hiding.

I wanted to stay away from the PATH Station, from the subways…anything. I had finally made my way back to the Holland Tunnel entrance and hitched a ride from someone who finally took me in and dropped me off close to home.

It was the weirdest feeling, walking back at night. I was caught in a tempest of desire for answers and a toxic brew of self-recrimination and scorn. *I had just killed a man!* I couldn't shake the guilt nor the memory. I didn't know who he was. But he was trying to kill Mohammed.

Maybe I should have let him. That thought passed through me like a fiery and wistful surge. He must have known about Mohammed too, right? Why else would he try to kill him? So many questions.

When I had walked to the Holland Tunnel just a few hours before, the twin towers soared into the sky overhead. I had stopped and drank in the view. They were like bastions of strength: soaring high like two twin sentinels, guarding America against the east. Briefly I remembered the

1993 parking garage bombing we'd heard about. We weren't in New Jersey at that time. But ever since we moved to Jersey, we could look out our apartment window over the Hudson and see these towers standing there, strong, tall, defiant against that attempt, and still watching over all of us there and here. They glimmered and glistened to their very crowns, and conveyed strength to me last night as I passed under their shadows, and now once more as I stared at them across the Hudson.

Be strong, Roland. Just like them.

Now I was home. I plopped myself down on my couch to just think, and to collect myself. At any moment I expected the NJPD or NYPD to burst in with guns drawn. They'd already been here once recently for Jake.

Jake. I stared down to where he had collapsed on my floor after the police took him down.

That detective had to know. She tried to call me, I'm sure, but I turned off my phone somewhere at City Hall Park. I didn't know if Penny had given her my last name or my address, or that I worked for News 12, but she was going to find me. I couldn't stay here.

A sudden urgency took hold of me, and I turned on the midnight news to see if there were any reports. Of course there would be, but I just couldn't stay here to see them. I switched it off. I needed sleep so very badly.

Scouring the apartment, I searched for whatever I needed for a life on the run. I was essentially already a fugitive. Good thing I hadn't taken my bike into New York yesterday or I would have left it at the hotel. Just another thing to identify me by.

Even now my mind raced.

I wondered what cameras I may have appeared on, or who may have spotted me. What news reels may have shown a man in a white t-shirt and jeans fleeing the crime scene. Whether anyone found my windbreaker. I laid my head back on the couch and ran my hands through my wet, sweaty hair.

I needed a shower. I had to at least manage that.

The shower done, I was cleaned and refreshed with a second wind. I quickly dressed and grabbed my things, glancing at the clock. It was now 1:14am on Tuesday morning. I had no idea where I was going to go, but I just needed to get to a motel or something…anything to get away from here. Dare I even bring my phone? I was scared to turn it on. Couldn't they track things like that?

I reached for some quarters. I could call my voicemail from a payphone at the very least, and see what messages might have been left for me.

Stealthily, I made my way down the path with my bike. I thought, if there's anywhere I could go, perhaps I could just ride it out and wait for the morning off of Hudson River Waterfront Parkway. There were a few coffee shops there, perhaps even one of the new Starbucks, and I wasn't sure if any of them were 24/7, but I could try. Or a 7/11 or something. *Man, I need sleep,* I groaned to myself.

In ten minutes I had biked to the waterfront. It was chilly out, and passersby were sparse. I was wary: on the lookout for the cops, on the lookout for hooligans, on the lookout for anyone and everyone.

I didn't want any white flashes, any nosebleeds, any episodes….any *anything*. I hated this gift right now, because it just wasn't that: *a gift.* I reviled what it was doing to me. It was actually a curse, and now that curse had enabled me to do something horrific. I knew Mohammed's name; I had no idea the name of the man whom I had killed. He was now nameless and faceless except for his Mets cap.

I could still see Mohammed's face, lying there on the floor and crawling eerily toward me. His thick accent echoed in my mind. I could practically smell the burning flesh of the Mets man, crying out in horror as his skin went up in smoke only feet from me. I still felt the wind racing against me as I fled from The Frederick.

There was a payphone on Sussex Street right before the Paulus Hook Pier. Dismounting my bike, I chained it up to a bike hoop and figured I'd walk for a bit. The Twin Towers twinkled from across the Hudson as I looked out, and it was breezy.

I dialed my own number and entered the pin. "You have - *fourteen* - new messages," the automated greeting said. I rolled my eyes and sighed. Fourteen, in the span of a few hours.

I stopped, wide-eyed. *Fourteen.* The number fourteen. What did that mean? I had seen that in my mind's eye this morning. What did it mean? I tried to parse through it but I wasn't coming up with anything.

Back to the voicemail.

The first was from Jenette, who had called me and had forgotten to hang up. I could hear her chattering, faintly, in the background with Amanda. The next few were that pre-recorded greeting from the Jersey City Jail. Penny had tried to call me.

And then the fourth call. There she was. Detective Roxanne Byers. It was during the assault yesterday when I didn't pick up. I could hear her curse into the recording when I didn't answer. Finally, she left a full message for me at 6:02pm last night.

Mr. Bishop, this is Detective Roxanne Byers. Her voice sounded hushed. *I'm looking for you. You need to meet with me. I know about the Frederick Hotel, Roland. I know what happened to the man you were following. It is in your best interest to call me right away at this number. I don't care what time it is. You need to call me. Please. Thank you.*

The voicemail ended. No mention of "turn yourself in" or "we're coming to get you?" It didn't sound nefarious. It sounded secretive. Could she know? Would she understand somehow? I warred with myself, struggling between suspecting entrapment and two choices: avoid her entirely and throw my Nokia into the Hudson, or trust her.

Wasn't that the right thing to do? Shouldn't I turn myself in? Shouldn't I trust her? Running just made me look guilty. She knew anyway. I wasn't going to get far, and I was incredulous that I was even still free.

And then a third choice presented itself to me.

Penny. I had to go see Penny. With everything that was in me, I had to ride this out and go see Penny as soon as humanly possible, perhaps one last time.

My skin crawled, suddenly. I felt someone watching me. In a reflex, I whirled around. On the other side of the street, a short, middle-aged Latino woman was standing there, watching me. She had thin black bifocals on, and was dressed in a red knit coat and a scarf.

"Kind of late to be out and about, isn't it?" Her eyes glinted at me suspiciously, but with a kindly, knowing smile. "Or…perhaps kind of early?"

"Right," I said, dismissively, in no mood to engage anyone. I glanced around, awkwardly.

"You look like you're running on vapors."

"Is that a fact?" I grunted. "And what does 'running on vapors look like, exactly?"

She chuckled, and didn't answer me. "I'm up here with my mother for a symposium. Couldn't sleep. My mother is in medical school down in Nashville. I'm considering it as well, and we thought we'd take a trip up to Manhattan together to see The Big Apple," she said cheerily, walking toward me, slowly, her hands in her pocket.

"Oh? Sounds interesting," I said, watching her curiously. "Your mother must be starting medical school late."

"She is. I'm thirty-six, almost thirty-seven. She's sixty-one. Never too old to make a change for the future, though, right?" She had drawn near to me and now eyed me curiously on the sidewalk.

I stared at her for a moment, assessing what she might want from me. "What can I do for you, ma'am?" I asked her, tentatively.

She smiled, graciously. "Oh, nothing. Just making chit-chat. You looked lonely and disheveled. You looked like you are running from something."

"Maybe I am, and maybe I'm not."

"Maybe you *are,*" she insisted. "But wherever you're running from or to, make sure and breathe." She looked out over the Hudson. "Peaceful, isn't it?"

I looked with her. "Yes, definitely."

The middle-aged woman turned back to me.

"I'm Roland. And you are?" I asked her, curiously.

"Rosie," she greeted me with a smile. "Well, look at that. Two 'Ro's' out for an early morning stroll. Except only one of us is running from something."

"I didn't say-"

"You didn't have to, kiddo." And she eyed me curiously. "I could tell from your body language and how you reacted to listening to your own voice mails."

"You're that perceptive, are you?" I said, suspiciously.

She hmmed and hawed it away. "Maybe. That's why I'm not sure about medicine. Something greater has always called me. Something not of this world."

I raised my eyebrows. I was sure I was dealing with a whack-job now. "Oh?"

"Yep," she said, sighing. "I'm a Christian. I serve God in Heaven. I'm just not sure if I'm supposed to serve Him in medicine, or, just in being where people need me."

"And is that what you think you're doing now? Being where people need you."

She smiled at me with a knowing smile, but didn't answer right away. "Maybe," she said at last. "I don't find the people. The people just seem to find me. It's nicer that way. Less pressure." She smiled and cocked her head at me through her bifocals.

I gave her an inevitable smile. "And did I find you tonight?"

"I don't know what you found, nor why. I just try to be where people who are in need….are."

I looked her up and down. "Well," I said at last, "sounds like you've found your calling. I really have to be on my way. It was nice meeting you."

"Somewhere you need to be at 1:30 in the morning?" Her question was loaded with sarcasm.

I chuckled. "Well, not really, but-"

She was ready to interrupt me. "My advice to you, though you haven't asked – and that's fine – is to stop running. Stop hiding. One day, something even bigger than what you're currently running from will come. And how you deal with this will determine how you deal with that."

I furrowed my brows, confused at the unanticipated advice from this unexpected stranger. "You sound like my psychiatrist. You wouldn't happen to know a Dr. Penny, would you?"

She shook her head. "I know only those the Father sends my way. And for some reason, this morning, here, He sent you. And that's what I'm supposed to say to you. Stop running, Roland." Her eyes twinkled in the night.

I didn't know what to say, but I gathered air into my lungs, stared down at her, and sighed. "Okay. Sounds good." I wasn't entirely sure if I meant that to get rid of her, or if I believed it. But it seemed to be enough for her.

"Okay. I wish you luck, Roland." And with that, she turned to walk away.

"Uh, yeah…good luck, uh…"

"Rosie," she said, over her shoulder.

I walked that waterfront back and forth for a few hours, wondering what to do, and pondering Rosie's words. Such a complete stranger, but I wondered if fate truly had her in store. She seemed wise beyond her years, and maternally sweet, just like Penny.

But my legs felt thick and my indecision weighed a ton.

My life was in limbo, and all I could do was stare helplessly out over the Hudson and watch the river flow by. That's all my life was doing now: my old life flowing by on the tides of time, off to somewhere else while I was stuck here in flux. I quickly grew tired of checking my watch, and stopped altogether. That allowed me a bit of surprise joy as I finally saw the first light of the rising sun spring up over Manhattan.

I found a coffee shop that opened at 7am. Visiting hours for Penny's block started at 10am today. I biked up to Grove and 7th and parked my bike. I was taking a bit of a risk, I figured, but I had to see her. She had to know, and I needed to know what to do.

As I pulled up, I noticed the baseball diamond across the street. I had seen it before, of course, but something had changed, or, at least I had changed and was now seeing it differently. There were kids playing on it, and their laughter brought an innocence to my ears and my soul that I think I needed. Once you've killed someone, and had someone killed in front of you, life sort of…changes.

I was inordinately tired, but I gathered myself together and took a deep, cleansing sigh before walking up to visitation.

Before long, I was seated there, and here came Penny once more. She practically ran to her little booth and snatched up her intercom.

"Tell me it isn't true," she said, leaning forward close to the glass that separated us.

I didn't reply. I didn't know what to say.

"Roland!" she whispered. "Tell me. Did it happen?"

"Penny, I-," I tried to play dumb. "I don't know what you mean."

"Oh, bollocks, Roland. You know perfectly well what I mean." And then she looked around her and up at the Guard behind me. "The Frederick," she whispered, and I tensed up. "The Frederick Hotel. Detective Byers visited me and told me. Did you?"

I suddenly lost all composure and felt the wind sucked out of me. A sigh forced its way out of my lungs and I shook my head mournfully. "Penny, I- I don't know what happened. It was all a blur."

"Was it the same way that it happened with your neighbor? The blue fire? The burns?"

I nodded.

"Only this time, you-"

I clenched my lip and just stared at her. "Is there room for one more in there?"

"Nonsense, Roland. It was an accident. Mine was intentional. You know that quite well. Detective Byers is a good woman. Has she tried to contact you?"

"Yes, many times. I turned my phone off."

"Whatever for?" she asked, her eyes widening, her face pressing further toward the glass.

"I don't know, Penny! Look!" I said, growing frantic and trying to keep my voice down. "I don't know what to do! If you saw what I did, your mind would be totally blown!"

"Listen to me, Roland Bishop," she hissed through her teeth. "I want you to go down and call Detective Byers back straightaway. Straightaway! You just might regret it if you don't, and it sounds like you really need an ally right now. Running only makes you look guilty."

I blew out hard air. "Tell me about it. I told myself the same thing."

"Well then?"

"Well then what? Penny," I said, lowering my voice even further, "they'll take me into custody right away. That man was trying to kill another man, and I stopped him!"

Her nose crinkled at the bridge. "What other man?"

"The man *he* was tailing."

"Wait – slow down," she said. "The man you tailed was not the one you told me about a few days ago, the one you saw in your vision with the planes?"

"No! It was someone completely different!"

"Oh dear."

"Yeah, *oh dear* is right! This new guy – he was wearing grungy clothes and a Mets cap – he was following someone, and that *someone* turned out to be the middle Eastern man I saw in my vision. Mohammed. But before I could get to Mohammed, the Mets cap guy had him in a chokehold on the ground in a room at The Frederick, and I got in and tried to prevent it, because I saw *his* attack in a vision too!"

"This is getting *decidedly* more complicated by the moment. So if I understand you correctly, you received a new vision for a new assailant – Mr. Mets Man – and you tailed him while *he* was tailing Mohammed to The Frederick."

I nodded.

"I wonder why he was tailing Mohammed just as you were previously."

"Exactly."

She paused for a moment, thinking.

"It doesn't matter."

"Pen-"

She stopped me. "Tut-tut!" she said, putting up a finger. "It's minutiae at this point. Insignificant for the moment. For now, your only concern is to contact Detective Byers at once. Is that clear?" She looked at me scoldingly.

I shook my head, incredulous. "I guess so. I mean, it sounds like I don't have any other option."

"You don't. Unless you want to fill your days tailing people who are tailing people. Sounds like everyone is tailing everyone out there while I'm eating shit on a shingle."

I stopped a guffaw. "What is that?"

"Deplorable breakfast food. Don't ask! What I wouldn't give for a biscuit."

I smiled at her through my frustration.

"Alright, I'll call her. Do *you* need anything?"

She looked at me sternly. "I need my clients to follow my directions. I didn't pay nearly a half-hundred-thousand dollars on a degree so that I could yip useless advice at passersby, Roland. Hmmph!" She clicked her tongue and looked away in what she would call a 'snit.'

I had to let out a chortle. "You know, you really are British, aren't you?" It wasn't a question.

"Irretrievably," she said, whipping her head back to me. "Now go call her, Roland. For your own good."

"Ya know, you've gotten pretty uppity since you've been in there."

"Just wait until I'm back out. We'll see how uppity I've become."

She shook her head, but I could see a trace of a smile in there wanting to jump out at me. And then she softened.

"Just look at us," she said. "My, how the tables have turned in just seventy-two hours. It used to be just me on this side of the glass. Now it might be you as well."

Her observation elicited a thick sigh on my part, looking at her, pressing that intercom up against my ear. "Can't believe it."

"Nor can I, Roland. But what matters now is *now*. What do you do with *now*?"

It was a good question. I knew exactly what I needed to do. Or, at least I knew what I needed to do to not get *tut-tutted* again.

My phone was still around sixty percent at least, so that was something.

It was now turned back on, and my fingers hovered over the *1* button to call my voicemail. I listened to her number again and noted it down, taking a deep breath. There would be no going back once I made this call.

I dialed her number into my phone but didn't hit 'send' just yet. I stared down at my little red Nokia, knowing full well the ramifications of calling her. It stared back at me apathetically, emotionless, with zero regard to what I had been through nor what I might go through after this.

Point of no return. My legs were trembling. My arm was spasming slightly. I made sure to stand close to my bike in case I needed to race out of there.

I pressed th-

My phone rang! My arm jerked back and my body quaked in surprise. Everything in me tensed up.

Reflexively, I accidentally hit 'answer.' I cursed in frustration, the phone at my side, but then slowly brought it to my ear.

"Hello?" I greeted slowly.

"Oh, thank God. Mr. Bishop, is that you?"

"Who's calling?"

"Mr. Bishop, it's Detective Roxanne Byers again. I'd like to meet with you. I know you're scared. *Please* don't hang up. I just need to meet with you. Where are you?"

I need to meet with you. My cynicism was on full alert. Was that cop-speak for *I'd very much like to arrest you now, if it's alright with you?*

Those words felt tinged with imminent betrayal: a lure with the good-cop routine, only to spring the *Gotcha!* bad cop routine and throw a net over me once she had me in her sights.

"Okay…," I slowly breathed in response.

"Where are you?"

"Jersey City."

"That doesn't exactly give me proximity. Where about?"

I sighed. "Listen, what's this about, Detective? I don't mean to be rude, bu-"

"I think you know what it's about Roland. Cut the crap. I've been trying to reach you all night. I'm asking nicely. Please," she said. The way she said *please* somehow had the ring of truth to it. I waited.

"Roland, are you there?"

I shriveled.

"Jersey City Jail," I offered glumly. "I just visited our mutual friend."

"No problem. I'll be there in five minutes. Please wait out front."

"Will do." I hit 'end.'

Nothing in me wanted to comply, and everything in me revolted. They were going to be here in five minutes. If they were going to take me in, she had my location, so why wouldn't she just call Jersey City Jail and have someone come out behind me, walk down the steps, and arrest me? I waited. No one came. No shouts of "Freeze!"

Penny strongly advocated for me to talk to her. Would Penny set me up? I didn't think so, but I began to suspect her of concealing dark designs now as well.

After all, she had hid them from her own husband, so why not me?

My view was colored. It had been colored blue yesterday with electricity. Now it was just colored green – green with suspicion and fear.

I thought back to Rosie on the waterfront. It was time to stop running.

"Mr. Bishop?" There was that Bronx accent again.

She stepped out of the Ford Bronco, and my legs were trembling. Trembling from fear, from lack of sleep, and now, from overwhelming beauty. She was ravishingly beautiful, stopping my heart with her billowing curly hair blowing in the breeze, and that tan blazer fitting her form perfectly.

And speaking of legs, hers were long, and every bit the looker.

"Detective Byers, I presume?" I asked tentatively.

She stopped just in front of me and looked me up and down. "Have you not had much sleep?"

"How could you guess?"

"Well, I know you were on the run, and you weren't answering my calls, and this sort of thing happens when someone feels guilty for something they did."

Feels guilty? I thought. *I am guilty, you hot-to-trot vixen.* I was gobsmacked by her immeasurably captivating looks, her figure, her power.

I started to speak, but no words came.

"Can you come with me, please? Time is pressing."

"Wh-where are you taking me?" I asked.

"I'm not *taking* you anywhere, Roland. I'd like to go somewhere with you. Please. You must be hungry."

What the hell was going on here? I had killed somebody. She knew that. What was with the cloak-and-dagger business? *If you're going to arrest me, just arrest me and get it over with,* I thought. My knees were shaking, but I followed her.

"I am hungry. Thanks."

"Let's go." Thankfully, she was alone. That was less intimidating than it might have been had she had a partner with her. She even allowed me to sit in the front seat.

She held the door open for me, and I looked under my eyebrows at her briefly as I passed by her, smelling her intoxicating perfume…similar to stuff that Jenette wore. Vera Wang 'Princess,' I think, or something like that. My eyes locked with hers, and there was understanding there. I think she also glanced briefly at my lips.

"What about my bike?" I asked her.

She shook her head. "We'll come back for it later."

"Will I be home tonight? I need to feed my cat."

"You'll be home tonight."

Maybe Penny was right after all. If we were coming back for my bike, that meant she wasn't arresting me just yet.

Or…did she mean that she would arrest me, and she and a partner would come back for it?

Maybe Penny was wrong after all.

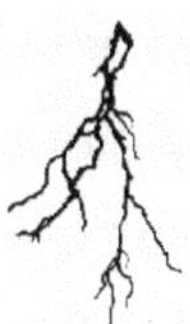

We had gone through a drive-through and she had bought me a few tacos and chips. I could barely even eat them, my nerves were so wracked.

"Is this the part where you say something? Or do I kick off our convo?" she asked me.

I looked over at her, sheepishly. "I don't know. You obviously know something, and this is a little too cloak-and-dagger for my taste."

She giggled maturely. "Cloak and dagger. You ever see that movie?"

"What?"

"*Cloak and Dagger.* Have you seen it? Dabney Coleman and the kid from E.T."

"N-no, I haven't," I said, furrowing my brows.

"Yeah. 'Jack Flack always escapes.' Cute movie. From 1984 I think. The kid pulled a 'crossfire gambit.' Like, a double-cross move and had the bad guys shoot at each other. They ended up killing each other off. Always loved that as a kid. Great movie. I'd love to try that someday."

"Interesting," I said nonchalantly. "Are there some bad guys we're about to talk about?"

She just looked at me without answering.

I'll take that as a yes.

"Where are we heading?" All I could tell was that we were headed back south.

"Certainly not The Frederick Hotel. But we are headed that way. We've got an office over there I'd like to take you to. Oh, by the way, here's your windbreaker. Thought you might want it back."

She reached behind the seat. I flinched. "Easy," she said. Byers fetched my windbreaker and set it in my lap. I looked down. Sure enough, there it was. Looked like it had some blackened marks on it that resembled burns. I gulped.

She reached for her car CB radio. "Byers to Armstrong, come in, over?"

"Armstrong here," came the answer over the CB.

"Subject apprehended, bringing him in, over."

"Roger that, see you soon."

"Yep." She clicked the CB radio into place once more.

"Apprehended?"

She smiled at me. "Just relax. *Keep your sunny disposition.* We just need to talk first."

A laugh inadvertently escaped my lips, and I snorted. She knew my tagline. Good detective work. "So, where's your office?"

"Manhattan."

My eyebrows flicked up. "Been there a lot lately."

"Yeah, it sounds like it."

An awkward few minutes passed as we drove through the Holland Tunnel and emerged on the other side. Once again, there were the two towers looming over us.

"Never gets old, does it? Just look at 'em."

"Yep, they're beautiful, alright," I mumbled back, tossing a glance her way, my eyes accidentally stealing to her legs. *Cool it, Roland. You're still married. Jenette might come take you back,* I thought. But an unsettling question steeped in me. *Did I really want her back? Did she really want me?*

I averted my eyes and sighed.

"Something wrong?" Byers asked me.

"Nope," I said, staring up at the towers and trying to focus on them, but instead visualizing superimposed long female legs pointing up into the sky.

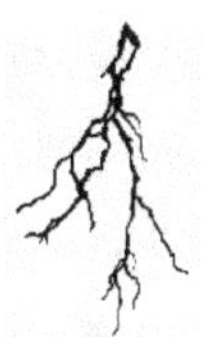

"Alright, we're here," said the Detective.

I looked around and took in the view.

"Please come with me, okay?"

I didn't say anything. Exited her Bronco and shut the door behind me. We were off Lafayette Street, entering a large white building with rusty garage doors flanking across the bottom. My mouth dropped open. It was the Wanamaker Building, all that remained of a legendary Astor Place department store that few New Yorkers remember. I had been here once only, on a brief New York sightseeing tour after Jenette and I moved here. Large, elegant letters rode high above one of the doors, which we passed, entering the double doors on the right.

I followed her silently through the doors. We stood in front of an elevator, not acknowledging each other. She depressed the floor button, and stared up at the descending numbers. I glanced over at her. She didn't glance back.

The door opened and we rode up together to the sixth floor. The bell dinged, the doors opened once more, and she motioned me out. And there, waiting for both of us, were two men in suits.

"Hey, Armstrong," Byers greeted him. He nodded back and then looked at me.

"Mr. Bishop?"

"Yes?" I answered nervously.

"Could you please place your arms out wide, sir?"

I did so, and the other agent advanced toward me, feeling through my shirt. My eyebrows muddled. Was he looking for a wire or something? What the hell? He felt all over, patting me down. "Ah, watch it, buddy," I said, as his hands patted up my inner leg.

"He's clean," my frisky agent said to Armstrong with a heavy New York accent. He took my Nokia and handed it to Armstrong.

"Hey – do I get that back?" I asked Armstrong.

"Chill out, Mr. Bishop," he said, but that did little more than test my patience.

"Why do they need my ph-"

"Detective Byers," Captain Frisks-a-lot acknowledged her to my right. "Come with me please."

Armstrong disappeared down another hallway with my phone.

I cast an awkward glance over at Detective Byers. Her face was nondescript, accustomed to this procedure, and she showed no signs of alarm or surprise, which I took as some measure of comfort. Nonetheless, this thing was getting more spy-movie by the minute.

After a seemingly interminable walk to the upper quadrant of the building, we were led into a suite, past a bank of cubicles, and into a collection of offices that looked north toward Astor Place. There was a conference table in a side room. Another agent was waiting there for us.

The previous agent, Captain Frisks-a-lot, motioned for me to go in. Byers followed me, and we sat down. They closed the door behind us. The second agent was seated at the conference table with a few file folders in front of him that he must have retrieved from a file cabinet that was situated against the wall close to the window.

"Could someone please tell me what this is all about?" I asked, trying to hide my nerves.

Captain Frisks-a-lot pulled out a tape recorder and sat down next to the seated agent, hitting record as he did so. "You don't mind if we record this, do you, for the record?"

"Well, actua-"

"Great," he said, and continued to record. The other one pulled out a notepad and began jotting down some notes. Then he turned to me.

I squirmed uneasily in my seat.

"Mr. Bishop," he said, with an equally heavy New York brogue, "my name is Agent Ryan Phelps, and this is

Agent Rob Fox." *That second one being aka Captain Frisks-a-lot. Got it.* "We're with the FBI."

That jarred me to attention. I flinched and eyed them in incredulity. My eyes traveled to Detective Byers nervously. "The FBI- what the hell is this?" Byers just watched me blandly. "You're with the *FBI??*"

"That's correct, Mr. Bishop. Please just listen."

"Listen, Roland," urged the Detective.

I tried to sit back and relax in my chair.

"Would you like something to drink, Roland?" asked Fox, and I didn't like the way he said my name so informally. I shook my head.

Fox looked back at Phelps, who continued.

"Mr. Bishop, Detective Byers was contacted by a Dr. Penelope Eggers who we understand is your psychiatrist, is that correct?"

I nodded.

"And that you've been seeing her following some abnormal episodes you've been having following a lightning strike that took place a few weeks ago in Millenium Park, yes?"

I nodded again.

Phelps paused. "You do speak English, yes?"

I let out a quick sigh. "Yes. I speak English, Agent Phelps. Could you please tell me-"

"Would it be safe to say that yesterday was the result of another one of these abnormal episodes?"

I didn't answer, just held still. I didn't want them to pry it out of me, but I also didn't care to feel any more like an anomaly than I already did.

"Look, I don't know wh-"

"Mr. Bishop," interrupted Fox, "you're not going to be arrested. I can imagine you're experiencing some fear and trepidation about what took place yesterday, and what the fallout will be. Let me assure you that you've been brought here because we need your help."

My head tilted seemingly of its own accord as my eyes narrowed. "Help…help with what? And where's my phone? When do I get my phone back?"

Phelps started up again. I looked over quickly at Byers who eyed me dispassionately and then returned her focus to the agents. "We understand that you've been having some visions, some *particular* visions, about a particular person, and we'd like to discuss that with you. Would that be alright?"

Mohammed. They didn't have to even say it. I knew. I gathered myself for a long breath.

"What does the FBI want with this man?" I asked.

Fox started to say something, but Phelps waved him down. "Please, Roland- Mr. Bishop, if I may. We have a lot to get through."

I shrugged my shoulders in acceptance. If they wanted to lead, they could lead.

"We believe the man you've been tailing is named Mohammed Atta." I flinched at the name. I knew it. I saw his face crawling toward me in The Frederick once more. "Born September 1st, 1968 in Egypt." Phelps opened a file folder, pulled out a dossier and placed it in front of me.

Mohammed Atta. That was him, sure enough.

"He studied architecture at Cairo University, graduated 1990, and studied at Hamburg University of Technology in Germany after that. While there he joined a mosque, and it's become apparent he is now part of a terrorist cell that had its roots there. Perhaps more than once he's been in contact with a man known as Osama bin Laden. Does that name ring a bell?"

The Al-Qaeda terrorist leader. I nodded. I had watched a documentary on him and knew that he had ties to the 1993 bombing at the World Trade Center.

"Osama bin Laden formed al-Qaeda in 1988 for the purposes of jihad. In August 1996 and again in February 1998 he declared *fatawa*, declarations of war, against America. He was indicted for the US embassy bombings on East Africa in 1998. He's regarded globally as one of the most dangerous men alive."

Fox cut in. "Yeah, FBI's got him on their Most Wanted Terrorists and Most Wanted Fugitives lists. And just two years ago the UN officially designated al-Qaeda as a terrorist organization."

"So, what does that mean for Mohammed Atta?" I asked. This time Phelps welcomed my question.

"I'm glad you asked. While in Germany, Atta formed a cell with several other men the FBI have been watching of late, and monitoring chatter." He flipped through Atta's dossier. "Marwan al-Shehhi, Ramzi bin al-Shibh, and Ziad Jarrah are some of the members of that cell whom we've been monitoring."

I heard a quick sizzle to my right and looked over. Byers had lit up a smoke. She recoiled, surprised. "You don't mind, do you?"

I shook my head. Somehow that made her even sexier.

"Atta, and members of the Hamburg cell, had been recruited by bin Laden as well as another man, Khalid Sheikh Mohammed, for an operation we believe will be here in the states, involving airplanes and possible hijack situations."

The wind was sucked out of me. I gasped. "Oh my- that's what I've been seeing. Those are the exact visions I saw."

"In these, these…abnormal episodes you've been having," said Fox.

"Sure," I said to him. I was beginning to dislike Fox. "Anyway, yeah, that's what I've been seeing ever since August 19th. I'm also now seeing *numbers,* though I don't know why. You guys think I'm crazy, don't you?"

Neither one of them nodded or shook their heads.

I'll take that as a yes as well.

Frankly, I was getting excited that some pieces were finally starting to fall into place. "Anyway, numbers. Today was fourteen. Yesterday was fifteen. I don't know."

"Fourteen. Fifteen. Could be a code of some kind. Do you have any lockers or PIN numbers that have that?" Fox asked.

"No, no, he said *fifteen-fourteen*, in that order," Phelps clarified. "That could be a mathematical equation, could be a countdown. We'll look at that in a bit. I would like to talk to you about your visions, specifically, Roland. What happened with them, and what happened *in* them?"

Byers blew out a long trail of smoke. Apparently she'd already heard this from Penny. I wondered if she even believed me.

"Well," I started, "I don't know what will trigger it except that it seems to be when I'm in close proximity with my target. Target- that's what I call them. Anyway, I starting having these…these white flashes, I get a heatwave pass through me, my head throbs, nosebleeds, passing out, the whole shebang. Before I know it, I'm on the floor.

"But," I paused, holding up a finger, "before I go down, in those shockwaves, I get all kinds of visual signals, like, I don't know, videos, of things that happened. Only none of them have happened yet. Detective Byers," I said, turning to her, "you know about the bank robbery where they killed the security guard and blew up the bank in Queens a week ago. And the twelve-year-old girl who got kidnapped out of Brooklyn and they found her body later?"

She nodded.

"I saw those too. I saw both of those incidents *before* they happened. I needed to talk to a shrink – sorry, psychiatrist," I said, remembering Dr. Walker's faux pas, "because I saw them on the news afterwards. Each time they had caught the suspect, and each time, I knew *that's* the suspect I had seen in my visions. I was near them only a day or two prior to their crime."

"So you have to be near them," said Fox, eyeing me curiously.

"Yeah. I mean, but don't mistake me, I don't know where they'll be, or when the images will strike. I've gotten all kinds of imagery lately. Just the other night I saw our neighbor killing his wife before it happened. And…" I trailed off, looking at each of them in turn.

"And what?" Phelps asked.

I glanced back at him. "I-I don't know, I was able to avert it somehow. I knew precisely how he'd do it, and who he'd do it to, so I took her in and kept her safe in my place. But eventually he found out where she was, and he barged into my apartment and tried to kill her. I," -here I took a deep breath, not knowing how much of this they'd actually swallow- "I somehow managed to disable him."

"Disable him? How?" Phelps asked again.

"I don't know exactly how. I don't know what happened to me. Like some lightning got 'stuck' in me, or something? I don't know. All I know is I grabbed his arm, and the next thing I knew his arm had burst into flame, and I was seeing white-hot blue vision and screaming with every fiber of my being and the fire of a thousand suns. It was electric. Powerfully electric."

They stared at me.

"Interesting," Phelps said, feeling the stubble of a beard on his chin.

Fox looked a bit incredulous, but was still at least listening.

"And this guy, this, Mohammed Atta," I asked them, "he was the same, a few nights ago. Only his hasn't happened yet. My neighbor Jake's happened within the span of a few hours. And the guy yesterday at the Frederick, well, his happened within an hour."

"So?" Fox asked.

"*So,*" I enunciated, "I think something in me is sensing that maybe the timeline is being sped up with some of them. I don't know. All I know with that guy is that he was trailing Mohammed Atta. I know that now because I-"

"You what?" Fox asked me quickly.

Answering his question, or completing my sentence, would potentially incriminate me. But they already knew that I had been onsite there. Byers confirmed that. She took another drag of her cigarette and blew it out heavily.

"Because he was there, Ryan," she said to Phelps. "He's the one who burnt your partner to a crisp."

I looked back at Phelps in horror. "Partner?!"

Phelps shrugged. "Not exactly. We're FBI, Mr. Bishop. He was a CIA operative working in coordination with us. You have to remember that there are some branches of us that don't exist and aren't supposed to. Agent Mulligan was tailing Atta and tracked him into his hotel. He tried to subdue Atta and take him out. That was his assignment."

"Wait, are you telling me I killed a federal agent?!" I asked in complete dismay.

They both sported blank slates. Maybe they didn't like Mulligan. Maybe he didn't technically exist and was expendable. Either way, they were expressionless. Perhaps they had just already come to grips with it and had moved on. Or maybe the FBI was just as cutthroat as I had always heard them to be: emotionless and all duty.

"Guys," I said, putting my hands up, "I had no idea. You have to believe me. I had *no* idea that's who he was. The vision didn't tell me who he was nor what he wanted. They…they don't give me any backgrounds or morality lessons on any of them. All I saw was him beating up and trying to kill someone else. I had no clue that someone else was Atta. And I had no idea that he was your partner. You gotta believe me."

They both looked at me quizzically for a moment. Fox spoke first. "We already know you were there. Nice windbreaker, by the way. Byers here tipped us off when she heard about your little, shall we say, 'gifts' from Dr. Eggers. So she told Agent Phelps here. In a very special kind of way, I might add."

"Special?"

"Fox, cut it out," said Phelps, briskly. "A little decorum, please."

I felt Byers stir along with him. "Ryan is my ex-boyfriend, Mr. Bishop. Got it?" I got it, but I wasn't happy about it. *At least it's 'ex,' I thought.* "So Penny tells me, I tell Ryan, Ryan thinks you might be valuable in finding out what our little Egyptian friend is doing, we bring you in. *Capisce?*" she said, sporting some Italian.

It made sense now.

"So you had no idea before hearing about it through Penny. Uh, Dr. Penelope Eggers," I clarified. She shook her head.

"Can we get back to the subject matter, people?" Fox asked annoyedly. "We're trying to stop Atta forward in time, not go back in time and recreate the love exchange."

Phelps rolled his eyes and pinched the bridge of his nose. "Mr. Bishop, what we're trying to tell you is that we have a potentially serious event about to go down in or around New York City at the hands of Mohammed Atta and others. We don't know what it is yet, but he and his accomplices have taken flight training here in the US. They obtained instrument ratings in May.

"We've tracked passports of other potential accomplices of Atta's who have begun their westward migration, coming into the states over the past year. People loosely affiliated with Atta but who could potentially be part of their next operation. We suspect they're going to hijack airplanes and take the hostages with them back home. Last month Atta himself flew to meet with one of the other terrorists, who we think is Ramzi bin al-Shibh. We lost Atta in Spain. Came back to the states eventually.

"And now," he continued, "over the past few months we see that he's been conducting what we assume are 'surveillance' flights, garnering information on whatever it is they're about to do."

"Wow," I breathed. "So, you think they're going to conduct a hijacking?"

"Confidence is high, yes," Phelps said.

"I'd like to come back to this numbering thing you mentioned, Roland," Fox said. "Maybe there's no rhyme or reason to it. Maybe it's not part of any kind of identifiable pattern. Might be random. But we should be looking at that too. You didn't see numbers associated with either of the previous crimes you previsualized?"

I shook my head. "No. Those were just the crimes themselves. But there have actually been *six* now, Agent Fox. The first two were the bank robbery and the girl from Brooklyn. Next came Mohammed Atta. After that it was Penny's – Dr. Penelope Egger's – husband. That turned out to be Penny herself, so my vision was incorrect… or… something. I don't know. Then my neighbor Jake, and now Agent Mulligan. None of those other ones beside Atta had any kind of numbers associated with them. The numbers thing just started yesterday. I can't really explain it yet. It's not like I saw the number six prior to my sixth vision or anything like that."

"But you think because some of them have been incorrect, or the actual tragedy differed from what you originally saw, that the numbers thing might be perhaps insignificant?" Fox kept at me.

"Not insignificant, but coincidental, certainly," I argued. "It's something that, again, I can't explain and that I, I don't know, hope gets clearer with time. In any event, they don't seem to correspond with the number of visions I've had. There's too much of a discrepancy."

"The reason I ask, Mr. Bishop," Fox said, "is because we had a bit of a surprise here ourselves that we can't explain."

"Oh?"

"Several of their guys had tickets purchased for Saturday, September 8th. Two groups of them booked together across two separate planes. Atta was with a group of two other men on one flight. An accomplice of his, Marwan al-Shehhi, was leading another group on a different flight. Then, a few days ago, on the 20th, something changed." He looked at me suspiciously.

"Something…changed?"

"Yeah. Something changed. There were no longer two groups on two different flights. There were three groups on three different flights. The two men previously listed, and then a third, led by yet another associate on a different flight. Hani Hanjour is his name. Another terrorist cell member."

I thought to myself. "Well, the night of the 19th is when I saw Mohammed Atta and the other man with him at the PATH Station. They had been on the subway with me before that. Maybe they changed their plans if they thought they were being tailed?"

"Maybe, maybe not. But then their plans changed again." I tilted my head as Fox continued. "After your little tussle with Agent Mulligan, and your subsequent encounter with Atta at The Frederick, the flights changed once more. Now there's only a single plane involved, and Atta isn't on it."

"How can that be? Did they call in and change the flight plans?"

"No. It's like they were booked that way from the very beginning. We're also tapped into bank accounts, and no further funds were exchanged, credited, or expended. That's why we've been having trouble pinpointing the exact date or manner in which they plan to conduct their hijackings."

I thought about both incidents. Both happened directly after my run-ins with Atta. And then both future plans changed. I was seeing the future! Was it possible that Atta was as well? Or was it possible that by intervening, I was altering the course of the future somehow?

No! I'm not that powerful! I thought. But that didn't explain the change of travel plans, or the fact that there was no financial or airline record of the change. That was a mystery that neither the FBI nor I could explain.

But there and then I found myself questioning *all* of the episodes I had had. Did I in some way accelerate or decelerate their transpiring? *No! It couldn't be!* There had to be an alternative explanation for it.

"I'd like to switch for a moment. Mr. Bishop, why don't you now tell us exactly what happened with Agent Mulligan at The Frederick Hotel yesterday," interrupted Phelps. "Did you meet Mohammed Atta? Are you certain that the man that Mulligan was tailing is the man pictured in the dossier before you?"

"It's him." I sighed, recollecting the haunting memory of that man crawling toward me across the floor. Of Agent Mulligan erupting into flames and burning before my very eyes. Of tearing out of there in a frenzy.

I walked them through everything I could, as best as I could recall, of how I tailed Agent Mulligan up Broadway, unaware that he himself was tailing someone else. What he was wearing. How I had the flashes and cried out in pain, and he stopped and looked back at me. Our encounter in the suite. What happened when I burnt him, and he erupted into flames just like Jake. Mohammed crawling toward me. What Mohammed had said to me. How I tore out of there.

"Got it," said Phelps. "And now, for the record, I'd like you to describe in exacting detail what you saw in your visions concerning Mohammed Atta."

I tried to think back to nine days ago on the subway, and then at the PATH Station. That sweet old lady who asked about me. The people bustling about. The sneers and disgusted look-aways because of my bloody nose. The heat. The sweat.

Mohammed.

I told them what I saw, as best as I could recall. And suddenly, as I began to prime the pump of my memory, I was seized with white flashes. As if on fast-forward, all the images came racing back, and my eyes fluttered.

Airplanes.

Large commercial airliners.

Fights high in the sky. Dark-skinned men, many of them. A middle-Eastern language.

A plane streaking across the sky.

No. *Multiple* planes.

People screaming.

Rubble everywhere. Smoke. Dust. Ash. The jet had obviously crashed into the ground, I figured. The images of the hijackers intruding into the cockpits of the planes. The visuals were jumping backward and forward with no cohesive timeline.

Screams.

Screams.

SCREAMS!

The anguished cries of thousands of people. Thousands? A massive rushing sound like concrete collapsing, pancaking one against another. Billows of smoke and dust. Yellowish ash clouds the size of buildings.

And then…blackened silence.

I was breathing hard as all of it cascaded before my eyes in a macabre montage of agony. My mouth was open, and I was sweating. I seemed to be floating in a black void.

I'm Roland Bishop, and I know where I am.

I'm Roland Bishop, and I know where I am.

I'm Roland Bishop, and I know where I am.

My heartbeat slowed. Gradually, as if through a fog, the mist cleared and I could dimly make out the shapes of Detective Roxanne Byers, Agent Ryan Phelps, and Agent Rob Fox, just staring at me.

The clock on the wall behind them read 6:17pm.

6:17pm?? How could that be? Had we been there that long?

Detective Byers had only just gotten us lunch on the way over. Had we talked that long? Or had my flood of visions taken me down some kind of wormhole?

Sweat trickled down my forehead, and I felt warmth trickling out of my nose. A cavalcade of images had just swamped me. I felt faint, still panting, looking at them incredulously.

"Th-they're going to hijack," I breathed out.

Byers reached out to steady me as I swayed.

"Hij-jack…multiple pl-planes," I said, and then I toppled over. Byers did her best to try and stop my fall, but it was too late.

I slumped over and then hit the floor hard on my already-pounding head.

As my mind faded, I reflected on the fact that I couldn't take many more hits to my cranium. Dr. Walker would have a thing or two to say.

So would Dr. Penny.

"Can I have my phone ba-" I started, but my tongue felt swollen and my lips failed me.

I dimly heard their voices calling for me. Someone slapped my face a little too hard, trying to rouse me. I bet that was Fox. All their voices seemed far away, too dim to hear through the lurid ringing in my ears.

There had been far too much in this day for me.

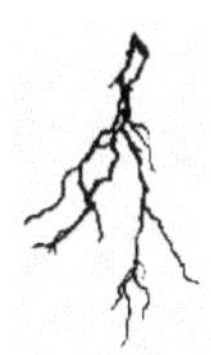

13 Days To Go

August 29th, 2001 • Manhattan, NY

Once more, I awoke feeling rested and calm.

Detective Byers was shaking my shoulder. "Good morning, Roland. How are you feeling?"

I felt nauseous, as well. "Not so good. What happened?"

"You blacked out."

"What time is it?"

"Almost 2am on Wednesday the 29th."

Dimly I took in my surroundings. She wasn't lying; the clock on the wall echoed the time. It was dark outside and inside. A dim corner lamp lit up another room in this cluster of offices. No sign of the agents or anyone else. There was a futon in here, and they hadn't pulled it out; I was just lying on the couch version of it, covered with a thin, knitted blanket that didn't really do much except snag your fingers. "Where is everyone else?"

"Home. Catching some shuteye. I took a nap and came back here to check on you. Armstrong is still downstairs, and other agents are on night shifts doing their own stuff, in and out."

"Does anyone else know the FBI has a field office here?" I asked her.

She shrugged. "Covert crap. Beyond my paygrade."

I groggily sat up and rubbed my eyes. "I thought you were sleeping *with* the higher paygrade though, ri-"

"I never said I was sleeping with him!" she instantly protested. "Watch it, Bishop."

I pulled my knuckles out of my reddened eyes and just stared at her. "Sorry. I didn't mean-"

"It's fine," she dismissed me. "Good Catholic girl. You assumed too much," she grunted, as she pulled out a smoke and lit it up, blowing a purplish-white plume out into the room. I waved it away from me. Never was fond of side stream smoke.

"Again, sorry," I said, and then I couldn't help it as a wild yawn escaped my lips and stretched my mouth until I thought it would rip. "Will I ever get my phone back?"

"Relax, Roland, you'll get your phone back soon," she said. *Yeah, if soon means 'sometime before Jesus returns' I thought annoyedly.* We sat there in silence, dimly illuminated by the glowing lamp.

"That was so odd. I've only ever passed out from the visions *during* the visions. Not while recollecting them. I guess plunging myself back into all of them jumpstarts the physical effects or something. So, what's next?"

"I don't know, exactly. Phelps and Fox will be back in the morning at 9am to debrief their superiors I think, and then they've got to file a report with Washington DC. Whatever directives come after that is up to DC."

"As in FBI Headquarters? Whoa," I breathed, taking it all in.

"Yep," she said in a monotone.

Another awkward silence for a while.

"Why did you say that?"

I turned back to her. "Say what?"

She pointed at me. "That thing you did, that *Roland Bishop I know where I am* thing. You said it three times. Is that something Dr. Eggers taught you?"

I nodded. "Yeah. She said it might help to 'center' me. Keep me grounded. Keep me here. Something. I don't know. I wish I could talk with her right now. This crap has grown exponentially far-reaching and crazy."

"Yeah, well, she's not going anywhere for a while. You can talk with her today. I talked with her last night after you blacked out."

"You did?"

"Yep. Told her you were safe, and that we were talking. Didn't tell her anything else. Classified, and all that." I swear she rolled her eyes at that last comment somewhat, and it made me wonder why she had dated Agent Phelps. "She sounded very relieved."

"How long have you known her?"

"Since '99. She was a good lady. Sorry. *Is* a good lady. Obviously made a very bad choice last week. But how can you blame her? She took back control of her life. They'll go easy on her. They always go easy on the battered wives." She heaved a big sigh as if she didn't approve. "I swear every time one of those comes across my desk, I already know how it's going to go down. Slap on the wrist. Not that I blame them," she said, adjusting herself in her uncomfortable side chair. "Sleeping with the enemy isn't something I envy. But neither is injustice."

"Injustice?"

"*Yeah*, injustice. You can't just kill someone because they're beating on you. There are a million and one things you can do beside that."

"Such as?"

"Gimme a break. Protective services. Witness protection. Restraining orders. Moving. Hell, using a tranquilizer gun instead of a *real* gun. But all of them seem to want to burn the beds of their oppressors. Goes against everything C.G. Jung said."

"Who's C.G....C.G....?"

She snorted, apparently offended that I didn't know. "*Jung.* Probably not your typical reading fare. He said, 'I am not what happened to me. I am what I choose to become.' I think that's pretty darn spot-on, Roland, don't you? All those people who take justice into their own hands and turn it into vengeance, well, they're becoming what happened to them instead of choosing to become something better."

"And you think that's wrong?"

"I'm a Detective, Mr. Bishop. It's my job to reveal the wrong that people do."

"Why are you opening up to me? Aren't I the perp, and you're the perp catcher?"

She raised an eyebrow at me. "Perp? Let's get something straight, Roland. You've been granted temporary immunity by the Attorney General. We'll see if it sticks. For now, they need you. We need you."

Please say 'I need you' next. The thought bounced around in my head, and then I felt guilty because I had also felt an attraction to Renita. And very little for my own wife Jenette anymore.

But she didn't say *I need you*. Instead, she looked away and blew out a plume of smoke, looking off past me with a thousand-yard stare. Until she realized that I was still watching her, however, and her eyes slowly drifted back over to me with the slightest hint of a seductive smile. That was enough to know that there were possibilities.

I giggled and looked away. That was sufficient for now. That, and wondering if something had happened to her that made her choose to become something else, like Jung had said.

"Crap – I need to get home at some point and feed Winston."

"Winston?"

"Our cat. I should have fed him last night."

"I can swing by if you give me your key."

I eyed her curiously. "Are you going to search the place?" I smirked.

"I can if you want me to."

That elicited a giggle from me. "Nah, I'm good. I wouldn't want you to find my secret stash of MMMbop cassettes and Britney Spears collectible magazines. Here you go." I handed her my keys and she was off with a wave of the hand. I thanked her, and laid back down to catch some more shuteye.

Just like clockwork, the agents arrived at 9am. Phelps and Fox strode in together, coffee in hand, wearing almost identical Savile Row suits. Both of them disappeared into another office, presumably to talk with DC, as Roxanne had figured earlier. I watched down the hall briefly to see if they would re-emerge, but they remained. There was nothing for me to do but lay back down and wait.

I awoke again at 8:37, yawned and stretched toward the sky, got up and paced around for a bit. There was a small bump on the back of my head, and it was tender to the touch. Dr. Walker would tell me that I was turning into a pickle with all of these bumps I was accumulating, and then he would owe his wife another quarter for telling me to relay that development to my shrink.

Someone had brought me coffee and placed it on the end table next to my pillow, along with a pack of Little Debbie's honey buns. I devoured them. My stomach had been rumbling from the moment I woke up.

Roxanne was nowhere to be found. I wrapped the light blanket around me and just sat there on the futon in the side room. I guessed it was her who had brought me the pastries and coffee. Staring out the window, I ruminated on how my life could have changed so much in such a short amount of time, shaking my head.

The lightning strike.

The visions.

Jenette.

Dr. Penny.

Mr. Eggers.

Renita & Joe-Joe.

Jake.

Mohammed.

Agent Mulligan.

Fleeing.

The FBI.

And then, crossing my mind briefly was the sheer audacity that I might have had something to do with Mohammed Atta changing his plans. How on earth was that even possible?

But then again, how on earth was a man receiving visions from the future after a lightning strike possible?

I shook my head to clear it off. I wished then that I had my bike and could just ride off into the wind and forget all of this. I wondered if it was still chained up outside Jersey City Jail, and whether or not someone had taken it, or whether I'd ever be coming back to it. I had no idea. I was now in the clutches of the FBI, and I had been imparted information that would not see me simply released back out into the wild to ride my bike freely once more.

Life had changed so much, and some premonition within told me it would continue changing.

My thoughts were drawn beyond myself as I furrowed my eyebrows. This was just my own life, centered around me. But what if Mohammed Atta and his terrorist cell should succeed? Who was he working with? Where was he now? Where would he go? And what about the others? Where were they? And when would they strike?

Without warning, I began to feel cold. I wrapped the blanket more tightly around myself and shut out the chill. As I did so, dimly in the halls of my mind came the number *thirteen*.

"Mister Bishop," said Agent Ryan Phelps. He held out his hand, and I shook it. His breath reeked of cheap convenience store coffee. Fox just looked at me without offering to shake my hand. "Did you get a good night's sleep? Nice to see you on your feet again," he said.

"Yeah, thanks. Nasty bump but I'll live. Do I have you to thank for that futon?"

He smiled. "Least we could do. You gave us some valuable intel last night and we're going to need more. Seems the best thing to do to get you ready would be to at least let you sleep off the initial intake."

I snickered. "Yeah, okay. Have you seen Detective Byers around here anywhere?" I asked, looking around.

Fox cocked a sly eye toward Phelps.

"No, I haven't."

"Well, is there any way someone can hook me up with a phone to call into the Jersey City Jail and talk to Dr. Eggers?"

"Sure, right this way," Phelps said. "Fox, meet you in the conference room in five." Fox nodded and was off. I fell in line behind Phelps on the way to a phone.

"Listen," he said, "don't worry about Byers and I, by the way. Fox likes to stir things up a bit. He can be kind of an ignorant meddling prick, but he's a good agent. He was friends with Mulligan, and Fox doesn't have many friends. So, he's less partial to you now than we are. Don't pay it any heed. Here we go," he said, leading me into his office. "Here's my landline. Jersey City Jail is in the book here. Just call the main line and introduce yourself as being with me and give them authorization code FFA926B. They'll put you on hold and then bring her up. It's not calling hours there yet, but this is sort of an override. Got it?"

I nodded.

"You find your way to the conference room we were in last night when you're done, yeah?"

"Okay, sounds good. Thanks."

"Oh! And here you go," he said, and then handed me a little sealed envelope. "Though you probably want to save your battery, I imagine. You can still use mine," he said, and sauntered off to the conference room.

I opened up the envelope. There was my little red Nokia, seemingly unharmed. What had they extracted from it? I wondered. But then, just as quickly, the thought came to me:

They're the FBI, idiot. Everything.

"Jersey City Jail."

Be professional. Be confident. You got this.

"Uh, hi, I'm calling with Agent Ryan Phelps for Penelope Eggers, authorization code FFA926B please."

"Say what?"

"Inmate Eggers. I'm using authorization code FFA926B." For a moment I felt like I was lowering my voice to sound more adult.

"One moment," came the curt voice.

After being on hold for a seeming eternity, there came a familiar voice on the other end. "Hello?"

"Hi! Penny, it's Roland. How are you?" I asked eagerly. "Are you doing okay?"

"I'm sorry, who is this?" She sounded muffled and withdrawn somehow.

I laughed in spite of her – and myself. "What? It's me, Roland. Are you okay? I might sound muffled because I'm on a differ-"

"I'm sorry, Roland *who?* Can I help you?"

I paused, uncertain. "*'Can you help me?'* What do you mean, 'can you help me?' Penny, it's *me.* Roland Bishop."

Pause, with nothing further from her.

"Hello?"

"I'm sorry, but you must have the wrong number. You've contacted the Jersey City Jail, and I am unfortunately an inmate here."

"Yes, I know. I-I just-" I faltered, losing patience and understanding. "Penny, what happened, are you okay? I know about Dr. Eggers."

She gasped. "What? Who told you? *Who is this and what do you want?!*"

There was an inexplicable certainty to her confusion. *She didn't know me.* And then it hit me – had her future changed as well? Something I said or did? I shook my head. It cannot be! I am *not* that powerful! "Listen to me. I am Roland Bishop, and I'm your client. What's up, Penny?"

"Please call me Penelope, sir. And what's this about 'client?' Client for what? I really should be going now."

"You're my psychiatrist and I'm your cli-"

"No. No! I don't know you, I don't know you! Never call me again, sir, please!" She hung up loudly.

I pulled Phelps' phone away from my ear slowly, staring off into the distance and wondering what had happened, searching with my eyes for answers that I would not find.

Penny didn't even know me. She had no clue who I was. My mouth dropped open and I swallowed hard with my eyes furrowed. Shock took over and I trembled, wondering what had been done – or undone – to make her completely oblivious to who I was.

I would not find an answer today.

"Welcome back. You okay?" asked Phelps.

I slowly trudged into the conference room, my mouth still cavernously agape. Bats could have flown out of there. I had no idea what had just happened. "I just, I-" I faltered. "I-I just got off the phone with Penelope Eggers in your office,

Mr. Phelps," I said, turning to him. "She didn't even know who I was. She didn't even…" I trailed off.

"Who?" Phelps asked.

I looked hard at him. "Penny. Dr. Penelope Egg-"

And then it hit me. He had no idea who she was, just as she had no idea who I was. My eyes turned slowly to Fox. His face showed he also was drawing a blank.

What the hell?

"Wh-where's Detective Byers?" I asked. "I need to find her. She needs to know about this!" I looked away from them, down the hall to see if perhaps she was on her way, those big flowing brown ravishing curls waving behind her shoulders.

I almost knew what they would say before they said it. A tremor ran through me.

"Detective who? What's going on? Are you feeling alright? You look a bit peaked."

"Oh my Go-" I started. "No. *No.* What do you mean, *Detective Who*, Phelps? Your ex-girlfriend. Detective Byers from, I dunno where she works. Jersey? Manhattan? What was that that she told me? I can't remember!"

I clutched my head. A white flash tore through me.

"I think she said Manhattan. But where in Manhattan, I have no idea. You're kidding, right? You don't know who I'm talking about?!"

Now I was just shaking. This was all too much. Penny couldn't remember me, and they couldn't remember Byers.

"No, man, we don't," said Fox. Well, at least some things hadn't changed; he was still an ass. "Who is this Dr., what did you say, Dr. *Egghead?*"

"I'm married," Phelps said, turning to Fox, lifting up his hands as if to swear on his own integrity. "I don't have a girlfriend, much less an ex-girlfriend. What are you talking about?"

My knees buckled and I crumpled into the chair opposite them. Phelps stood up to try and steady me. Fox simply sat and gawked at me. "What's going on?"

I stared at them with narrowed eyes. Heat passed through me. I felt like I was starting to sweat. "Why did I just use your phone, Agent Phelps?"

He stared at me blankly for a moment. "You… said… you wanted to call your father back home and tell him you were okay. Did you get ahold of him? Was it something he said? What's going on, Ethan?"

My heart froze. *Ethan.* Ethan? What the- I leaned toward the table and propped my elbows on it, cupping my mouth in my hands. I stared wide-eyed at them. Suddenly, in an impulse, I reached into my pants pocket and pulled out my phone.

My blue phone. It said 'Motorola V60' on the front of it, and I nearly dropped it in fright, yelling and backing away. It was a flip phone, totally different than my Nokia! *Where was my little red Nokia??*

I looked slowly back up at them in dismay.

"Tell me everything about last night. Tell me *everything* I told you. Please. *Tell me everything! Tell me now, please!*" I yelled at the top of my lungs, frantic. The tears were coming. I felt like I was having a breakdown. What was going on!?

Fox put up his hands. "Whoa, whoa, settle down Mr. Stiles. We'll get this worked out."

I froze in horror again. "Mr. *Stiles??* What do you me-"

I stopped mid-sentence and stood up quickly. Fox mirrored me and reached for his gun. "Hold it!" he said, but Phelps restrained him. "Rob, wait!" he said.

I dug my wallet out of my slacks – *slacks! I was suddenly wearing slacks and not jeans, what the hell?!* – and ripped open the Velcro on it.

There, in plain sight for all of us to see, was my license, clearly displaying the name *Ethan Parker Stiles.* My DOL picture was right next to it.

But it wasn't me.

"Take a picture of me," I said.

"What?"

"Take a picture of me and let me see it!" I yelled. Fox reluctantly did so, and held his phone up to me.

That was not me in that image. I was older, with graying hair, about late fifties with a five o'clock shadow, thick eyebrows and a solid jawline. "What the hell?" I felt around my face, up and down. The man who stared back at me looked familiar somehow. I just couldn't place him.

"Mr. Stiles, what's going on?" Agent Fox asked me in a flustered tone.

"Ethan!" cried Agent Phelps.

I crumpled to the floor in a heap.

Once more, I was unconscious, in agony and fear.

3 Days To Go

September 8th, 2001 • Manhattan, NY

Something shook me to my left.

I awoke out of a mesmerized trance, standing there in Central Park.

"Hey, Roland," said Detective Byers. "You okay? You got this, or do I need to call another clairvoyant?"

I stared at her. "B-byers," I breathed in amazement. "Roxanne…you're-" I stopped, mouth agape.

"What the hell, Roland? We're gonna lose him, are you with me or what? Get in gear, knucklehead!" She pulled out her gun.

Get him? Get *who*? And how was I Roland Bishop all over again, and not Ethan Stiles? What the *hell* had happened yesterday? Was she talking about Mohammed Atta? Were we tailing him together?

"I need you to tell me when you sense him. This is where we got the APB."

It *was* Atta. I sighed, shaking off what must have been the most barbaric state of delirium I had ever encountered, and gathered my wits, snapping to attention. "I'm- yeah, ok, I'm-I'm ready. Let's do this," I said. "Do I get a gun?"

"Not a chance, man. Get up there and see what you can feel out," she said, smiling at me with an adventurous look. "Be careful, hotshot," she said seductively once more.

I cleared my vision and nodded. I pulled my eyes away from her beautiful flowing hair – it suddenly struck me how much she looked like Andie MacDowell in *Groundhog Day* – and tried to expel the heavy air that had settled into my lungs, steeling myself for action. *I am not what happened to me. I am what I choose to become.* And then I changed it. *I'm Roland Bishop, and I know who I am. I'm Roland Bishop, and I know who I am. I'm Roland Bishop, and I know who I am.* That ought to keep whomever this 'Ethan Stiles' was at bay for a while.

And with that, I was heading deep into Central Park, trying to find a terrorist. I cast a glance back to see her, and the officers with her, leave the Bethesda Fountain area heading for Wagner Cove. Suddenly my head was filled with memories of a conversation that I don't remember having. Standing there at the Fountain, their plan, she had said, was to go around north and then hem them in south. I was to proceed south toward the Naumburg Bandshell and then head west through Skater's Circle and Le Pain Quotidien, straddling the Sheep Meadow to its north as I moved toward Warner LeRoy Place. That's where someone reported a potential sighting of Mohammed Atta.

I had been to Central Park a few times with Jenette – I hoped to God that was still her name – and just remembered the trees. There were so many trees.

Suddenly, I remembered my cellphone. With widened eyes I reached down into my pants and pulled out a familiar object. My little red Nokia. I accessed the contacts and quickly found Dr. Penny. Jenette. Amanda. Thank goodness. Things were back to normal.

Concentrate, Roland, I told myself, stuffing my phone back into my pocket. I needed to relax and focus. I needed to see what I could see and feel around me, searching for signals for the terrorist that they were looking for.

I tried to calm myself.

Breathe, Roland. Breathe. You got this. He's somewhere around here. You can find him. In and out, big guy. Nice and slow.

I paced, steadily, walking westward. I tried to breathe as slowly as I could, channeling my focus and my vision into one steady stream of consciousness.

But the flashes didn't come. No flashes. No nose bleeds. No sudden pangs of anxiety. No heat waves. I was confused, and a deep-seated desire to talk to Penny was welling up inside me. *Well, the last thing I would suggest in good conscience would be to tail anyone you suspect as a malefactor. You could be placing yourself in considerable danger.* She had said that to me nineteen days ag-

Wait. *Nineteen days?* I looked again at my Nokia.

Sure enough, the date read 9.8.01 and 3:16pm on the screen. But how was that possible? Yesterday was August 29th! How was today September 8th?

I was losing my mind. I suddenly felt nauseous. I had to talk to Penny. I tried to focus, to breathe, to do whatever I could to keep my radar up and see what signals I could receive that might possibly lead to where Atta was.

And then the memories came flooding back. Memories from the past ten days – from *this* timeline, the *real* timeline – flooded back. Memories that had happened, but in my mind had not. Not as Ethan Stiles, or any other name, but as Roland Bishop, my real name.

Jenette calling me on the 3rd to tell me she had filed for separation and was now back in Seattle.

Being very near one or both of the terrorists on Labor Day, September 4th, and passing out yet again after a series of visions seeing four planes hijacked again. That number kept growing, seemingly. And bodies…bodies falling.

Roxanne getting shot on the 4th but recovering.

Phelps – seeing him gunned down on the 4th by an unknown assailant, and a car veering off, leaving me there with blood splatter on my clothes. Seeing Fox killed.

Running into Mohammed Atta again on the 5th. And then tailing Ziad Jarrah on the 7th as well, one of the other terrorists Phelps had originally mentioned.

Me on the run again on the 5th. I felt funny while I was running…my legs felt different. My chest felt different.

Awash in these 'memories,' I began to see the number three. *Three.* Why three? Walking through Central

Park, trying to visually scout around for Mohammed Atta, why was I now seeing the number three?

I didn't understand. I just didn't understand any of it.

And then, suddenly, as I drew near to Tavern on the Green, I heard a ringing in my ears. My heart fluttered. My eyes blinked in a series of spasms. A cold wave passed through me, followed by heat.

And then the flashes.

They were here. Somewhere.

The nosebleed started.

My phone rang. Byers. "Bishop, what's your 20?"

"Huh?" I asked her.

"Your location! Where are you, Roland?"

"I'm getting close to the Tavern on the Green. And close to them, I think, Roxanne. Detective Byers, I mean...I think one or more of them are- *ow!*" I clutched my temple. Flashes of white. Back-to-back and searing. I could see the planes lifting off, all four of them in tandem. There were four now! They were flying and launching together, all of them eventually diverging outward toward different destinations.

Suddenly, in stark clarity, I got an image of a strange building with five sides. But it was smoking, charred, and burning in one quadrant. Something had rammed into it like a missile with a vengeance from hell. A triangular gash had been torn through it, and all of the support structures in that area had collapsed.

The Pentagon.

I could see it clearly now, as from above. But then, as my eyes were narrowing on it and the unabating white flashes took hold once more, everything was obstructed from view in a dense cloud of yellowish-white ash and dust. A billowing, blustery cloud enveloped all, shrouding the Pentagon from view.

"The Pen-Pentagon," I stuttered, stumbling. "That's one of their targets," I breathed.

"Stay there, we're coming!"

I looked around wildly to see if she was in fact coming, and if so, from where. Sweat pooled in the small of my back. The lower ends of my hair above my neck were sopped with sweat. It was only sixty degrees outside, but I began to drip. I didn't have a handkerchief, and now my nose flowed freely. I kept my phone pressed to my ear.

And then I saw him. There he was! Clear as day, Mohammed Atta was walking briskly, looking back over his shoulder toward the north. He had two other men with him. They were all neatly groomed.

"Attaaaa!!" I cried at the top of my lungs, and everyone around me must have heard it. Atta stopped and stared at me, rooted to the ground.

And the world whirred around me. I felt dizzy and spasmed. As if by some supernatural force that spun the earth like a top, my vision swam. Everything flew out of view and was replaced, dizzily, by something else. The entire scene was exchanged in a crazy patchwork. The latter took the place of the former, the new substituting the old in a dizzying trade, as a wild, howling wind rushed around me.

I toppled to the ground, my nose bleed unabating, and my head throbbing with pain. There was thunder in the wind, and there was lightning in the thunder. A rising tide of swollen undulating tone permeated everything around me. Rocks cracked around me in the vibratory pulsations.

My hand gripped my phone to the point of crushing; I couldn't bring myself to let go, and my mind would not will my hand to do it anyway.

White flashes.

Lightning strikes, all over again, zipping through my flesh, carving out domain in my blood vessels, seizing my peace and shredding it into ribbons, replacing it with agonized cries of sheer pain. I felt suspended and whisked about, nearly ready to vomit.

In ten seconds, it was all over, and I was dropped to the ground, breathing hard, covered in sweat and vomit and blood. People moved away in disgust, murmuring "did you see that guy?"

I took off my outer shirt and wiped away my sweat, my vomit, my nose, and gathered my senses. I looked up.

Atta was gone, along with his accomplices. The temperature felt more like a balmy seventy-two. Rain clouds were on the horizon.

I glanced slowly down at my hand, knowing full well what I found there would not be what I wanted or needed. In my hand I held a blue Motorola V60 flip phone.

I grimaced, burying my face in my hands, breaking down and crying right there in the park. Detective Byers was nowhere to be found in Central Park. She was nowhere to be found in my life, or anyone's life for that matter, and I was nowhere to be found in anyone else's.

I wept out of pure insanity, not knowing where I was nor who I was.

I'm Roland Bishop, and I know…
I'm Roland Bishop…
I'm…

I couldn't even complete it, and I crumpled to the
ground, my body prostrate, my face in my hands.
Sadness took me, and I left.

PART TWO

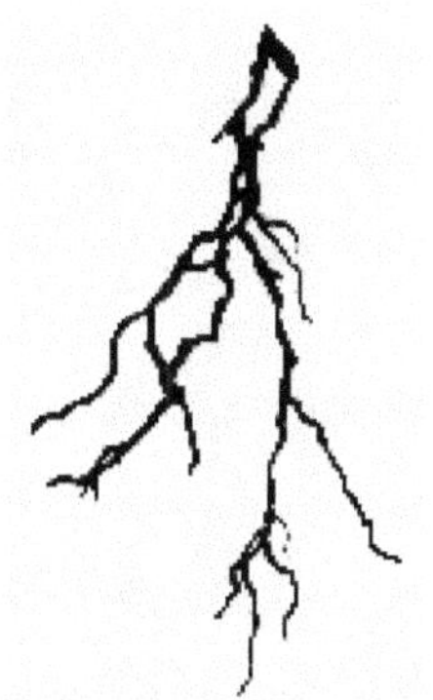

9 Days To Go

September 2nd, 2001 • Manhattan, NY

I didn't know what to think anymore. I was starting to lose everything that was me.

When the lightning tornado subsided, I didn't know where I was at first. The images around me blurred and colors were muted. There was a familiarity about the air and the noises, and that's all that I had just experienced: *noise*. The peace of this new environment was beyond compare, and as the images unblurred and coalesced into clarity, I realized I was sitting on the edge of my bed, back in my own apartment.

However, my disorientation still deepened.

Maybe it was all just a bad dream. One horrendously realistic and politically-charged bad dream, loaded with clandestine spy thrills and frenetic tension. I took a long breath to push out the past, and shook my head.

Just then my phone rang, and I looked down. As I did so, I glanced at the clock. 9:09am.

Jenette. I gasped. I lifted up my cellphone, and it was my little Nokia again. I shook my head and gritted my teeth, fighting between surprised joy at Jenette's call, and the unexplainable phenomenon of having memories I sadly didn't remember.

"Jenette?" I asked.

"Yeah, babe, hi…hey, Amanda was wondering if she could come over tonight for dinner so you could finally meet her. I could make her my world-famous white bean turkey chili. What do you think?"

Tears streamed from my eyes, and I didn't know why. Was it that we were still married, and apparently happily so? Or was it that I seemed to be in a moment of peace here from all the hysteria? Maybe a combination of both? I just had no clue who even knew me anymore, let alone whom I knew. Somewhere out there was a Dr. Penelope Eggers, and I needed to know if she still knew me.

"Uh, sure, hon, that sounds great," I said, muscling up a smile, and the tears continued to flow. I was so confused, and tears were the only clarity.

I wiped my eyes, and as I did so they were drawn to the counter to see if Winston had eaten his food. A can of nine lives was sitting there unopened. "Oh, come here, buddy," I said. "I forgot to feed Winston," I told Jenette.

"Aww! He'll live. He'll be fine. Okay, so, can we plan for 6? I figure we can chat for a bit after that. She just needs to be home by nine."

"Yeah, hon, that sounds just fine," I said. Something tingled my skin. I called out for Winston and clicked my tongue to summon him. A tiny gray lump burst up on the counter. He had already smelled it as I cracked open the can, and heard the *pshickt* of the can opening. "Can I pick up anything from the store for you?"

"Uh, sure, if you want, Jellybean. I think I'm out of Tropicana."

Jellybean?? My face scrunched up for a moment. She had never called me that, to my knowledge. "Huh? Since when do you call me Jellybean?" I laughed.

"What are you talking about? That's your nickname," she said cutely, and giggled. My skin tingled again for some reason. Was it cold in here? "And can you pick up some more chamomile tea please? I think I'm out."

Whatever. "Sure, hon. No problem." I was just glad to be doing normal things again with no psychiatrist, no lightning, and no FBI. "I-I love you," I stammered, and it came out weirdly.

"I love you too, Jellybean. Be home soon. Oh! Are you swinging by the library?"

Just like Jenette. My lip curled up at the end. She always remembered things right before she hung up.

"I can."

"I forgot to return the books that I got from the library for Joe-Joe, you remember him? The little boy next door?"

"Uh, *yeah*, I remember him." She had no clue, of course, about what happened a few nights ago.

"They're on my nightstand. It's the Nine Lives Series. About cats. I thought Amy could read it to Joe-Joe."

Something in me flinched, and I stopped scooping out the cat food into Winston's bowl. I looked at him, and he stared up, perplexed, licking his lips.

"Who is Amy?"

"*Amy,* silly! Amy and Terrell next door? Joe-Joe's parents! Are you okay??" she asked, confused.

I was not okay. I was not okay at all.

"Hon, are you there?" she asked.

My skin started to tingle, and I could feel my blood pressure rising. The phone fell out of my hands and clattered to the floor. Winston hissed at me and retreated under the bed in our room. I could hear him from far away growling at me as I steadied myself against the countertop.

Amy and Terrell? What the hell happened to Renita and Jake?

I heard Jenette's muffled voice coming from the floor out of the tiny earpiece on my phone. "Hon? Hon! Are you okay?"

I felt like I was going to vomit. My stomach started to churn violently. My vision swam as if I had been on a boat for hours. And then the flashes began.

A string of flashes, one after the next. And always, every single one of them, tinged with a number.

Nine.

September, the ninth month.

9:09am.

Nine Lives.

Jellybean had nine letters.

So did chamomile.

So did Tropicana.

Nine.

Someone was trying to tell me something. *Someone* out there was trying to send me a sign.

Fox's face came into my mind. As from a photographic memory, his words rang back through my mind with crystal clarity. *I'd like to come back to this numbering thing you mentioned, Roland. Maybe there's no rhyme or reason to it. Maybe it's not part of any kind of pattern. But we should be looking at that too.*

And then – just then – I started to awaken to the truth. Slowly, as a fog enveloping the land, it rolled over me, revealing truth after truth about my situation. My jaw dropped and my skin tingled, nervously. Suddenly, *I knew.*

In desperation, I snatched up my phone from the floor and hung up on my wife. "Call ya back," was all that I said. Winston hissed again.

I grabbed my coat and called the Jersey City Jail. I was rolling inside, but I tried to gain my composure and steady myself. I was getting more nauseous by the moment. Sweat dripped off me. I lost my balance as my legs buckled underneath me.

As I fell backward, my right hand shot out to grab onto something. From my palm emitted a blazing blue light, and a bolt of lightning arced from my hand to the lamp on our end table. The bulb burst and shattered, sending shards everywhere.

"Jersey City Jail," came the greeting.

Come on, you can do this. I breathed in carefully. "Hi, this is Agent Ryan Phelps. I need to speak with inmate Penelope Eggers. Authorization code FFA926B."

"One moment."

It was more than one moment. Flash after flash hit me. Wave after wave of nausea.

I couldn't hold back. Vomit spewed out of me all over the countertop, and I was about to pass out. *No….NO…* I willed myself to stay awake, and alert. I couldn't let any more time pass.

Whatever loop I was stuck in was consuming me, but I knew the truth and it couldn't stay here. *Must… stay… conscious…*

All of them. Nine.

"Hello? Sir, are you there?"

"Penny! Is this Penny?"

"Well yes, of course it is…? Is this…Roland? I thought it was Agent Phelps again."

"You remember me!"

"Well of course I remember you, you nitwit! When are you visiting me again? Have you heard from Detective Byers? I certainly hope you are keeping your sunny disposition!" She chortled.

"Oh Penny, you're too much. I'm coming to you. Stay right there."

"Yes. I'm in jail. I shall remain right here. Brilliant idea, Roland."

I rolled my eyes and tore out of there. *Hiss at me all you want, Winston. This has got to stop.*

"Oh, man, Penny. You have no idea how good it is to see you, and for you to kno-" I started to say, but she would have no idea what I was even saying. I'd have to tell her about my new bike even. I had a blue BMC before. Now, suddenly, I had a green Schwinn. I didn't even notice it until I hopped on it. It was as if some little elves had unlocked it from in front of the jail, switched it, and brought it back here to me, transformed entirely. Now I had this one instead. Just like how my phone kept changing.

I swear I was losing my mind.

"I'm losing my mind, Penny. Seriously."

"Whatever do you mean?" She tilted her head and looked at me quizzically. Her eyes squinted. "Has something happened?"

My eyes went wide and I gasped in laughter. "Has something happened? Ha!" I couldn't repress the sick humor of it all. "*Has something happened!?* Well, yes *and* no! A lot *and* nothing, Penny! I don't even know what to think anymore! It's like nothing *and* a double serving all at once, backward and forward, side to side, and I don't even get to drive."

My laughter faded as she just watched me, unsure what to think, and waiting for the slow unraveling of my thoughts. My eyes gradually fell down to her left arm. There, as a testament to a sure past that I could at least rely on for the next five minutes, was an iron-shaped burn. I sighed and shook my head.

"You're not going to believe any of it."

"Try me," she said instantly. "There are three things in life that you should never discredit, Roland. They are one, a woman, two, the elderly, and three, the British. I'm an elderly British woman. So try me if you dare."

I took a deep breath and just watched her. Her mouth was pressed into a pulled-back smile, clenched and ready for whatever truths I was prepared to unfold upon her.

"Okay. But don't say I didn't warn you."

I don't know what that authorization code thingy did, but it granted Penny a visit far outlasting any of the other inmates in her block. It wasn't just to reach her at any time; it was to give her – and me – all the time we needed. I didn't understand the power of it, but I was thankful for it.

We spent hours talking about the most infinite details of what had happened since she and I had last seen each other on the 28th, which was five days ago, and yet it was also eleven days ago.

I began to lose count of the many *fascinating!* and *how intriguing!* and *spellbinding!* and *riveting!* and every other adverb she could conjure up as she listened, hanging on my every word, captivated and enthralled. I was positive that there was no psychology or psychiatry course that covered any of it. She was in uncharted waters just the same as me.

Her incredulity was matched only by her good humor for the sheer inanity of it all.

"Wild, huh?" I asked her.

"To put it mildly," she grunted. "But it is not outside the realm of possibility, Roland. I said before that this was a gift. I mean it! But just look at all the gifts that came with it."

"Oh, Penny, I'm still not convinced this is a gift. This has been a whirlwind of upheaval. First I'm married to Jenette, then I'm not, first I saved my neighbor, then I didn't. Do you have any idea how many different phones I've had this week alone?"

She cocked her head.

"Every time something changes, I get a new phone, or a new bike…or a new wife….or a new name! Or…it's something else! *Something* changes. I get a number that changes every single day. It's so odd. It's like every time we get closer to Mohammed Atta, something in the future – or the past – changes, and has to adapt. Whoever is running all these timelines has got to have their head spinning by now."

"Hmm," was all she could say. "That *is* fascinating, truly. You should indeed get that to the agents straightaway. If you're correct, we still have some time. But not much. The clock is ticking, Roland."

"Have you ever heard of C.G. Jung?"

She shook her head, squinting her eyes at me, her fingers to her lips.

"He said, 'I am not what happened to me. I am what I choose to become.' Detective Byers shared that with me in one of the timelines, though now I don't remember which one anymore. It could be any one of them. Or all of them. Or, tomorrow, it could be none of them. I seriously have no idea." I took a long, cleansing sigh. "I'm losing it, Penny."

I cast a quick look up at the clock. I nodded her to it. She sported a confused look and turned around to see what I was seeing.

5:27pm.

"I think you missed chow time."

She turned back around, smiling. "Roland Bishop, if you think this right here isn't food for my soul, you've another think coming. And if you think jail food is actual food, you've yet another lined up beyond that one. I think all of this is marvelous. A ripping good time hearing how you've been faring out there. Quite apart from the nosebleeds, that is."

"A *ripping* good time, did you say? Ha! That sounds appropriate. It sounds as though there's been a rip in the space time continuum or something like that."

"A very astute observation." She looked at me hard and just held my gaze for a moment. It was almost as if she was trying to hypnotize me. My mind recalled being back there in her front room while she stared at me curiously over the rim of her mug. Life was simpler then.

"Here's what I would suggest, Roland.   Keep something with you at all times: something you know to be constant. Something that will never change."

I tilted my head at her.

"By all appearances, you seem to be running on parallel tracks of time all streaming into the future full steam ahead. It doesn't appear that you'll know which one you will be on at any given point in time, and your choices seem to be altering your trajectory *and* the trajectory of others. If what you currently possess is changing frequently, day by day, this might be a grounding element. It might stop the erratic jumps and keep you on a straightforward track. It also…"

She stopped, and I crinkled my brow at her. "What? Also what, Penny?" She appeared sad.

"Well, I daren't jump too far ahead or project us into any far-fetched doomsday scenarios, but, well, I'm a psychiatrist, Roland. I've seen patients enter a state of psychosis. It's not pleasant. They lose the best part of themselves in the process. I don't want anything like that to happen to you. You are my friend, Roland." She smiled at me, motherly and kind.

"You always told me to say that thing to myself. *I'm Roland Bishop, and I know where I am.* I actually twisted it the other day. I said I know *who* I am. I needed to. I wasn't sure if I was Roland Bishop or Ethan Stiles. It was eerie."

"Hmm. That may be all it takes. But I encourage you to find something tangible. Something that is uniquely and irrefutably *you.* Carry it with you at all times. It would be a disagreeable tragedy to lose you, Mr. Bishop," she said, leaning forward on her elbows and staring at me endearingly.

I smiled back.

"Is that my psychiatrist talking, or my British friend?"

Her smile grew wider.

"Well, I was an Amazonian enchantress wielding a staff of light in another life. You may address me as Lady Divinitus," she said with a giggle. "So I'm part friend, part psychiatrist, part superhero myself."

"Wow," I said, and I couldn't hold back the chuckle.

She laughed a gentle laugh and stowed her laughter. "In all sincerity, you have full right to call me 'Penny' until the end of days. Yours or mine." And then she put her hand up against the glass pane between us, fingers outstretched.

A warmth spread through my chest, radiating from her heart into mine. This was a special lady who had conquered her own pain and used it to turn the tide against the cause. I was so proud to know her.

I slowly reached out my hand to touch hers through the pane. Simple glass couldn't separate us.

She pulled her hand away and started right back in. "Now. Tell me about the numbers. How they keep changing. I'm especially interested in that. They're not going to let me talk much longer, and I'm starting to feel a bit peckish."

"Oh, Penny, it's insane. The numbers I've been seeing! Today, I got *nine.* It's September 2nd. On August 27th I got *fifteen.* When I jumped forward to September 8th, I got *three.*"

She stared at me blankly.

"Penny, don't you see? It's a *countdown!* I have to get this to the Detective and the FBI guys. It's a countdown, Penny. With each new day I get a new number, and depending on which day I'm on, that tells me when the hijacking is supposed to happen. I'm almost sure of it.

"It's *September 11th,* Penny. That's when they're going to do it. It all makes sense. The more days away from September 11th I am, the higher the number. The closer I am to September 11th, the lower the number. I put it all together in my head today when the number *nine* kept appearing out of thin air during a call with Jenette."

Penny still didn't say anything. She had stopped moving. *What?* "Penny?"

And then…flashes. White hot flashes. Electricity shooting through the transparent surface, connecting us and bridging the gap with pulverizing light and energy.

I couldn't pull away.

On the other side of the glass, it seemed Penny was retreating, being slowly pulled back by a tether, dwindling into the distance, all the while frozen in time, frozen in a maternal expression of interest in my story.

A vortex opened up behind her, glistening with rotating light and color, flashes of iridescent and spatial light emanating from it, shooting out like galaxial emissaries, seeking me with some connecting message of love from her.

Yet, somehow, Penny was continuously being pulled magnetically backward, and I couldn't move toward her. I was stuck in a fixed position, immovable, paralyzed. The glass acted as an eternal barrier: translucent and impermeable.

I watched as Penny's arms stretched endlessly, stuck to the table while the rest of her withdrew into the recesses of time and space.

Keep your sunny disposition, I heard a faint voice urge me. Was that just me? Or had she whispered that to me from the other side of time?

And then she was gone. Her mind, body and spirit: gone. My counselor was taken from me.

I didn't know what to think! I had just lost Penny, and thus, a little piece of me.

1 Day To Go

September 10th, 2001 • Jersey City, NJ

I woke up today feeling frightened and tense.

Uncertain of the future, and unsure of who I really was in all of it. Would there even *be* a future?

What had I just witnessed? Penny had literally evaporated, *dissipated* into thin air right before my eyes on the other side of that glass. It was calmly brutal and brutally calm, the taking of my counselor. I had no idea what to think.

I rolled over to check my clock on the end table. My eyes felt glossed over and clouded. I blinked hard to clear out the night's gunk and the confusion, and tilted my head up at it.

September 10th, 2001. 1:01am.

That couldn't be right! No! I bolted up in a pang of fear, awash with tension. How could it be only one day to go?

Tomorrow was when the frightening and intense attacks would hap-

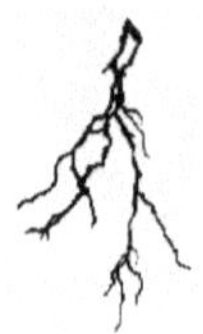

1 Day To Go

September 10th, 2001 • Jersey City, NJ

My eyes opened and I gasped in frustration.

Everything seemed to freeze for a moment. In the dim morning light streaming through the window, dust particles hung in the air, unmoving and ambivalent to my dream.

I was in a cold sweat, and my muscles were tensed as I panted heavily.

What a horrible dream! I had this knowledge in me that was more of a curse than a blessing, equipping me with neither realization nor awareness. No. Instead, it kept saddling me with caution and anxiety.

I let out my breath slowly. I still had time. It was okay; it was just a nightmare. Pain stabbed through my head fleetingly, and I closed my eyes, swallowing hard and attempting to regulate my breathing.

That's when I saw the number *one* dimly appear in my subconscious, and my eyes slowly opened once more, ringed with alarm.

I whipped over to the clock and saw the readout clearly:

September 10th, 2001. 1:01am again.

No! It wasn't a dream! Not again!

My eyes closed and I gasped, still here, trapped in this damned frustr-

8 Days To Go

September 3rd, 2001 • Jersey City, NJ

I woke up, hung my head and cried.
It was just like the old song:

The other night, dear, while I lay sleeping
I dreamed I held you in my arms
But when I woke up, I was mistaken
And I hung my head and cried…

Penny was gone. Dr. Penelope Eggers, my friend, counselor, murderess, witty sage, bastion of encouragement and direction, taken from me without warning. But what caused it? I hadn't seen any warning signs, no premonitions or visions, nothing to hint that she was departing.

Nothing.

The only constant friend I had, the only thing that seemed to remain, was Winston. He was rubbing up against my leg, and his tail was slicing the air against me, twitching. He looked up at me and meowed. I managed a meager smile, reaching down and scratching the scruff of his neck. The soft purr was audible in the deafening silence of the empty apartment.

None of it made any sense, the least of which was this. In the middle of it, the number *eight* appeared dim yet resounding in my mind. Had Penny moved to the other side? Was she now at some 'Clock of Life,' pushing on the hands with steadiness, using all her might to preserve forward momentum?

I didn't know. I just didn't know anything anymore, and here I was all over again at the starting line.

When I came to, it was 3:08pm. The very first thing I did was call Jersey City Jail and ask if they had an inmate named Penelope Eggers there.

"What was that name again?" asked the jail operator. I repeated it for her.

No such inmate here by that name.

Penny truly was gone. Either that, or she was trapped in whatever vortex everything else had been swirling around in, perhaps under some other name, and maybe her own knowledge was compromised as the others' had been. Another timeline owned her…at least for now.

A phone call for me this time. The ringtone sounded different. I looked at it. I wasn't sure I was ready for whomever it was, but as I lifted my phone to my face to see the display, it was a Motorola V60 flip phone. The same phone I suddenly had when the agents called me *Ethan Stiles*. Where was my little Nokia again?

It was an unlisted number. My mind scrambled for a moment, trying to think back to that whole *Jellybean* business yesterday with Jenette. I wondered what nonsense today would bring.

"Hello?" she asked. It was Jenette's voice.

"Yeah. Oh! Hey, hon."

"Please don't call me that."

My eyes squinted. "What?" I asked tiredly.

"I just called to let you know that I filed. The paperwork has been submitted like you requested. I tried to send you a text but it-"

"Like I requested? What paperwork?"

"Seriously? Are you drunk? Please don't make me spell it out for you."

"Hon, I don-"

"*Don't* call me that! I'm back in Seattle. Don't try to find me. I'm not coming back. I filed the paperwork. You should hear from my lawyer within the week."

"Seattle. Seattle? What?" I asked briskly, getting irritated. "What? You tell me that *I* requested that you file, you ask to have Amanda over for your white bean turkey chili, you call me *Jellybean* and ask me to get your Tropicana? What is all this? None of this makes sense!"

She paused: enough time for my blood pressure to rise dramatically. "What? What are you talking about?"

"Oh yeah. *Yeah. I'm* the insane one. Whatever happened to *Jellybean* and your friggin' *chamomile?!*" I screamed into the phone at her, turning and hurling it against the wall. It shattered into a few different pieces. Winston scampered away once more in fright, making for the bedroom.

I threw myself down onto the couch.

A soft knock at the door. I sighed, shook my head, cursed, and got up. With any luck it would be the Mormons. Good. I needed someone to beat up.

"Who is it?"

"Uh, hi, it's Renita and Jacob, your next door neighbors?"

My eyes widened, and I opened the door.

The woman standing outside was not Renita. The baby in her arms was not Joe-Joe. The man standing beside her was not Jake. My heart sank. How much longer would this go on?

"Hi, we're your neighbors. I'm Renita and this is Jake. And this little guy is Joe-Joe. Say hi, Joe-Joe," she teased, and the little baby leaned against her shyly, his pacifier bobbing in his mouth. "We were, uh, just getting ready to head out for dinner and we heard – whatever that was. Are you okay? Is everything alright?"

I gasped and snorted. I looked down at the floor for a moment. How in the hell could either one of them have known that people with their same names had been so prominent in my life only a week earlier, ending in his tragedy? They didn't look like Renita, Jake or Joe-Joe, but they had their names. I was truly going insane, I was convinced of that now.

"Um, I-I'm," I tried. "I'm fine. Really. Thanks. I just… bad conversation with the wife. *Ex*-wife, I guess."

"Oh, no, I'm so sorry." She sucked her teeth in. "If there's anything we can do to help?" she asked tentatively.

"Yeah, we're just right here," Jake said, pointing to their apartment.

Yeah, I know, man, okay? I just killed you a few nights ago, I thought.

"Yeah, I appreciate it. Okay. Thanks. Everything is fine. Just…blowing off some steam I guess."

They both looked at me as if yearning for an alternate explanation. "Okay, well, just let us know," said Jake, extending his hand toward me. "Take care, man. It's, uh, *Ethan,* right? I saw your name on the mailbox."

I had begun to extend my hand out toward him but then it jerked back seemingly of its own accord.

No wonder Jenette didn't call me Roland, I thought. *She had been married to Ethan.* No wonder her number didn't show up. Somewhere in the grand scheme of parallel timelines, someone was messing with Roland and Ethan's tracks and couldn't keep things straight. Some sadistic, celestial killjoy was tampering with my life, and it was a sick game of chaos theory or the butterfly effect. Sooner or later, I was going to wind up being either Ethan Bishop or Roland Stiles, and either would be in a straitjacket. I didn't care which anymore. I was just starting to get pissed off.

"Alright, fine. Thanks," I said, closing my door abruptly on them.

I was going to get answers. I was sick and tired of being messed with. In a fit of rage I swept the planter off of our little dining table a few paces from the front door, shattering it and spilling dirt everywhere. I cursed again, and pulled on my own hair, nearly yanking it out. I passed the kitchen and happened to look over.

There, on the ground, was my little phone, in pieces. I shook my head. Now I couldn't even call anyone. I couldn't call Jenette back, not that I would. I couldn't call Detective Byers, not that she would even believe me.

And I couldn't call Penny because she didn't exist.

My sunny disposition was becoming a rainy, contemplative thousand-yard stare, devoid of connection.

"Screw it," I said, disconnected and ambivalent.

I hung my head and sighed, and just went to sleep.

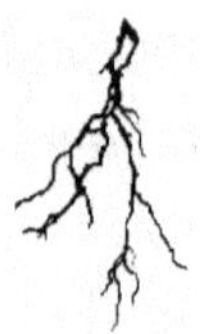

7 Days To Go

September 4th, 2001 • Jersey City, NJ

The future and the past were blending together in a seamless blur, hazy and confusing.

I awoke to a new day. The number *seven* almost jumped out at me from the walls. Spooked Winston. He fled to his usual haven of seclusion: the far recesses below our bed, closest to the corner of the room.

I shot out of bed feeling a resolve I couldn't explain, except for the fact that I was just tired of the inconsistency bullshit. I had to get back on my own track and find my way back to me. To life. To purpose.

To Detective Byers. I needed to call her.

Before I even got dressed, I went out to see if it were even possible to make a call on my pho-

There it was, sitting on the counter. *On the counter.* Last night it was in fragments on the floor. Yet there it was, my old Nokia 3310, lying there, fully intact, as if it had never once been thrown and never once been a Motorola V60. I picked it up and just stared at it, finally grunting and setting it back down. Why was I not even surprised anymore?

There were no guarantees in waking. Not anymore.

I wondered if Jenette had still filed. I wondered if Renita and Jake looked like their old selves…or if Jake looked like death embalmed. I wondered if Penny was still there.

Winston! That was the constant that I needed. That was one of the last things that Penny urged me to do before I lost her. *Carry it with you at all times.* So that's what I did. I took Winston's collar off him and looked at the ID tag that I had made so many years ago before we moved here. It read, clearly, *Roland Bishop*, and my phone number. But beyond that, there was a strange logo, an R and a B together, in a stylish fusion: something I had worked on in my spare time. That was *definitely* me. I loosened it a bit more, and then fastened it around my wrist.

God bless you, Penny. I won't lose this.

I moved with purpose and tightened that cat collar around my wrist until it hurt. It would be a sensory reminder that I could not ignore, and would be with me at all times.

I grabbed my stupid transforming cellphone.

I picked up Winston, scratching his chin and kissing him hard until he protested.

I threw on some clothes and a Yankees baseball cap, slamming the door on my way out. It was time to see Detective Roxanne Byers, if that was even her name.

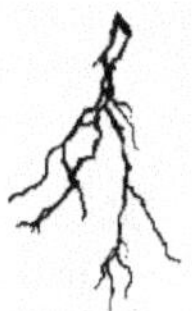

Thankfully, she was in my contacts. "Detective Byers, it's Roland Bishop. Are you at your office?"

I had just gotten out of the Holland Tunnel and was riding slowly up West Street along the waterfront. It was a beautiful, sunny day, though the wind was brisk and gusty flowing down the Hudson with the water. There loomed up the two towers, gleaming proudly.

"No, I'm not, Roland. Hey, where did you go last night? You just disappeared." She sounded like she was in the middle of something urgent and was speaking quickly.

"Disappeared?"

"Yeah, *disappeared*. You were here in the office and then it was like you just got up and left. But no one had seen you exit the building."

"I wasn't at your office yesterday. I didn't see you at all, Roxanne."

Pause. "What? Is this some kind of a joke?"

"I'll explain later. Where are you?"

"Central Park. Got a tip that Atta is there. And Ryan says there are *four* planes now. There used to be just one, if you recall. Somehow their flight plans changed again."

A chill ran down my spine. Had that timeline been changed? I had seen him there on the 8th. That's when the whirlwind hit me. But that date hadn't come yet! It was still only the 4th! Whatever I was doing kept changing the timeline and the events leading up to it. But this one remained consistent. Why?

"Wait – Byers!"

"Hold *on*, Roland!" I could hear her talking to a fellow cop over her walkie-talkie in the background. She concluded with a "10-4" and then she was back on. "Gotta go, Roland. Stakeout. Talk soon."

"No wait, Byers, don't!"

Suddenly, the images of Detective Byers getting shot, of Phelps getting gunned down, of Atta and his colleagues in the park careened wildly through my mind.

The nosebleed started instantly. It was on replay this time, but it was still the same vision. I wasted no time.

I got on my BMC and increased my speed. I suddenly registered that the bike wasn't my Schwinn bike anymore. I shook my head and just dismissed it. I had to save Byers! I pedaled faster. It would take me at *least* twenty minutes to get to Central Park. I had to save her.

The wind sliced through my hair as I raced up Empire State Trail.

I broke off at West 52nd Street and careened through traffic. A car just missed me at 52nd and 11th, and smashed into another in the waiting intersection. A cop on horseback saw all of it and began to pursue. "Shit!" I exclaimed, whipping out my phone and frantically trying to steer my bike while calling Byers again. It rang and then went to voicemail. "Dammit!"

I pedaled harder. The sweat was building in my hair and on my neck. I could feel my shirt getting damp, but the wind mitigated it.

Only a few more blocks to 8th, and then I could head north again! A helicopter rushed by overhead, and I looked up. I traced its trajectory. Sure enough, it was heading for Central Park. I tried to call Byers again. Nothing.

I willed my legs to pump harder, and as I clenched the handlebars of my bike, Winston's collar dug into my wrist. That reminded me of who I was and where I was, at least. I adapted it. *I'm Roland Bishop, and I know who I am. I'm Roland Bishop, and I know where I'm going. I'm Roland Bishop, and I know what I need to do.*

Yellow cabs were everywhere, yellow blurs whizzing past me as I screamed north.

I slashed through 10th, and then again through 9th. 8th loomed up before me, and there was a large truck and construction working there. A few guys in orange jackets were milling around and the road at 8th and 52nd heading east was cordoned off with cones. I zipped through, and went right underneath a bulldozer. They screamed at me and hurled insults.

I had lost the first cop, thankfully, but there was another one on horseback, and he called after me, raising his horse to a gallop and pursuing me up 8th. I saw cop cars over on 7th, and then a blinding flash tore through me.

Man, I wish I had a motorcycle, I thought to myself. I had to get there! My hair was sopping now as I pedaled hard. Up ahead, a long line of cars was stopped at 8th and West 55th St for some reason. Honks sounded in a dissonant symphony of noise. I did the only thing I could do and screamed out into oncoming traffic, dodging cars right and left. One of them clipped my rear wheel as I weaved to the left, passing briefly under a long awning flanked by scaffolding and netting as workers improved the façade of the building at the intersection of 8th and 55th. Someone screamed at me. "Get the hell out of the road, ya moron!"

I spotted a yellow cab up ahead, heading north. Nothing but green lights. I flicked my head back. The cop on horseback was gaining on me. *Come on, legs.* I pumped them as hard as I could and caught up with the cab, grabbing onto the trunk edge where it met the window, and desperately trying to keep myself pointing straight. I kept my eyes on my front wheel.

Too low. A sidewalk vendor jutted out too far into the street and I almost lost my head against a cooker housing falafels in the making. My right leg clipped his stand, spinning his countertop somewhat. It all happened so fast.

I looked back. The cop was dwindling. Just then I heard yelling from inside the taxi. The driver was now aware of me and was railing at me with angry hand gestures. But he didn't slow down.

The taxi finally started to slow as we were almost to Columbus Circle. By then, I was starting to hear a ringing in my ears.

That's when the flashes started. I clutched my head in agony. White flashes zipped through my mind. I inadvertently let go of his cab as he banked around the circle and sped away. My bike wobbled, and I grabbed ahold of it. I felt nauseous. The trees loomed up and I lost my vision momentarily, swarmed with heat and flashes. I moaned in pain, clutching my temples once more. I lost my presence of mind and let go of the handlebars, and I went crashing into the trees in the southwest corner.

Dazed, I stumbled up. I had to get moving. It wouldn't be long before the 10-foot-cop caught up to me. Mounted police officers had a reputation for, ahem, *impatience.*

I ditched my bike and ran, careening through the trees onto West Drive, whipping out my phone. *Come on, Byers, pick up!*

More flashes. More searing pain. More nosebleed. I could hear the helicopter, and I looked up. It was north of me, maybe about a mile. That's when I saw other flying shapes. Four of them. The hijacked planes.

There were four of them again.

Without warning, the haunting visions flooded my mind. Shouting in the sky. People falling from above. Ash and smoke. Horror below as bodies pummeled the pavement. But where? Where were they falling from? From the airplanes?

I crashed through Heckscher kickball fields and bolted across the softball fields next, heading for East 65th Street. "Byers! Detective Byers!" I called, but my voice choked as a burst of flashes racked my brain. A series of them collided together, enveloping me in back-to-back stings. The aftermath was utterly throbbing. I wiped my nose as I hurled myself forward again. "Byers! Byers!" I called frantically.

I passed the Sheep Meadow right across the street. If she was anywhere on the south side of the park, she should be able to hear me from there. It was unobstructed. It was also where everything changed for me on the 8th, in what was for me only three days ago, despite the fact that it was only the 4th today.

More flashes, and more visions.

Before I knew it, I was racing up East Drive, my feet flying with the wind.

Flash.

Someone with a handgun jumping out of the trees, firing wildly into Phelps' chest.

Flash.

Fox lying nearby, his head blown apart, and a pool of blood pouring from him.

Flash.

Another assailant shooting at Byers as she returned fire. And then she was on the ground, but still moving.

The chopper was almost directly overhead, drowning out my cries of *Detective Byers! I need you!* I called with all of my might, but my voice was getting hoarse. I also knew that I would be drawing that mounted policeman to myself.

No reply. All I could do was keep running and calling for her. People veered out of my way. Pulling my phone to my ear once more, I tried calling her one last time before I sprinted full-tilt for the other end of the park. I thought I heard a noise behind me as I crossed the 79th Street

Transverse cutting around Turtle Pond and making for the softball field in the great lawn.

Before I knew what happened, something struck me in the leg. I winced in pain and was down on the ground instantly, choking and breathing hard. The ringing in my ears grew louder and I started hyperventilating. I was just shy of the softball field, sprawled out across the path.

I groaned in agony and looked back, reaching down for my leg. Blood streamed from it. The mounted police officer was running up toward me, gun drawn, talking into his shoulder radio.

And just then, another noise behind me. Men, five of them, running. Off in the distance, I saw a thick head of billowing brown hair leaping over a hedge and chasing after them, other officers in tow. The woman cried out, "Freeze!"

The mounted officer called out "Freeze!"

I lost it. Byers was in danger. My visions happened; they became part of history after I saw them. I would not let her die. Or Phelps. Or Fox. I turned around and summoned up every bit of emotion as I was racked with white flashes and pain. Planes flying through the sky. Planes slamming into buildings. Buildings! One of them, very large. Another plane slamming into a green mass of Earth, carving a commercial jet-sized cavernous hole two-hundred twenty feet wide as a fireball engulfed my vision.

Blood streamed from my nose as I tried to stand.

"Get down on the ground, now!"

I'm Roland Bishop, and I know who I am. My skin tingled. My heartbeat raced. All I could see was hot blue coming from my eyes. As a note starting on the lowest end of the scale but escalating in pitch, blending with a crude harmonic, a hideous noise welled out of me and turned into an ear-piercing cacophony. I could feel my own ears bleeding.

The sun was blotted out by gathering clouds. The weather overhead changed. Briefly I caught a glimpse of the helicopter floundering, regaining its composure, and then vacating the area.

"Down on the ground or I will fire on you again!"

I looked at him, and his jaw dropped. He was covering one of his ears as he had his gun trained on me. But his gun was lowering as he gaped. I don't know what he saw, but I know what I felt.

I arched my back. I whipped my head forward as a tremendous pulse of energy snapped outward from my core, expanding in an unlimited and vicious diameter of radiating ire and heat.

The cop was suddenly blown backward and his gun went flying. He grunted, collected his wits and glared back up at me in shock and awe.

I raised my arms with my palms to the sky, and arcs of lightning burst forth from them, connecting with every bit of iron, steel, aluminum, titanium, and every other metal around me, seeking a grounding connection. My mouth expelled heat and I was engulfed in blue flame.

I'm using my gifts, Penny. This is my sunny disposition. I'm Roland Bishop, and I know who I am.

I could feel myself lift off the ground, and I turned back north, hovering up and above the trees as arcs and flashes of lightning emanated from my core and connected with random conduits for each burst. Through a blue mist I could see the Detective racing after someone. A few men fled from her presence.

And then, further up, I could see two men in suits sprinting back south to cut them off as they ran. Shots were fired. People fled in all directions. A whirlwind was around me and the vortex swirled chaotically, sending shrapnel, litter, loose branches and dust and dirt spinning off in all directions. I could feel the cop's eyes watching me along with others. Yet I only had eyes for Byers as I wafted over the trees, my arms outstretched.

There she was, her own gun drawn and pointed at an unknown assailant concealed in the trees. I descended upon him with wrath, bolts of lightning pulsing from my mouth and my eyes. The air swirled as I dropped to the ground. Byers looked over at me in horror as the wind whipped her hair up into a frenzy.

And then, the gun fired. I saw it, as if in slow motion, speeding out from under the trees and across from her toward the Alexander Hamilton Monument, slicing through the air. Without so much as a word, I grimaced, and a band of current traced from my fingertips, intersecting with the path of the bullet. Byers dove behind a tree. The bullet exploded in a micro-burst of shrapnel.

Phelps and Fox returned fire, downing one of the assailants. Another stood there and opened fire at them. Two more fled.

The two agents dashed for cover close to Byers. All three of them were pinned down.

Something Byers had said to me earlier. What was it? Through the blue haze and smoke, I remembered her words.

The kid pulled a 'crossfire gambit.' Like, a double-cross move and had the bad guys shoot at each other. They ended up killing each other off.

With every pulsing fiber of my distorted being, I flew between the gunner and the gunned, drawing his attention. It was Mohammed Atta himself. I faced him, swirling to my right as he watched me in dread. I held his gaze. He turned his gun on me. I moved between he and his fleeing assailants. They were now aware of me. Suddenly, all of their names flashed before my eyes.

Marwan al-Shehhi.

Nawaf al-Hazmi.

Khalid al-Mihdhar.

The two fleeing terrorists, al-Hazmi and al-Mihdhar, whipped their bodies around and opened fire, sending a volley of ammunition racing eastward at me, as Atta emptied his magazine of his remaining bullets westward in my direction.

I closed my eyes and breathed, lifting my head toward the sky. As a passing wind, I was gone, and so were the terrorists, killed in the crossfire gambit.

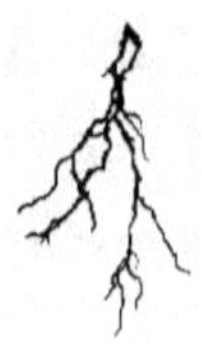

The cop dug his knee into my back and held me down. Winston's collar dug further into my skin as the dirt pressed it inward. "Stay down, d'ya hear me? Suspect down, suspect down," he spoke into his radio. "Move back, everyone, stay clear! Central, I'm at the 79th Street Transverse. Just west of East Drive before the field, over?"

"Roger, on our way," came the reply.

"Don't move, punk. Don't even breathe," he said firmly, and I could feel the cold steel of a barrel in my neck.

Footsteps running. Running. Men and women allowed to come closer. "I got him!" shouted the cop. "This who you're looking for?"

"Yeah, that's him!" yelled a man, breathing hard, and holstering his weapon. I recognized the voice. Phelps.

"Hold him down, he might spring," said Fox. Both men came over and forcibly pulled my hands behind my back, cuffing me.

"What the hell are you doing, Fox?" My voice sounded strange. Thick and weird. My mouth tasted like blood. They jerked me up and held me before them, finishing the handcuffs and hauling me eastward, presumably toward 5th Avenue and a waiting police car.

Phelps was alive. So was Fox. I looked around desperately. Where was Byers? She had to be still alive too!

There she was! She came running down from East Drive to meet the Agents as they led me to their car.

"Nice try, mister. Almost outran us. Your buddies weren't so fortunate either. Might wanna make plans without them for the rest of their lives."

"Byers, what the hell are you doing?"

"Shut it. I got him, guys," she said proudly. The mounted police officer rode off. They walked me eastward. It was the strangest sensation…I didn't know what was happening. Had I hurt someone? No, that wasn't it. Had I damaged public property? Almost certainly. That wasn't it either. And then I felt it.

My leg. It was perfectly fine. I looked down. No rip in my jeans. No bullet hole. No limping. It was gone.

Everything changed. Again.

I turned to Byers. "Detective Byers, you have to believe me. I'm not-"

"Shut it, Atta!" Phelps said. "I don't wanna hear it! Just get in the car."

We reached the car. I whipped back around to Agent Phelps. "What did you call me?" I asked, wincing from disbelief. My voice spoke with an accent that was not me.

"Get in the car, *Mohammed,*" he hissed. He searched me, extracting my phone from my pocket. I saw it. Splitting the front of the phone face in half was a large tactile flip keyboard, and a monochromatic screen. A Kyocera QCP-6035 smartphone. I had never had one of those before! I had never even bothered with a Blackberry.

My eyes froze upon him and a wave of fear passed over me. The squad car opened and I was thrust violently inside, my head hitting the opposite door handle. Blood streamed down my forehead.

Atta. He called me Mohammed Atta.

I glanced through to the front seat and noticed the cop's computer display. It read 2:42pm. How long was I electrified? How long had all of that taken?

I had no answers, and this was not the change I was looking for.

Byers, Phelps and Fox were alive, but now, I *myself* was the enemy.

The truth and the lie had blended together in a
seamless blur, unnerving and terrifying.

6 Days To Go

September 5th, 2001 • Manhattan, NY

It was all starting to make sense to me now.

This whole terrorist plot was *going* to happen. It was inevitable. And I was caught up in the inevitability of it. We all were. But whatever I did seemed to have the most bearings on it. No matter how much I changed things, or interfered, the hijackings were going to happen and the terrorists would have their way.

I shook my head, thinking back to that damned hotel where Agent Mulligan had Atta in a chokehold. I should have just let him strangle him. Just let him kill him.

Shoulda coulda woulda as they say. That was now all in the past.

And now, they thought I myself was Mohammed Atta. Hell, my face felt different, my accent was different, and I had all kinds of memories that I never remembered, once more, fusing with the ones that I knew to be true. I was Roland Bishop *and* Ethan Stiles *and* Mohammed Atta all rolled into one. The one I knew the least was Ethan Stiles. At the very least, I remembered where it was that I had seen Stiles before, but that brought me no comfort.

Maybe Atta and I could sit down to a nice cup of tea someday and discuss trading lives in a nice Arabic language. I laughed grimly to myself. This whole thing was ridiculous.

And what the hell had happened to me out there? I thought the first episode was bad. This was much worse.

They had patched up my bleeding head, treated my nosebleed, and then tossed me into a small, windowless room at the FBI office after pulling into the parking garage and thrusting a bag over my head. I rolled my eyes. *I've already been here, fellas. I could tell you about the futon, the file cabinet at the end of the conference room, Phelps' office, and his authorization code. Been there, done that.*

Once inside, they pulled the bag off my head and searched me before slamming me into a dark office, tying me to a chair, shutting off the light and locking the door. That was at 6pm. Agent Phelps pulled out my cellphone, that strange Kyocera smartphone again. Finished with that, he examined Winston's collar on my wrist and laughed scornfully at it, shaking his head. "Nice jewelry, Atta."

I grimaced at him. *It's more than that,* I thought, angrily.

Fox fiercely extracted my wallet and held it up to my face. "See this? This is what a scumbag looks like. You'll find out what we do to scumbags."

I just stared at it, firm and unwavering.

There, on the license, right before my eyes, was the name *Mohammed Atta*. My thin, pursed lips. My bushy, chestnut hair. My piercing black eyes set under thick black daunting eyebrows. My scratchy neck. My downcurved cheeks that hinted at disapproval. My slightly drooping left eyelid. My white T-Shirt and black button-up pulled high up my neckline.

It wasn't me, but it was me.

Just like that wasn't me, hovering there in Central Park, shooting lightning out of my ass at everything and everyone. But it was me.

It was, unfortunately, all me.

That was last night.

Now, I was sitting here, awake and alert, staring at the floor, wondering what to do in the early morning of September 5th, 2001. The number *six* kept appearing dimly, cascading before my eyes in the thick ink of that dark room, sometimes zooming into me and startling my vision.

Six days until the hijacking. I knew it. I just had to make *them* know it.

I didn't know what time it was, but there was no noise outside. Everyone must have left for the night except for the agents.

I sensed something.

My wrist throbbed. The cuffs were digging into my skin, and my arms were growing tired from being looped around the back of this chair.

And there, in the darkness of that room, I heard a voice calling to me dimly. It was a sweet, gentle voice that could be firm at times, coming across in tones both tender and resolute. A maternal voice, beckoning to me from the deeps of time and space. There was a yearning in that voice, of some kind of longing unfulfilled, some wrong never quite righted. I knew it well.

Penny.

Was she alive? Hope kindled in me and erupted into a fire, yearning in return for that sweet voice. Could it be that she had never existed in one timeline because of the choices that I had made, and yet now that everything had been flipped, she was alive again?

Anything was possible, I told myself. I had to see her. I strained my shoulders back to adjust my cuffs and stop them from cutting into my wrists, when I felt it.

There, in the dark, with no light, working by feel, I felt Winston's collar on my wrist.

I pressed it firmly. *I'm Roland Bishop, and I know who I am.* It was almost an incantation now, firm and secure, an anchor for my timeline. And just as swiftly the thought came to me, *What if I control my own timeline?*

What if I'm *in charge? Instead of things happening to me and around me, what if* I *happened to* it *and* I *happened around* it?" I tried to wrap my brain around that.

The hijacking had to be stopped, whether Atta was a part of it any longer or not. These terrorists didn't operate alone. Perhaps I could even infiltrate their midst and gain valuable intel that would make the FBI, Byers, anyone, believe me. After all, Phelps and Fox – and maybe even Byers – owed me their lives. If I hadn't done my lightning thing at the park, they might be dead. I averted that future for them. They just didn't know it yet.

I remembered what Byers had said to me, that C.G. Jung quote. *I am not what happened to me. I am what I choose to become.*

My breathing slowed. I closed my eyes, blotting out the dark and the reality. I projected myself outside this cell.

It began quietly.

A faint rumble.

Winston's collar starting to feel so hot against my skin that I grimaced.

A ringing in my ears that grew in volume.

Slowly, the room started to glow around me in a faint hue of azure. Cerulean swirls, vaporous sapphire and eddies of cobalt fused together around me as my little prison blazed with light. As before, I felt dizzy and spasmed. My eyes were closed, but I could see it all. My breathing was measured, though I was buffeted with wind.

Once more, the world whirred around me. What I couldn't even see – the dark of this room – spun like a top around my *Mohammed Atta* shell sitting there in that cell, and the black flew out of my view. Once more, there was thunder in the wind, and there was lightning in the thunder. Once more, the latter took the place of the former, the new substituting the old in that same frenetic patchwork exchange, as the wind howled around me. Light filtered in through chinks in the dark, and the dark gave way in shifting segments that slid and moved out of the way to accommodate the new reality around me.

Blood streamed from my nose and ran down my adopted lips, and this foreign head I was now trapped in throbbed with pain. I didn't know the body, but I knew that cranial angina. *Mild intracranial hematoma*, Dr. Walker had said. *Oh, if he could see me now.*

The heat from Winston's cat collar burned through the strong metal of the cuffs and sent glowing embers flying as I wrenched my hands free. Scalding liquid metal dripped to the floor from their remnants.

I looked out of my cell, from a different building in a different town.

The small table to the right of the door had my Kyocera phone sitting there, turned off. I grabbed it and stepped out of my old cell into a new world: a different building in a different town. But where was I?

The heat hit me first. Hot scorching heat, and my clothes felt way too thick. Vegetation everywhere. There were bronzed hills and caves stretching for miles around me, dotted with evergreens, oaks, almond trees, pine and fir. Treeless steppes extended to the north. Uninhabitable deserts scrolled away to the south. To the east, montane conifer forests with shrubs, herbaceous cover and open woodland went as far as the eye could see.

All over, the image seemed glossy; softened edges around everything, somehow, out of a vignette. Hazy and murky, distinct from reality. Even my very air seemed manufactured.

But where I was, there were caves. And where I was, there was one not thirty feet from me. And where I could see, there was a six-foot-four-inch man with an olive complexion. He was dressed in a traditional Yemeni keffiyeh under a green army field jacket with no insignia. He had a gold shawl draped over himself. His foot-long beard stretched below piercing eyes and a hooked nose with high cheeks, outlined as he approached me.

He greeted me. "As-salamu alaikum," he breathed, and wrapped his arms around me. "Welcome, Mohammed," he said, and I smiled in a reflex, though I hadn't intended to.

"Nahar, Osama," I said, and the language came freely from my lips, though I'd never studied.

There, before me, stood Osama bin Mohammed bin Awad bin Laden.

Winston's collar made its presence known, hot against my wrist, but concealed under my black shirt. bin Laden did not notice, hopefully. I was sitting with him and his Taliban and al Qaeda militants in the Tora Bora caves. Stunningly, I could discern their speech. We were eating late in the day, taking in some of the cool evening air of Afghanistan.

They talked about their immense plans for 'The Great Satan,' as they called America, and as I listened to them, it all became suddenly clear to me.

In six days, jihad would reach an apex as they prayed to Allah the Omniscient for the restoration of Sharia law. They would move on Allah's behalf to strike The Great Satan at the core of its pride, in three key geographic areas.

Financially, they would attack the World Trade Center. The 1993 bombing had not done enough. The buildings must be leveled to the ground.

Militarily, they would attack the Pentagon.

Governmentally, they would attack the White House.

All three of their targets were now plain for me to hear, and their brothers in America were already moving. Pieces were already being moved into place and I, Mohammed Atta, was one of them.

They named all of the jihadist pilots who were already in America. Astonishingly, they named me, though I was sitting right there in the midst of them.

Mohammed Atta.

Marwan al-Shehhi.

Hani Hanjour.

Ziad Jarrah.

They even listed flight numbers, corroborating what the brothers in America had previously confirmed with them. Mohammed Atta was to take American Airlines Flight 11. al-Shehhi was to take United Airlines Flight 175. Hanjour was to take American Flight 77. Jarrah was to take United Airlines Flight 93.

I, Mohammed Atta, would strike the North Tower of the World Trade Center.

al-Shehhi would strike the South Tower.

Hanjour would strike the Pentagon.

Jarrah would strike the White House.

And all of this would take place on September 11th.

Allahu Akbar! they shouted into the night. *Allahu Akbar! ALLAHU AKBAR!!!*

That unending bellow, that deplorable din, that hideous battle cry permeated my soul and barraged my conscience. White flashes yet again, and pain, pain, *pain.* I could feel my eyes hot with tears and rage.

In a flash of a second, I saw buildings topple amidst wild explosions that sent New Yorkers, and the nation, and then the world, into a roiling panic. I saw them fall, two bastions of American strength, collapsing into a vicious cloud of all-consuming dust. And then I was propelled backward in time and caught glimpses of bodies… people… human beings, desperate to avoid being burned alive and taking their own final moments heroically into their own hands. I saw passengers storm up an aisleway to break cockpit doors and wrest control away from hijackers. With horrific clarity I saw all of it.

It was too much. Too barbaric. Too obscene.

I struggled with Winston's cat collar, gripping it and holding it to me, kissing it against my burning lips, and crying out. bin Laden and everyone else gawked at me in confusion.

White flashes. Heat waves. I stared at bin Laden and he stared right back, perceiving me and the threat of an infidel in his midst. I spasmed. He started to approach me, slowly and cautiously, making his steady way through his crowd of deluded disciples.

Visions of helicopters, one of them crashing. High triangular walls around a compound. Soldiers infiltrating a multi-tiered house. An explosion from the courtyard. Shots fired.

bin Laden looked at me in horror.

And then, I woke up screaming in the middle of the night in a cold sweat. My eyes were ringed with fear, and I called out for anyone who would heed my desperation.

It all made perfect, deadly sense now.

PART THREE

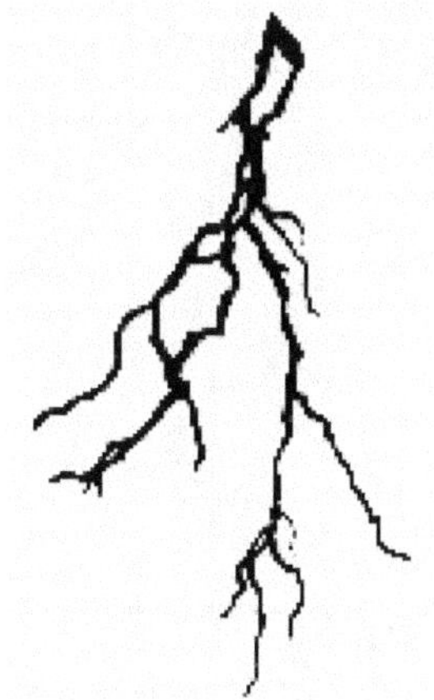

5 Days To Go

September 6th, 2001 • Jersey City, NJ

No more dreams.

No more visions.

No more hope.

All those people!

I just wanted quiet. I just wanted to think.

The terrifyingly vivid nightmare passed, and I was back to myself.

I don't know where I went off the rails and collided with Atta, but everything was so incredibly realistic.

I didn't know who I was anymore, whether Roland Bishop or Ethan Stiles or Mohammed Atta. I didn't want to be *any* of them anymore.

After the vision I was exhausted to my very core, like a weariness had crept into my very bones. I was sapped of any desire to do anything, and my arms hung limply at my side on the couch as I stared off into the nothingness that awaited all those poor people. I looked wearily at the clock: 5:05am. I desperately needed sleep.

I had had so many forward jumps and backward jumps and even *side* jumps…I was in a pinball maze designed by a very cruel maker. The only definite thing that I knew was the certainty of the cat collar around my wrist. But whether or not it would be there tomorrow, I had no clue.

That vision utterly racked me. Who was I, so tiny and insignificant, so powerless, so scant, so bereft of resources, name, ability and even identity, to avert the coming history? Who was I to do anything at all?

Revelations came to me of two giant, square pools, filled with the waters of sadness, though I had no idea where they were. They contained tears. Tears of all those who mourned all those who fell. The number *five* materialized as through a mist, and I took that to mean that there were only five days until this unspeakable tragedy would unfold. *Five days*. And then, I received different flashes, as I buried my face in my pillow, seeking to soak up my tears.

Two thousand nine hundred and ninety six.

I knew in an instant that that number meant the body count. I didn't have to ask or guess. I knew with absolute assurance that in five days, that would be the total. The people in those four targets had no idea what was coming.

Sixteen hundred victims from the North Tower, including all those who tried to rescue those dead or dying, and those on the ground.

One thousand from the South Tower.

One hundred twenty five at the Pentagon.

Two-hundred sixty-five passengers aboard the four planes that were used as missiles.

And six nameless faces somewhere throughout.

On top of that, faces rushed past me of all those in the future who would die from cancers, emphysema, exposure to dust and toxins, and other chronic lung conditions. The damage would be horrific.

The terrorists would not be hijacking the planes to kidnap the passengers and exact some unreasonable ransom. They would not be holding them as collateral to ensure their military and political demands were met. They would not be kidnapping them indefinitely. Nor would they be commandeering the commercial jetliners and dropping them off at some remote airport to release hostages once their horrendous wishes had been granted.

No.

They were going to use them as *missiles*, and drive them into the structures that epitomized American strength and resolve, taking innocent American lives with them. They were going to attempt to bring the United States of America to its collective knees through terror, and they had lain their plans bare before me.

The results would be catastrophic. I had to do something, I just didn't even know where to start.

Winston rubbed against my leg and purred softly, looking at me quizzically. I burst into tears at his oblivion to the carnage that was about to unfold.

And so, having no clue what to do, where to go, or who to be, I wept.

And weeping was all that I did.

All day long, I wept and wondered, wondered and wept. Wept as if it had already happened, mourning for souls whose names I would never know.

All those people!

No more hope.

No more visions.

No more dreams.

4 Days To Go

September 7th, 2001 • Jersey City, NJ

There was no time for mourning what might not be.

Four.

I shot up in bed at 4am the moment the alarm went off. Winston had been perched on my neck. He freaked and leapt off of me, arching his back.

Four.

Haunted by the dream of Osama bin Laden and his jihadists, knowing what they were about to do in the future, I let my mind travel back to the past.

Just a few days ago I had visions of Byers being shot and wounded. Of Phelps being gunned down. Of Fox's head rendered a pulp of tissue and exposed skull and brains. Of Mr. Eggers murdering Penny. Of Jake killing Renita. Of Agent Mulligan taking out Atta.

Yet none of them came to be.

In some way, in some small part, I had managed to alter the course of the future. Through my own meager interference, the tides of time carried other sands to the shoreline instead of what was to be.

Could it be that my dream of bin Laden would be formative to what would happen in their future as well?

The number *four* kept pinging my brain. Four days to go until the attacks. My eyes were opened. I was filled once more with fierce purpose. I had to get information to Byers, as well as to Phelps and Fox.

I reached over to my wrist and felt Winston's collar digging into it. Winston himself eyed me curiously from across the room, unsure of what to think of the insane human staring down at him, wondering why he hadn't been given food.

A brief thought of Jenette passed through my mind, but I didn't sense that she was part of my purpose. I felt nothing for her. I hated that, but it was what it was. I spooned some Nine Lives into Winston's bowl and tore out of there once more, throwing on a grey Old Navy sweatshirt.

I entered Manhattan. I was on the PATH train once more, heading into upper New York. In my hand I clutched a familiar Nokia 3310 red cellphone, a priceless treasure from the continuity of days gone by. I had no idea how much longer I would have it, but I held it close and dialed Detective Byers.

She answered nearly immediately.

"Byers."

"Roxanne! It's Roland Bishop. Listen, I know what the terrorists are going to do, *and* when they're going to do it. Are you at the FBI headquarters?"

"Yes, Roland - oh man, dude, we need to lojack you. Where did you go *again*? We caught Atta!"

"What?"

"Yeah! We caught him in Central Park. Almost gunned us down. Somehow he got away. Phelps and Fox have no idea how. I'm scratching my head as well."

I had an idea how.

"Never mind that now. I'm on my way to you. I can be there in twenty minutes."

"I'll meet you there."

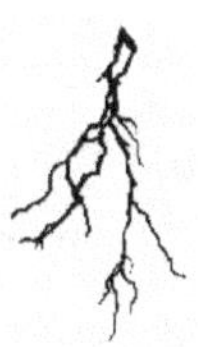

I had no bike, so I took the bus all the way to Lafayette and sprinted up to the Wanamaker Building. There was Roxanne's familiar Bronco parked outside.

Armstrong was outside having a smoke.

"Armstrong!" I greeted him.

"Don't ever say my name out here, you idiot."

"Nice to see you too." I waved him away and headed inside the building. He looked at me in disgust, taking a heavy drag on his smoke.

Byers was inside waiting for the elevator. "Well, hello there," she greeted me.

"Hey. Boy do I have a story to tell you guys."

She shrugged, and her billowing hair bounced in tandem. "Can't wait to hear it. I hope it explains how you keep vanishing right out from under our noses. Did you teach Atta that little trick?"

I snickered, but said nothing, looking up at the dropping elevator numbers.

"Ya know, I think we're gonna have to start all over here at some point and figure out what's really going on with you. Penny is as just as confused as I am."

I turned to her in surprise. "Penny's- she's still there?"

She smirked in amazement. "You really are a head case, aren't you?"

Warmth radiated around my heart. Penny was back. I mean, why shouldn't she be? I was starting to figure it out and get back on track with myself. I was no longer Atta, or Stiles, or anyone else, other than myself. I had kept Winston's collar solidly on me as a talisman, and it kept me here. Maybe in so doing it brought her back and kept her here too. Or maybe she had her own talisman. Either way, the notion that she had returned brought me hope.

"My ex-wife thinks so."

"Well, maybe she and I should go shopping together sometime. I could learn a thing or two."

"You wanna learn a thing or two about me, Detective Byers? I'd be happy to introduce you to the real Roland Bishop," I said, looking at her slyly. Whatever reaction I was hoping for didn't materialize on her face.

"Weirdo," she said, turning to face the elevator just as it dinged and opened, and I swear she almost winked. Her voluminous hair bobbed slightly in her frizzy pony tail.

We entered and went up.

Phelps and Fox were in their offices. Byers pointed to me as we walked through the hallway between them, and they both bid farewells to their respective calls, following us in. I took a long heave of my lungs and moved into the same conference room I had met them in on the 28th, only ten short days ago. We said nothing for a moment after they closed the door.

Phelps raised his hands in annoyance. "Well? You wanna tell us just what this is all about?"

"Yeah," Fox sounded. "And how you and your little Middle-eastern buddy managed to slip right through our fingers a few times now."

"Fox," Phelps scolded. Fox didn't apologize.

"He's not my buddy." Fox just scoffed.

I cleared my throat. "I know when and where they're going to strike," I said gravely. "I've seen it, and I need you to trust me. I *know*."

"Okay, let's have it," Phelps said. "Have a seat."

Fox pulled out his tape recorder once more, setting it on the table in front of me. This time I didn't mind. We all sat.

"You guys remember I've been receiving *numbers*, right? Strange numbers in my visions."

They nodded.

"They're a countdown. Today I got the number *four*. Yesterday it was *five*. The day before it was *six*, and so on and so forth. All the way back to when I had my first vision of Atta at the PATH Station on August 19th, when I got the number *twenty-three*. Don't you see? Twenty-three days from August 19th is September 11th. Four days from today is September 11th. Six days from two days ago is September 11th. Each day I get closer, the number drops. For me, a bit ago it was 9 days to go. Then it was 1 day to go. Then it was 1 day to go *again*. 9-1-1! Don't you see?"

"Could just be a coincidence," Phelps said.

"I had a dream."

"Well that's nice," said Fox. "So did MLK Junior."

"You're not hearing me," I protested. "I had a dream that I was with Osama bin Laden *as* Mohammed Atta. I was *with* them in Afghanistan. I was given names. Targets. *Flight numbers*. You have to believe me."

"What were the flight numbers?" Phelps asked furiously, scribbling down into his notepad and waiting for me. I sighed and recalled them from the frightening dream.

"They were speaking in Arabic. But I understood all of them."

"What, you speak Arabic now?" Fox squealed. "Your little friend Atta teach you that?" Phelps yelled at him. "What?! They're both pullin' the same stunts, Ryan, vanishing right under our noses."

"Give me the damn flights, please, Roland!" Phelps yelled, pounding his fist. "Rob, *shut it!*"

Fox sneered and turned to face out the windows.

I thought back. My head was pounding at the memory, and my wrist flinched, cut by Winston's collar.

"United Airlines 175. American Airlines 11. American Airlines 77. United Airlines 93. All leaving on September 11th from various airports up and down the Eastern seaboard," I told them, pounding my fist on the table. "I checked them all! United 175 departs from Boston this Tuesday. American 11 departs from Logan. United Airlines Flight 93 departs from Newark. American Flight 77 departs from Dulles. They're doing this so as to not arouse suspicion. You guys have to believe me. Every single one of these jets is going to be aiming for targets."

Both of them stopped, staring at me intently. Byers started to say something and then stopped mid-sentence. Blood trickled from my nose. "What is it, Byers?" I asked her. She didn't say anything; just stared at me. "Byers?"

I looked back at the agents. They hadn't moved a muscle. Frozen, as if catatonic, both of them. I grunted in confusion, looking them both over, back and forth. Fox had his pencil in his mouth. "Agent Phelps?" Nothing. "Fox?" I asked. Again, nothing.

Comprehension seized me.

"Oh, shit," I said with a gasp. "Now they know. I get it. Of *course* everything changes once they know everything." I stared at them, frozen there in suspended animation. It was like the Windows Blue Screen of death, and nothing could restart it except for a reboot. A system had crashed somewhere.

I reached over and pressed Byers' shoulder. It was hard as a rock and icy to the touch. Indeed, my own breath in that room seemed to be visible before me. A chill swept through. A brief thought passed of punching Fox in the jaw. He would never know it was me.

Think, Roland. Now you're going to have to explain this to them all over again. They won't remember any of this. I tried to think of where the reboots had been. They weren't exactly uniform; they had taken place in multiple locations and at diverse, inconsistent times.

But the *major* reboots – those had happened at Central Park. Going home wouldn't reset anything until seemingly the next day.

And in any event, having to tell them the same revelatory information every single day wouldn't serve any purpose in us locating the terrorists where they were *now*, nor would it give us enough time to avert their dastardly plans for the morning of the 11th. They might already be at the airport ready to launch.

I was stuck in a loop. The Inevitability Loop.

But how could I get out of it? How could I jump ship and get out of this loop, making sure to stay 'me' in the process, lest I too was swallowed up and frozen by the same space-time continuum reboot loop?

Think. Who else had been there, returned in an altered form, and yet re-emerged as themselves?

Her name jumped out at me. *Penny.*

      Everything had frozen without the escape hatch of sleep, and it was a long ride back to Jersey City Jail. People were standing in the middle of the street. New York was a noiseless metropolis of a bustling standstill. A ringing was in the air, like a pent-up compression engine under strain, and it was slowly rising.

      But the New Yorkers heard it not. Cars were everywhere in mid-stream, the blur of their activity trailing behind them. I stole some poor guy's bike right out from underneath him, and that was a surreal task. He stayed there, levitating, without the slightest trace of annoyance, and was in for a rude awakening once the timer ran out.

      Once again I was screaming through the streets of New York City, but this time heading south. I swear I passed the 10-foot-cop that had shot me, now riding around the waterfront, his horse frozen in mid-gallop. I passed quickly through the Holland Tunnel and emerged on the other side, heading up to the Jersey City Jail.

      Everyone, everywhere were stopped in their tracks. Motorcyclists in the streets leaned dangerously to pass around other cars buzzing down Hudson River Greenway, stopped entirely in a pocket of gravity. I glanced up. A commercial jetliner was up there, flying who knows where. Suspended between earth and sky, lifeless, and yet full of lives. My heart was heavy at that sight. But…I needed to press on.

I made it to Jersey City.

No one greeted me at the reception counter of the jail. I broke the glass on the attendant's security window and depressed what I thought would be the release button to allow me back into the cells where I might find Penny. By that time I was drenched with sweat and completely out of breath. But the Winston collar held fast.

I rounded a corner and traced down a bank of cells. The last one on the right had a little light streaming out of it. The heaves of my breath sounded loud and clear against the walls of those cells. Inmates in varying stages of undress were in their cells, lying about, reading, writing, or on the toilet. Two female inmates were showering together, and the rivulets of water ricocheting off their naked bodies held fast in the air, suspended in time and space as they stood completely still under the warm, frozen downpour.

And there she was. She was reading, a book in her hands, her thin readers adorning her face, with a steaming Styrofoam cup in her hands as she read. She eyed me playfully over the top of it.

"Whatever took you so long?"

"Welcome back, Lady Divinitus."

"I see you found what makes you...*you,*" she said, pointing to Winston's cat collar attached firmly around my wrist. I just stared at her. I knew her, and she knew me.

And then, there I was again, lying on her bunk, just like old times. There was a female inmate on the bunk above us, frozen in time, completely unaware of the sheer joy we were both experiencing at being reunited.

Penny sat opposite me on the cold aluminum shitter, drinking her tea and asking me questions. I answered all of them, much to her heart's content, while she listened intently and took mental notes. Pencils were not allowed in here; they all too easily made cunning shanks.

She would answer no questions about herself until she was thoroughly satisfied with my accounts of everything that had transpired since the last time we had seen each other on September 2nd.

It was so good to see her again. I had to be careful, however. I didn't want to risk sending her back through some ill-timed release of information that would necessitate a reboot. Or...was she immune to it? I wanted to prove my theory, but if I mentioned the date, or the specifics of the flights, or both, it might jumpstart that loop again.

"Penny, do you remember leaving? When you drifted away? What happened?"

She quietly sipped her tea and then pensively stared at the floor. "I don't know, Roland. I truly don't. It was the most bizarre thing I had ever experienced. You were talking, and then you just...froze."

"*I* froze? I thought *you* did!"

"Strange. I could see you, but I could not speak to you. Or, rather, you could not hear me. And then, things got very dim and, sort of, stretched away from me. Elastic and ungraspable."

I nodded, remembering.

"I waited for a while, and then pounded on the glass to catch the attention of the guard so that they could help you. But I grew frantic, I must confess. A bit gutted. The whole thing was dodgy. I was growing quite inconsolable, and a guard behind me came and had to physically remove me. I was hysterical, Roland, if you should like to know the truth. Hysterical."

Now it was my turn to *hmmm*. "And what happened after that?"

"Well, nothing, really, except I settled down in my cell and they told me that they removed you and took you away to the hospital. That was the last I heard of any of it."

"Utterly bizarre. On my end, *I* was still here and *you* were gone. I felt devastated. Exhausted. Drawn. I went home and just cried."

"Oh! You poor thing. It appears that we are both in need of counseling."

"Indeed," I said, mimicking her. She caught my impression and smiled endearingly. I wished that I could tell her the details, just to get it out of me.

"There's more to be said, isn't there," she asked, reading my inner thoughts. "You have something you wish to tell me."

I nodded. "I do. But I'm worried what might happen if I do."

"Well, out with it then. Surely, it could not be much worse than the last time you froze us and you thought I no longer existed. Or are we just making chinwag here?"

"What's a chinwag?"

"Stay on topic, Roland!"

I sighed, and sat up quickly. "I'm worried," I said, "about losing you again. I mean, all these people aren't going to stay motionless forever. Something's eventually gotta give, and the clock will have to reset, and things will be in motion once more. I'm just counting my lucky stars that you're back and that we could talk."

"Bollocks. If you think I went to the great beyond and came back all knackered and bereft of wisdom, you're certifiably mad. Besides, you've dropped enough bread crumbs now for me to decode the rest on my own, Roland."

"I have?"

"Yes! Of course you have. Have you even taken a look at my book?"

My eyes narrowed. *Her book?* She extended it to me. It was a black book with gold letters. I read the title.

The Only Plane In The Sky. An Oral History of 9/11.

I looked up at her and gasped.

"Take a look at the back cover, Roland."

I turned it over. There, plainly for me to see, was proof that she knew.

Avid Reader Press / Simon & Schuster (September 8, 2020).

I gasped again and stood up, staring hard. "No way…where did you… how did you… where did you get this, Penny?"

I stared at her in amazement. She giggled.

"Lady Divinitus has her ways. If you want to know the truth of the matter, I don't know. I wandered aimlessly for a while in dark hallways. Only slowly did I become aware that I was meandering through what must be the galaxy's greatest library. Full of treasure troves of books upon books to the power of books. Fiction, nonfiction, biographical, memoirs, autobiographies, reference books, romance, western, science fiction, fantasy, history, all of it. I cannot tell you where it was, nor where I was. All I knew was that I was somewhere…*else*.

"And that's when it hit me, Roland, and I became quite chuffed, really," she said, smiling. "I was *ecstatic!* I realized that I, too, had been given a gift. For whatever reason, I was transported here for answers. Not just for me, but for you. I, in my Jersey City Jail jumpsuit, roamed that hall for what seemed like years. There were dim lights and tables to read at. There were rolling ladders to access the upper shelves. Strangely, there was no one else present. I had an unencumbered visit, shall we say?

"At any rate, I proceeded to the history section to see if you were correct. I never doubted you for a second, but I wanted to make sure for myself and to know precisely what happened. I found this book, Roland. Published in the year 2020. And so, as when I counseled you that you should take something with you that is uniquely you, I made the book uniquely me. I tore out this page." She showed me the inner flaps of the book. Just as she said, page 83 was missing. "Just a random page, no less, but I did something to ensure the story's passage with me. *I ate it.* Yes! I balled it up and ate the dratted thing. It tasted of knowledge,

Roland, don't you know?" She was talking faster now, excited and mesmerized by her own experience.

"Anyway, it's still in here, somewhere," -here she rubbed her hand across her belly- "and so I have it with me. I began to feel something *sliding.* Not the floor, or the ladder, not the weather…but…*time.* Time itself. A strange wind began to course through that library. It buffeted me and pushed me backwards. Colors swirled around me. Blues, mostly. There was a tremendous rushing wind that carried me out of there. I tell you here and now that I clutched that book to my chest like there was no tomorrow. *Because there might not be*, I thought! And then, before I knew it, I was back here. Right back here. Clutching this book to my chest. The guards almost confiscated it as contraband, for goodness' sa-"

A thrill ran through me. "What day was that? The date!"

She searched her memory. "What? When they tried to confisca-"

"No, no, Penny, the date you came back!"

"Ah. Let's see, it was three days ago. September 4th, Roland. Right around 2:30pm in the afternoon."

My legs quaked, and I fell onto the bunk. The inmate above us jostled lifelessly. "What is it? Whatever is the matter?" asked Penny.

"Of course. That's when I was in the park and I became Atta. Things changed. Everything changed right there. I saw the same wind."

"You became Mohammed Atta!" she shrieked.

"Long story. I can't explain it. I'm not even sure I would want to try. It was the most bizarre thing. But that's when I felt that wind – and the colors – and it plunged me into change. For the second time, I should add. And then, I was in Afghanistan, with Osama bin Laden and his jihadists. I thought it was a dream, but I can't explain the transition, nor where it happened. And then the next time I tried to explain all that to Byers and the FBI, they froze too."

"Yes but don't you see?" she asked me. "There's no risk of that with me, now, Roland. I found it out on my own. I read here that it will happen on September 11th, four days from now." My eyes widened. I reached for Winston's cat collar. "Relax, I'm not going anywhere, Roland. I know all about the history of it. The names you've shared with me, those are all in here. The history is not set yet, because not all the pieces have fallen into place, and you keep changing things. And I'm sensing that there is still more to do. You have a part to play in all of this yet."

She stiffened, and stuck out her chin. "I'm going to give you reverse counsel now. Something I cautioned you against before. Your power is evident. That much is clear. Your ability to recreate history is also growing. So I suggest you engage it. Nurture it. Go out there and see what you can find. There's still time to change the past, Roland."

"You mean the future."

"I mean both. The future *contains* the past. The present is what you have to work with to influence both. You're outside of both. So, be the change! You have your feet in both worlds, apparently. I counsel you to straddle them carefully, and to go see what you can do. Just hold onto that cat collar." She looked at it. "What is your cat's name?"

"Winston."

"Ha! A most British name. Jolly good. That really is a very great comfort to my mind."

I breathed a sigh of relief to have her back, and to expel the pent-up incredulity that continued to settle upon me. This was all far too incredible. Penny must have sensed what I was thinking. She took a sip of her tea and leaned toward me.

"Roland," she whispered. "Go be the change."

It was 4:13pm, looking up at the clock as I walked out of Jersey City Jail.

For whatever reason, I felt compelled to avoid Atta. I couldn't be sure where *any* of them were, but I didn't want to go whisking off to Afghanistan again, and he was the FBI's primary target: I might get shot. Who else should I pursue? New York City was such a huge metropolis. Where would I even find any of them?

More hot flashes. And this time, they were *welcome*. I spasmed, standing outside the Jersey City Jail, thinking and waiting. White. Blinding flashes of light that traveled from the back to the front of my brain with scalding heat. My pores opened up to expel the perspiration within. And then, suddenly, I was whispered a name.

Ziad Jarrah. He was one of the lead hijackers that Phelps had mentioned and whom Osama bin Laden had confirmed. And then I saw him! There were three other men with him, and they were all disembarking a plane, walking up the passenger boarding bridge. But when? And where? The number *four* appeared in my mind's eye again. I clenched my jaw and gritted my teeth. *Four still means today*, I thought. Was I supposed to tail them now? That didn't answer the question of *where?*

More flashes. A cockpit being burst into with a beverage cart and fire extinguishers. A plane flying out of control. Green grass looming up. The number *ninety-three.*

I opened my eyes. That was it. That had to be it. Jarrah was the lead hijacker for United 93. The four men were getting off a plane at an airport, preparing for their hijacking. But where? I clutched at my cat collar and tried to breathe.

My knees buckled from a revelation so powerful it racked my spine. I nearly collapsed to the ground. Out of a plane window, through the eyes of an unidentified soul, I could see the World Trade Center in the distance. There it was. Both towers as solid steel fingers pointing up into the sky in defiance of what was to come.

They were arriving at an airport. But what airport was within sight range of The World Trade Center?

My eyes opened wide. I grabbed my stolen bike and raced off. Newark International Airport was forty-six minutes away. I had to get there.

The sun was setting when I finally rolled up to Newark International Airport.

I was panting and sweating. The wind had served to mitigate some of that sweat, but now, slowed to a halt, my body was heating back up, and my damp clothes were paying for it.

I looked back.   Far away now, I could see the World Trade Center like toothpicks, brightly illuminated and reflecting the distant setting sun.

I had no idea where to go. I had no idea what to do. People were everywhere, still frozen and statuesque as though someone had hit a celestial 'pause' button. Birds were suspended in the sky in flocks. The crests of water usually rippling along the Hudson formed tiny stabbing peaks, deadly to dive into.

Deadly – that was the word to describe the people I was seeking. They were here…somewhere. I had no idea where to look.

It had to be after 5pm now. I glanced at my watch. It was no longer there. *My watch was no longer there!* Winston's collar was still there, but memories brewed in me of never having worn a watch. *Impossible.* I knew the face of it, knew its hands, but it had disappeared entirely. Had I lost it? Or had it been stripped away in one of these mysterious interludes between the certain and the strange? Or had I just forgotten to slip it on that morning?

It was a good bet it was the former, not the latter.

Dread seized me, wondering if this was the beginning of a change I could not resist or rebel against. Change that might steal Penny from me. Or Byers. Or justice. I cast my bike aside and ran inside the airport.

I didn't have much time. I had no idea where to look, or if they were even still here. I just knew I had to find them.

I wondered if any of the people around me could still see. If they were able to perceive the one human in motion sprinting everywhere throughout the airport. I raced with all of my heart, fueled by adrenaline and raw fear. I examined every single terminal, checked out every single face, every single gate, every single baggage claim, restrooms, airport lounge and security screening area that I could.

The worst part about all of it were the flashes, and the nausea. And the nosebleeds. All throughout the airport, I became repeatedly stricken. Searching for the faces of these terrorists, I drew near to countless souls whose future held horrors. They were beyond count. Either my intuition and power were growing stronger, or the concentration was greater. In either case, the depravity of future man was on full display here. I was repulsed and disgusted. There were far too many to alert to the authorities.

Sadly, I had to face the moral quandary of whether or not to take any action. Could people survive rape? Yes. Could they survive being robbed or kidnapped, or sexual assault? Yes. But could they survive murder? No. I had to leave these people behind, and it was the hardest thing I had ever done. One particular face, as I drew near, disgusted me so much I wanted to gut him. The visions I saw that that man would commit…were unthinkable. I would have to return to him afterwards.

It's not your mission to save everyone, Roland. Just 2996 of them.

Finally, I gave up hope and stopped in the middle of the Alaska gates, my hands on my knees, my form doubled over. I was crying from the horror of all that I had seen, out of breath and spent from the miles that I had run. Exhausted and drained, I was a dog-tired and ragged wreck. I couldn't remember when I last ate, and now I was paying for it with all my calories expended and my heart broken.

I couldn't find them. They simply weren't here. Perhaps they had already left the airport and were on their way to their final destination, preparing to hide out until the morning of the 11th. Perhaps it was already far too late.

I needed food desperately: something. Anything. In a dazed stupor I found the nearest restaurant and stole myself some already cooked Argentinian Choripan and a bottled water. I held it up and said 'cheers' as I walked out, and dried my sopped hair on some poor sap's sweater, making sure he didn't topple over as I did so.

I sat and ate. It must have been a good half-hour. The black of night draped over the airport outside. I decided to go back for more as long as this time suspension worked to my advantage. But on my trip for seconds, I stopped. Halfway back to the restaurant, an idea gripped me, and I paused. I abandoned my pursuit of food, and raced back up to the main ticketing counter at the front of the security checkpoint. Newark had never looked busier with all of these people in here packed together and motionless.

I shoved a ticketing agent aside and fiddled my way into the computer system, trying to find where to go. It was easy enough. I touched the mouse and recoiled from a spark, which surprised me. Tentatively I returned to it, and I heard whirring and clicking as the computer returned to life from its dormant state. I clicked 'Search' and my fingers tapped the rest.

Jarrah, Ziad.

Within an instant, the computer had found what I was looking for. I was amazed that it, too, was frozen, but maybe it reacted to my touch. Perhaps the electricity still living in me had jumpstarted it. Whatever happened was irrelevant. What I saw on the screen, however, was.

Jarrah, Ziad S, M. FC, Spirit FLL > EWR, Arrival 1933pm, B-2.

Easy enough to decode. Ziad S. Jarrah, male, First Class, Spirit Air, Fort Lauderdale to Newark, arriving at 7:33pm at Terminal B, Gate 2.

I quickly scanned the rest of the names.

Saeed al Ghambi.

Ahmed Ibrahim al Haznawi.

Ahmed al Nami.

Ziad's fellow jihadists. His musclemen.

They were all almost here.

My eyes were drawn to the clock at the bottom right of the Windows 2000 interface.

6:48pm. I had forty-five minutes until Jarrah would arrive. I had to trigger the reactivation. I had to get things moving again. That plane had to land. Jarrah had to exit and come out so I could report him to the authorities. But how? *Think.*

What was keeping me centered and keeping everything else at bay? What had triggered the pause the first time around? I remember being back at the FBI office with Phelps, Fox and Byers. I was telling them the flight numbers and the date.

Then, everything froze.

Be the change.

I heard Penny's voice crystal clear in my mind… urging me… guiding me. Almost as if she was standing right beside me. How could I be the change?

Suddenly, my cat collar began to glow again. It pulsed and itched, heating up my wrist, hot to the touch. I wrestled with it and unclasped it, feeling the burn as I did so.

I wrenched it off of me and stared at it, breathing hard. My wrist sported a slightly reddened line spanning it. Suspending it there in front of me, I saw my logo. *RB.* There it was. *Something uniquely me.* And I was supposed to go be the change. That's what Penny had said to me.

Not even really knowing what I was doing, or if it would work, much less if it would do irreversible damage, I stared at Winston's collar. I'm sure he was somewhere at home, watching out the window, tummy rumbling and wondering if he would ever be fed again.

But here, miles away at Newark airport, I had to de-center. I had to become part of the running timeline again. I had to step back into the loop. That meant releasing that which grounded me to where and who I was.

I had to get away from everyone so no one would see it. I had to make sure that I was cleared of security and in the gate waiting area, or I would be prevented from entering and possibly accosted. I ran to the men's room and jumped into an unoccupied stall.

I sighed, and tried to summon whatever it was that I needed to do. I thought of Penny. Jenette. Byers. Atta. bin Laden. Winston. Jarrah. Phelps. Fox. The cop. Dr. Walker. The sweet elderly lady on the subway. Renita. Joe-Joe. Jake. The taxi driver. The frenzy of all of it; the whirlwind of these past few days. A tremor ran through me as I tensed my muscles and flexed my core, trying to feel every bit of emotion at what had taken over my life.

It was working.

Suddenly, I breathed out in a reflex, and hot vapor distended the air around me. Waves of heat scorched my vicinity. Winston's collar began to sizzle. I grabbed it hard and stared at it as everything phased to blue. Energy took me. I took it back. With my left hand I held his collar, as I extended my right up toward it.

A single arc of blue light shot out from my index finger and transformed poor Winston's collar into burning metal. The energy bolt vaporized it, and it melted in an instant to the floor at my feet.

As I did so, everything and everyone suddenly screeched back to life, as if a record had skipped and then realigned. The end of *Where The Party At* by Jagged Edge and Nelly was playing inside the terminal. It faded out and then *Hanging by a Moment* by Lifehouse started blaring through the speakers. *How appropriate,* I thought. *Tragedy was truly hanging by a moment here.*

"What the hell?" the man in the stall next to me shouted. I looked down and saw trousers around ankles.

"Sorry," I feebly said, exiting the stall. A group of men were all looking toward my stall in amazement.

"Do *not* eat the Choripan!" I warned them, pointing to my stomach, and walking briskly out of there. I think my profuse sweating was the clincher for them.

Be the change.

I had done it. That plane would land. Jarrah and his men would be here. Now, it was just a waiting game. I glanced at the clock again.

Only thirty-five more minutes until Jarrah's plane arrived.

The taxiing lights eventually pulled around the corner, and a yellow commercial jetliner's nose emerged from out of the black mist outside, pulling up to the passenger boarding bridge.

Soon, they were all exiting out of the gate. The terrorists were in First Class, but for some reason they didn't exit. They were in first class! They should have exited by now. Maybe they were hanging back to see if anyone was accosted, or if federal agents were coming for them, and if so, this way they could remain on the plane, commandeer it, and take off for an alternate destination.

Oh no, I thought. *I changed something again! Where are they?!*

Just when all hope seemed lost, the familiar white flashes seized me once more. *There he was.*

Ziad Jarrah. And a white flash of heat.

He was followed by his henchmen. Those who, presumably, would fight off any opposition while he assumed control of the aircraft and began their deadly flight. I tried to think back to where he was supposed to strike. The White House? Yet I didn't see the White House in ruins. Only the Pentagon and the two towers of the World Trade Center.

Then I remembered the hole in the ground. A commercial jet-sized cavernous hole two-hundred twenty feet wide, and the ensuing fireball.

Was their mission thwarted? I *had* seen passengers ramming the cockpit of United 93. Was that mission thwarted? Were Jarrah and his men rendered a failure?

There was no way to be sure. And even more frightening, there was no way to be sure if my presence here would alter that. Still, I had to try.

They exited the passenger boarding bridge with all the nonchalant confidence that the jihadist life could afford them for their suicide mission. They hardly looked around, putting distance between each other as if to make it appear that they were cellular and disconnected one from another.

How You Remind Me by Nickelback was playing as I began my pursuit of them. I tried to ignore being seen. Thankfully, my bloody nose had abated for now, and I took up my pursuit behind them with my sweatshirt hood pulled up over my head.

The flashes continued, and my wrist spasmed. I looked down, missing Winston's collar. As Nickelback's song continued, I was myself reminded of my poor cat back home, and I wished I could be there to feed him.

They continued on at a decent clip. For a moment I wondered if they would be heading to baggage claim, but then the cold truth slapped me in the face: they weren't staying long. What baggage? This was a one-way trip for all four of them.

At one point, one of them suddenly looked back and noticed me. It was the shortest of them. A flash tore through me, and the name *Ahmed al-Nami* flew through my vision. That was al-Nami! They were all following in lockstep with Jarrah further ahead.

I tried to avert his gaze and attempted to hide myself behind a large man walking in front of me, but I made the mistake of peeking out behind him so that I wouldn't lose any of my targets.

al-Nami was still watching me. He did a quick double-take, and then moved up closer to his partners. I could see him leaning into them, muttering something in Arabic.

All four of them began to move at a quickened pace, each in turn looking back in my direction.

Suddenly, they broke into a run.

White flashes! My head lit up like the sun. Visions of The White House exploding in flame and ruin. A tailfin sticking out of it, and a shower of rubble flying in all directions. Blackened smoke miles high into the air, carried away by the breeze.

Shit! I messed it up!

I started running after them.

More flashes. People fleeing and screaming. Someone trapped under concrete, pleading for their lives. And everywhere, people burning. A blackened American flag lying on the ground in tatters.

People, aware of the commotion, started to look around wildly in fright. Five men rushed past them for an unknown reason, one in pursuit of the other four, and the last one appearing disheveled and bloody.

They raced down the concourse.

I did the only thing I could. "Help! Security! Terrorists!" I yelled at the top of my lungs, screaming into the air as we all hurled our way up to the top of Terminal B where it split toward Baggage Claim and Rental Cars.

They kept running. People screamed.

The terrorists were putting distance between them and myself now.

I could see one of them up ahead lift a phone to his ear. Jarrah was calling in for evacuation: someone on the receiving end of that call was their driver who would usher them to safety. I continued to yell in hot pursuit.

A security guard leapt out of nowhere and brandished a weapon. "Thank God – security, those men are terrorists!"

"Get down!" he screamed, and he trained his gun on me. "Hands behind your head! Get down on the ground *now!*" he hollered.

"What? No!" I said, hitting the deck. "Those guys ahead, they, they're getting away!" He flicked his head back in Jarrah's direction, and then spoke into his shoulder radio. "Dispatch, possible terrorist activity, Terminal B, merging with the concourse." He turned back toward me again.

"You stay right there!" he barked at me, and I nodded compliantly. He raced off after Jarrah and the others, informing one of his colleagues where I was.

But I wasn't going to stay there.

Don't you know I'm part of the Inevitability Loop, buddy? I got up as soon as he was out of view, cautiously trailing both him and them.

I could see all of them up ahead. The guard was calling after them and telling them to freeze. People were scattering and running for cover. He ordered them to halt and pointed his weapon. Jarrah and his men moved behind columns and through passengers as if they had done it a thousand times before.

All of them were moving toward Level 3 and the loading/unloading zone. If they got into their transport vehicle it could be all over for all of us, and they would get away. I was starting to lose control. Getting hot, getting tired, still hungry, and desperately thirsty. The anger began to course through me as I wanted to be closer to them, to tackle one of them, to do *something*.

I'm trying to be the change, Penny, I said in my head. *I'm Roland Bishop, and I know who I'm supposed to be,* I encouraged myself.

My feet started to slow as my energy ebbed. I couldn't keep it up. I had no way to get them, and no way to catch up, and no way to even try.

Jarrah and his men raced out of there, and the cop slowly fell behind. I couldn't see them. They were getting away.

My head flashed painfully and I clutched my temples.

My mind was going. Blackness was taking over the white flashes, and I grew dizzy from exhaustion and mental strain. Gradually, as if the foreground blurred and fluidly retreated, gelling into the background behind it, the rear image replaced the former in a murky swap. Hazily, I could see The White House, completely intact, remaining solidly present as Jarrah and his men escaped in their getaway car.

I looked around in a daze, exhausted. The sweat pooled in my back, and my hair was drenched. My knees buckled and I fell to the floor. I heard the security guard, huffing heavily, making his way back to me, his weapon drawn once more.

Jarrah and his goons were nowhere to be found. It was late, and darkness was descending upon New York with only three days to go until unspeakable tragedy.

My mind was fading, and wicked bolts of discomfort were shooting through my brain! My vision clouded over, and I didn't even have my Winston collar to center myself.

I was out of time, mourning what still would be.

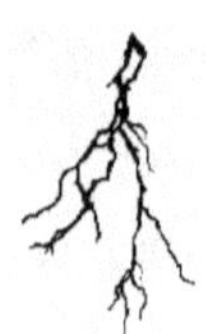

1 Day To Go

September 10th, 2001 • Newark, NJ

The darkness was receding, and light was coming in.

I had been unconscious for a few days, in a mild coma, the voice said, and it had a familiar ring to it, though I couldn't place it. It echoed through the caverns of my muddied and contorted mind as I strove to listen clearly.

"You had quite the nasty fall at the airport. Doctor says you have a hematoma, and you had already had one that this was building upon. Lots of swelling going on in that cranium of yours. Sounds like you were causing a bit of a stir at the airport, too, yeah?"

I knew that voice.

I groggily opened my eyes and looked at her – there were her thick, voluminous brown curls, cascading down her shoulders in unrestricted, wild locks desperate to make a statement.

"Good to see you."

She stifled a surprised giggle, and looked down at me, her eyebrows furrowing. "Uh, good to see you too."

Oh, I see. Trying to play hard to get.

The TV was playing softly, suspended in the far corner of the hospital room on Channel 1. It was playing a preview of the upcoming *The Lord of the Rings: The Fellowship of the Ring* movie, coming to theaters this December. I wondered who would be around to see it, and if there would be any interest following the deadly tragedy that was almost upon us in two days' time.

Byers spoke again. "Do you remember anything that happened at the airport?"

I reached up to scratch my head and look around. My mouth felt parched and sticky. "Is there any way I can get some water?"

"No, there is no way. Do you remember the *airport*?" she reiterated with some edge this time. I returned my eyes to her and showed my surprise at her tone.

"Uh, no, well, yeah," I said. "Kinda. I was tailing Mohammed Atta. Wait – no, sorry. This time it was Ziad Jarrah. And his goons. The guys from United 93."

"What are you talking about?" she whined. "Who?"

I was in the middle of stretching my mouth when I stopped and looked over at her in disbelief. I brought my wrist up to my face and glanced at the hospital ID tag.

Stiles, Ethan P. M / 53 / Cauc.

I threw my hand back down on the bed with some force, cursing. My arm skimmed the roll-up food cart parked next to me on the other side, bouncing the ginger ale dangerously about.

"Whoa! Easy there, Mr. Stiles. You're going to make *one* helluva mess there."

"Shhhhhit! *Whatever.* It doesn't even matter anymore," I mumbled. "I failed."

"What doesn't matter? And…failed at what?" she asked me, frustrated.

I clicked my teeth and rolled my eyes, wondering if Penny was still who she was. I wished briefly that I had swallowed my own book and kept it with me. *The Book of Penny.* That way I would always have her with me. Never before had I felt so ungrounded and uncentered.

"You wouldn't believe me if I told you."

"Try me."

"No." I shook my head. "Not even *I* believe myself anymore."

"Well, the passengers at the airport sure believed you, running around and screaming about terrorists, chasing phantom bad guys. You caused quite the stir. I'm afraid that's what the cuffs are for."

I hadn't even noticed them. I guess I thought that I had some phantom sensation of Winston's cat collar and assumed it was that. But no: glancing down, I saw the cuffs and lightly tugged against them, rattling the bed rail.

The nurse came in and checked my vitals. I asked her for some water. "*Oooone* minute, Mr. Stiles," she said dismissively, heading back out, her loafers swishing on the floor. My mouth felt thick and pasty.

I grunted in disapproval and turned back toward Byers. "So, what now? Arrest? Public disturbance? What?" I said in a blasé tone.

"One thing at a time," she said, holding her hand up. "You mentioned you were tailing somebody. Who was that?"

"Ziad…Jarrah. Terrorist."

She stared at me blankly. "Is that one name? One terrorist? More than one?"

"There were four."

"The…guard that apprehended you said you were running by yourself. That you were alone."

"I was alone. No one was with me. I rode all the way to Newark from Jersey City Jail."

"That's where you're at now. University Hospital in Newark. That was the one closest place to take you," she clarified. "But the guard said that you were one. There were no 'four people' you were chasing. Just one. You."

Why the hell do I keep hearing the number one, I thought. "Wai-wai-wait a minute," I said, waving her down. "He said those guys weren't even there?"

She nodded.

"No. That can't be. Check the manifests. It was a flight from Fort Lauderdale to Newark. I'm not crazy here. It was one plane" -here I noticed the number one again…*what the hell?*- "with four of the 9/11 terrorists on it."

"9/11?"

"Sorry," I grunted, exasperated. "No one calls it that yet, I guess. September 11th. It's one of the terrorists that Phelps and Fox talked about. The attacks happen then."

"September 11th, you mean *tomorrow? What* attacks?! And how do you know Phelps and Fox?" she asked, approaching a frantic tone. "Talk to me!"

"No-no-no…today is Sunday the 9th. The attacks happen on Tuesday."

"No, today is *Monday* the *10th*. September 11th is *tomorrow*."

I stared at her blankly. "It can't be." My jaw dropped. In a reflex I grabbed the remote and flicked the channel until I saw News 12 pop up. In a ticker on the bottom, there it was. Monday, September 10th. My eyes went wide. In a moment of seizure, all was made plain, and the number *one* appeared through bursts of blinding radiance in my mind, drifting past me.

We had one day left, and less than that! The attacks were going to happen tomorrow morning! I was out of time.

"Byers. Byers!" I nearly shouted. My blood-pressure monitor started to beep a warning. "You gotta get me outta here. My name is Roland Bishop. Not Ethan Stiles. *Roland Bishop!* You gotta tell Phelps and Fox that I know when they're going to strike. When *and* where! I know all of it now!" I shook my handcuff against the bed vigorously, and she stood up and backed away. "You gotta get me out of here. *Please,*" I begged.

"No way! Stiles, Bishop, or whatever you think your name is. You're not getting out of here. I'm supposed to hold you until the FBI arrives."

I grunted and laid back in my bed. Penny's words came back to me then and there, as if from a shadow of my past, dim yet rising in clarity as they progressed.

The present is what you have to work with to influence both. You're outside of both. So, be the change! You have your feet in both worlds, apparently. I counsel you to straddle them carefully, and to go see what you can do.

I needed to straddle them carefully, indeed. If I was Ethan Stiles, I was in an alternate timeline and in an alternate identity. I had to get back. But if I told her the truth about all the names, and the flight numbers and all that, that would cause another system crash, and this freaking Inevitability Loop would suck me – or her – right out of the present. If I stayed right where I was and slept, I might never ever wake up as Roland Bishop again. And if I did either, would I lose Penny and Roxanne in the process?

I needed to straddle carefully. *Think, Roland. Think. There might be one way.*

And just then, the number *one* flashed through my mind. All these one's. I should have been paying attention. *One* meant, as all the other numbers had before it, the number of days left. Only one day left. There might be a way.

"Byers," I asked her. "Okay. Okay. Fine. What time is it?" I gritted my teeth in hope.

She looked at her watch. "2:28pm. Why?"

"I need to make a call to my neighbor at least. Her name is Renita. Or Amy. Can't remember."

"You don't even know your neighbor's name?"

"Byers! This is serious! Anyway, she said she would feed my cat. At least let me make sure that Winston is taken care of. *Please.*"

Byers stared at me with a silly sneer. "Winston?" she asked skeptically.

"Yes! I know it's a silly name. But it's a silly cat from a silly ex-wife. I do love him though. If they're gonna come haul me away, please at least let me call her and make sure she gets in."

She shook her head, still in disbelief. "Fine, Ethan. Take care of your silly cat. They confiscated your phone, though, so how are you going to do that?"

I sighed. "I can use the room phone here." I pointed to it sitting over on an end table by the wall. Byers raised an eyebrow at me and walked over toward it. She bent over, and picked up the phone.

I began my deep breathing.

She studied it for a moment, looked at me, and then started walking it over to me.

I dredged up every angry memory I had.

She handed me the phone. "Make it qui-"

I grabbed her with my free arm and pulled her on top of me, hugging her close as my body began to tense and pulsate. She elbowed me in the ribs, which only made me angrier. The handcuff on my right arm sizzled and smoked, burning me as arcs of lightning began to flash out of me. Byers screamed.

"Help! Someone, help me!"

"I'm sorry, Roxanne, I'm sorry!" I called out in wrath, my whole body buzzing with frenetic energy. "I'm sorry!"

In an instant, everything melted into a cobalt-indigo shade. All waved and flickered in the heat, and the walls around us shifted. Right on time. Byers continued to scream for help, elbowing and kicking backward into me. I took every blow. "Let go of me!" she yelled, and then screamed again as she witnessed what I was witnessing.

She turned her head to look at me and screamed once more — I couldn't tell you how horrifying I must have looked because I've never looked in a mirror while it was happening.

The cuffs melted and I was free. I wrapped my other arm around her in a bear hug and I could hear her wheeze. I was not letting go. This was my new centering and my new grounding, and she was going to straddle history and future with me. At the same time I gripped my hospital ID tag hard to make sure I had a hold on it. I wasn't letting go of that either.

The vortex claimed both of us, sucking us in as Ethan Stiles kidnapped the Detective and emerged on the other side as Roland Bishop.

The light then receded, and darkness took us.

4 Days To Go

September 7th, 2001 • Jersey City, NJ

There we were, together, just the two of us.

Byers was on top of me on my bed, frozen in shock, having watched her entire present vanish in a lightning haze and tumultuous whirlwind. My only regret was that we were both clothed…but that could wait.

Words failed her, and she could only form grunts. In a flurry of movement, though, she was off me, jumping out and down the hall into the kitchen, staring back at me in alarm.

"What the *hell* was that?!" she screamed.

I would answer her in a moment. I reached to turn my nightstand clock toward me. To my everlasting joy and relief, there was Winston's cat collar firmly digging into my wrist. I took it and kissed it. Next, I checked the alarm clock. There, plainly displayed for my joyful eyes, it read:

Friday 9.7.01.

It was the 7th all over again. Hopefully, I wouldn't have to relive all of that chase. But, taking heart, I accepted the fact that I bought us some time. I had straddled the line of the present to influence both the past and the future. I had carried her with me into a *new* present, and now she would believe what I told her, because her eyes were now opened. The running date was now a variable for her as well.

Byers would know with certainty that we had skipped through it, diving in and out of the never-ending flow of Time.

Roxanne stood there now, perplexed, panting hard, hands outstretched at her side. She gawked at me out of the corner of her eyes, her face contorted in freakish misery.

"Seriously! What the hell was that?"

"What…when…who…where…all of it is pretty irrelevant, Roxanne," I said. "But I can prove it to you-"

"Yes! Please! Prove it to me *right now,* Ethan!"

"Well, first, my name is not Ethan Stiles. It's Roland Bishop. And I *was* chasing Ziad Jarrah and the other jihadists last night at Newark. They were there."

She said nothing.

"They confiscated my phone, right? Do you remember the color?"

She nodded. "Blue?" she asked, nervously.

"Tell me what that is right there," I said, pointing behind her. She turned and looked. On the counter behind her was my phone, once again a little red Nokia 3310. She turned back to me. Winston skittered across her path, and she jumped in fright. "That's my cat. Winston. Whose name you like so much."

Her eyes followed him, and then she looked around in fear. "We're in my apartment in Jersey City. Where I end up after every single one of these episodes. At least, except for one." I saved the detail about Mohammed Atta and Afghanistan for later. Not too much all at once.

"Look at your own watch," I urged her. "Go ahead, look."

She pensively brought her wrist up and her eyes finally left me and moved to it. She gasped. Apparently her phone read the same time and date as mine.

6:13pm · September 7th, 2001.

"B-but," she started. "It was 2:28 on the 10th…"

"I don't know how it happens, Roxanne. I don't know *why* it happens. But I've been jumping in and out of this time loop for weeks now, straddling multiple running storylines, always ending at the inevitable attack on the World Trade Center this Tuesday. Tomorrow you'll be in Central Park. You were there already in a previous timeline, chasing Mohammed Atta. Do you remember that at all?"

She shook her head. "No, yesterday I just happened to be at Newark following up on a lead when I got the call about you."

"Nope. Think, Roxanne. That wasn't yesterday, that was three days from now on the 10th. Yesterday, for you, was the *8th*, and you were in Central Park with your officers tailing Mohammed Atta. It hasn't happened yet, of course. We went backward in time."

"You mean you kidnapped me and *took* me backward in time!" she yelled at me.

"I had to, Roxanne. You have to believe me. Look at your watch. Look at your phone. Look at my hospital tag!" I held it up for her. "See? Read it."

She leaned in close and peered at it. "You gotta be shittin' me," she said. "Bishop, Roland J. Male, 28, Caucasian. *No…way,*" she breathed in utter disbelief. "I put that tag on you! I gave them your name from your wallet!"

I pulled my wallet off of the counter behind her by my phone, and flipped it open. She read my driver's license and closed her eyes. *Bishop, Roland J.*

"Tell me I'm not going crazy," she said, her eyes pleading with me. "Tell me that this isn't a dream."

"It's not a dream. If anything, it's a terrible nightmare – or will be in a few days. For whatever reason, I was struck by lightning and given what Penny insists is a gift – a *few* gifts - and now I'm just trying to use them as best as I can. I used it yesterday, summoning up all my emotion and opening up that wormhole, taking you with me. I don't know how. I just have to get really hot and bothered, and, I just, I don't know," I ended lamely. "It just happens."

We looked at each other in silence for a moment.

I put my wallet back on the counter.

She breathed lengthily and dropped her head. "Ya know," she said, "I wouldn't have believed you at all except that you looked so damned familiar, lying there in the hospital bed. I was fighting with myself the whole time, knowing I knew you from somewhere. I left that hospital bed so many times and walked out," -here she started pacing- "then walked back right in to lean over your bed rail and see who the hell you were! I've known you before now. I've known you as Roland. I just didn't know that I knew you."

I smiled at her, seeing her take it all in.

"In any of those times, did you happen to lean over and kiss me?"

"You wish," she said, pacing again and putting her hair up into a pony tail. "I was looking at your face and realizing maybe God had a sense of humor after all."

"Oh, thank you."

"It's the Catholic in me." She huffed, putting her hands on her hips and turning around to gawk at me.

"Dr. Penny chose wisely," I said.

"Did she?"

"She did indeed. Come here." She didn't resist me. Roxanne Byers slowly paced over to me, stopping a few inches short. I could still feel the heat from Winston's collar, but I was now feeling a different type of heat altogether.

So was she, because our stopping and staring turned into something different altogether. I leaned in, slowly, and my lips met hers. She had on cherry Chapstick, and I could taste it, as I thrust my lips deep against hers.

It was the most wonderful taste I'd had in a long time, especially after so little food yesterday. That night, we ate food together, this good Catholic girl and I. It was the food of love that we ate, while we drank deep the nectar of life.

There we stayed, together, just the two of us.

1 Day To Go

September 10th, 2001 • Jersey City, NJ

The number *one* flashed before my eyes again.

We had one day left to avert tragedy. Three days ago, we thought we had all the time in the world.

It was 5:37am. Roxanne lay still, quiet, beside me, her mind dead to the world. Yet mine was teeming with energy, full of information streaming through me: facts and data that I had never read yet somehow knew to be true.

This Inevitability Loop was carrying me through a portal of history, as if I had read the very book that Penny had swallowed.

History now played out before me in my mind, as if *all* of it had already happened:

August 6th, Atta and an associate rented a white, four-door 1995 Ford Escort from Warrick's Rent-A-Car, which they returned on August 13th. Atta booked a flight on Spirit Airlines, also from Fort Lauderdale to Newark as Jarrah had done. He left on August 7th and returned on August 9th. He went to Central Office & Travel located in Pompano Beach to purchase one ticket for a flight to Newark. He was scheduled to leave on August 7th in the evening, and scheduled to return in the evening of August 9th. But he did not take the return flight.

On August 7th, Atta checked into the Wayne Inn in Wayne, New Jersey. He checked out August 9th. On that very same day he booked a one-way first-class ticket on America West. It was Flight 244 from Ronald Reagan National Airport heading to Las Vegas.

It was clear now that Atta traveled twice to Las Vegas. These flights were known as 'surveillance flights.' They were for he and the other jihadist cells in America to plan and rehearse how to carry out their attacks that were going to happen tomorrow. It was also now clear that the other hijackers also traveled to Las Vegas at various times over the summer of this year.

Throughout this past summer, Mohammed Atta met with Nawaf al-Hazmi to bring him up to speed on the status of their upcoming attacks. They met monthly for updates.

On August 23rd, Atta's driver license got revoked. It was revoked *in absentia* after Atta failed to show up to traffic court for an earlier citation he had received for driving without a license.

The same day, the Mossad, which was the Institute for Intelligence and Special Operations in Israel, provided his name to the FBI. They said that Atta was one of nineteen US residents that they suspected were preparing to plan an imminent attack against the United States. The only four publicly-known names they provided were Atta's and fellow accomplices Marwan al-Shehhi, Nawaf al-Hazmi, and Khalid al-Mihdhar. No one knew if every one of those nineteen names were all initially going to be part of those who would carry out the attacks tomorrow.

More flashes burst through my mind. I was receiving information on the future again! As I was receiving, I felt the slow trickle coming out of my nose, and I got up to stumble to the bathroom for some Kleenex.

On September 10th – *today* – Atta would be picking up al-Omari from the Milner Hotel in Boston. I could see their car: it was a Nissan Altima. They were talking. I heard them! They were heading to a Comfort Inn in South Portland, Maine. They were far away. Cameras would pick them up pumping gas at an Exxon station in Portland later this afternoon.

I saw a number on a hotel room door. *Room 233.* I saw a bank ATM. They were making withdrawals. The logo for Wal-Mart flew through my vision. They were picking up supplies there. I saw box-cutters. The logo for Pizza Hut flashed into my vision. Atta was eating there.

And then, suddenly, it was tomorrow: September 11th. I could see Atta and al-Omari, together, driving. I watched them arrive in the early morning hours to Portland International Jetport. They abandoned their Altima in the parking lot. They boarded Colgan Air at 6am, heading to Logan International Airport in Boston.

The connection between the two flights at Logan was within Terminal B, but the two gates were not connected within security. There were two separate concourses in Terminal B. The south one was used mostly by US Airways; the north was used mostly by American Airlines. I could see Atta becoming belligerent with a ticket staffer once he was told about additional screening requirements in Boston.

6:45am flashed into my mind. 6:45am at the airport in Boston. Atta lifted a phone to his ears. It was his fellow jihadist, hijacker Marwan al-Shehhi from United 175, confirming readiness to begin.

I could then see Atta checking in for American Airlines Flight 11 just as I had experienced in my previous visions. He once again passed through security, and he boarded his flight. He was sitting in business class. I saw another number. His seat number. 8D.

The plane lifted off at 7:59am from Boston to LAX.

It had eighty-one passengers aboard.

All of them were going to die.

We had less than one day to go. I sat on the toilet clad only in my boxers, steeped in thought, my head in my hands and Kleenex stuffed up my left nostril to staunch the bleeding. How were we ever going to stop four groups of terrorists in four different planes from four different locations? I couldn't even relay all these details to anyone who could do a damned thing about it without freezing time all over again.

It was now 6:28am. Roxanne stirred in my bedroom. I heard her let out a soft moan in her sleep. She muttered something incoherent about time travel.

Winston jumped up on the bathroom countertop and meowed demandingly. "Come here," I said to him, scooping him up. Poor thing hadn't been fed properly in I don't know how many days. "When were you fed last, Winny, huh? The year 1792? I know. Daddy's all over the map," I said, setting him down and cracking open a can of Nine Lives for him once more.

And then it hit me. I stared at that can for what seemed like time immemorial as visions flashed into my brain of possible outcomes.

Over the span of the past few weeks I had lived three different lives. I was Roland Bishop *and* I was Ethan Stiles *and* I was Mohammed Atta. The lightning lived on for each of them, and they were all connected.

But what if they could be *dis*-connected? What if I could be in three places all at once?

But that would take care of only *three* of the groups.
Roxanne made four.

Roxanne also knew. She made four! She could now head one of the groups off at the pass as well. The four of us could work in tandem.

We had to get Phelps and Fox and the others to know, or we'd never make it. We had to find a way to get all of these four lives in different locations at the right times.

But I had only just received information about Atta. I didn't know where or when the others would arrive. I just knew the flight numbers.

The flight numbers! Of course. How simple! Those that would tell me and everyone else where they would each be. That is, unless by trying to intervene the flight numbers had changed, and the hijackers would now be on a different flight. But then, wouldn't Penny's book have changed? Wouldn't I be receiving visions of *different* flight numbers for tomorrow?

In my mind's eye and in my memory, the flight numbers had not changed. Maybe they were fixed, and all of us were variables around them? Were they, being inevitable, the only fixed, grounded and centered points other than Winston's cat collar and Penny's book?

We had to intervene, Roxanne and I. Even if we were the only two who knew, we had to do something and try to stop them. And we had one day left to do it.

But we wouldn't be the only two. There would be *four* of us, and I knew who they were.

American 11 would depart from Logan at 7:59am. It would crash into the North Tower of the World Trade Center at 8:46am.

United 175 would depart from Boston at 8:15am, slicing diagonally into the corner of the South Tower in a grisly inferno seen by the entire world at 9:03am.

American 77 would depart from Dulles at 8:20am, drilling into the Pentagon like a missile at 9:37am.

United 93 would depart from Newark at 8:42am, though they were supposed to leave earlier but were delayed on the tarmac. I could not see its end result.

Four locations. *Four* of us.

I raced into the bedroom. "Roxanne, come on, get up." She moaned again and flipped over angrily on her side. It gave me a chuckle. *Not a morning person. Noted.* "Roxanne, come on, you gotta get up. I have an idea. I need your help."

"Whaaa-?" she asked, sitting up and throwing a mess of her own hair out of her face. "What are you talking about? What time is it?"

"Almost seven. I need you to come with me. Now."

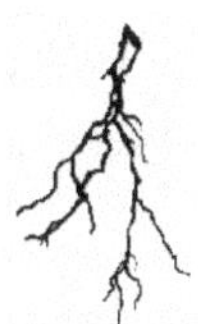

She didn't stop grumbling, but she did come with me. To our amazement, heading outside, there was her Bronco with us. I was thinking we would have to take the bus, but this was an added bonus. Maybe the stars were aligning. Maybe we would have a chance.

I was talking quickly as she drove. "Straight to the FBI office. We need to tell them in person because we need to take them with us."

"Take them with us? You mean like-"

"Exactly. You hold onto one, and I'll hold onto the other. You can take Phelps if you'd like since you guys used to be an item. I'll take Fox. I have a mind to squeeze the life out of him anyway. Maybe I'll grab him and cut off his circulation as a little payback. Should cut off the blood to his brain. He doesn't use it much anyway."

"Roland, don't."

I rolled my eyes. "I'm kidding!   I wouldn't. We need him. We need *both* of them."

We were racing through Jersey City heading for the Holland Tunnel. It was now 7:15am. I reached into my pocket and pulled out my Nokia. I smiled. "Hey! Would you look at that? I'm still me." I showed it to her, and she looked at me and smiled crazily.

"I don't know how you're still sane, dude."

"Me neither. Let's hope we both stay that way." I looked down at my phone and called information for the numbers to the two airlines. "Man, I wish someday we had internet on our phones so we could just verify this kind of information in a browser."

Roxanne scoffed. "Ha! The internet in your hands in a phone? Yeah, like that'll ever happen." She returned her eyes to the road and sped toward the Big Apple.

We reached the FBI Office. Once more, the agent stood out front. Only this time he looked different.

"What's up, Ostrom?" Roxanne asked him as we scurried inside.

"Who the heck is Ostrom?" I asked, hurrying in behind her.

"Don't ask. I remember Armstrong too. But now I have this memory of Ostrom that I didn't ask for. So just… don't ask."

I shook my head and exhaled, following her into the elevator and up to the office where Phelps and Fox were waiting.

"Phelps! Fox!" she cried. They each emerged from their offices, coming down the hall toward us.

"Where the hell have you been, Byers?" Fox asked angrily. "I thought you were on the job at Newark four nights ago and then you vanish without a trace and don't return our calls?"

"Can it, Fox! Both of you, get in here!"

She motioned angrily for them to follow her into the conference room. Like obedient children or dogs with their tails between their legs, they followed her in.

"This is serious," she began. I was going to lead the way, but she was more fiery, and they felt it. "Bishop here has news, he has *proof* of when Atta and his goons are gonna pull everything off. We know the date, we know the times, we know the flight numbers."

Phelps' jaw dropped. "How? How did you get all that?"

"Never mind that right now. I just need both of you to stand right here."

"What?"

"Just do it, Fox!" she yelled. "There's no time! Both of you, please, come over here. This is not something we can just explain to you – it's something you have to experience." I watched her as she shepherded them further into the room on the other side of the conference table."

"Roxanne, I really don't see-"

"Shut it, Ryan! You have to trust me on this."

My cat collar began to get hot. Of course it did: we were changing the future and the past all at once, with less than one day to go. I glanced up at the clock. It was now 9:36am. We couldn't delay.

"Okay. Just stand right there." Phelps and Fox were side by side, casting awkward glances at each other. "Roland, come here." I obliged. "Stand in front of Ryan." I did so, not sure where she was going with this.

I was eye to eye with him, and we both turned to look at Roxanne.

"Okay, Ryan. Now hit him."

"What?" Phelps asked, flabbergasted.

"What?" I asked at the same time.

"Go on, hit him!" she insisted. *Oh, now I get it,* I thought, as I started to return my gaze to Phelps. *She wants me to get angr-*

Oooof! Phelps smashed his fist into my gut and I doubled over.

Oh boy, did that piss me off. I couldn't breathe for a moment, and my body was tingling with anger. I furrowed my brow and sought for air. "Don't do that again," I choked, staring angrily at Phelps. "Roxanne! Stop. It doesn't work that way."

"But you said-"

"I know what I said! That's not what I meant though. *I* have to start it off."

"Oh. Sorry."

"If you need me to do it instead, let me know," Fox offered. I shrugged him off and walked away.

Straddle the line, I told myself quietly, reaching over and grabbing my cat collar. I faced away from them, and started to breathe hard. My stomach still roiled, and I wanted to turn and punch Fox. Good. I was getting angrier. Winston's collar started to burn.

"What's going-" Phelps started.

"Shh! Just wait," Roxanne urged him.

Flickers of blue at the corners of my vision. *Straddle the line*, I said again softly to myself. I brought up every emotional thought I'd ever experienced. Every grudge, grievance, frustration, bitterness. I dredged it all up. I went all the way back to being a child under my mom's strict control. My brother Burt. The frustration of being dictated to and never heard. My dad's absence. Things I had never even told Penny. Everything from the past few weeks and the stress of it all: I summoned it to the surface.

"*Byers?*" Phelps asked nervously.

My skin began to get hot. I was churning inside. I clutched Winston's collar and dug it further into my skin, pressing the heat into my epidermis.

"Wait for it..." Byers whispered.

The wind began to blow. Both of the agents' ties fluttered, and they looked down in amazement. The clouds outside faded to a burnt auburn, underlit and eerie. Traffic seemed to slow to a grinding halt.

But for me, all I saw was glowing blue. Flickers of angry blue flame erupted out of my head, and the agents recoiled. I clutched my temples, trying to stay grounded. *Straddle the line! Straddle the line!* I heard myself yelling.

"No, Fox, don't!" Roxanne yelled. "Stow your weapon! He's not going to hurt you!"

In a reflex, my head was thrown back and I couldn't contain the buildup anymore. Blue flame burst forth out of my mouth with every word as I screamed:

I'm Roland Bishop, and I know who I am!
I'm Ethan Stiles, and I know who I am!
I'm Mohammed Atta, and I know who I am!
Straddle the line! Straddle the line!

A vortex erupted around us. The agents howled in dismay, and Roxanne screamed. Loose papers flew around the room. Before I knew what was happening, a dissonant shriek shot from my soul and split the room's air asunder. My hands went out wide and arcs of lightning connected with every piece of metal. The gun in Fox's hand was seized by an arc, and then it flashed and burst in his hands. His right hand had been completely blown apart. His chest was splattered with his own blood.

Fox screamed in agony and I could hear Roxanne trying to help him.

One by one, the glass windows blew out around us as I continued to shout.

I'm Roland Bishop, and I know who I am!
I'm Ethan Stiles, and I know who I am!
I'm Mohammed Atta, and I know who I am!
Straddle the line! Straddle the line!

Tracers of white hot light burst from me and incinerated points of the walls around us. The conference table caught fire. They were all powerless in the midst of it.

But not me. I was full of power. I channeled all of my emotion and all of my strategy into a triumvirate of focused concentration and will. It demanded everything from me. At just the right moment, I let go of Winston's cat collar as a blinding light took all of us.

For a moment, all was silent.

Briefly, everything around us was stilled. I dropped to the ground, heaving in the inky blackness. I turned and looked around me as stray remnants of the vortex danced on the periphery, fading away, rescinding into nothingness. Light filtered back in, and I saw them standing there, panting, looking all around in dismay and awe.

We were all in my living room, back in Jersey City.

The number zero flashed before my eyes as they noticed me on the ground.

All three of me.

Phelps drew his gun, recognizing one of me.

Roxanne stopped him. "Ryan, *no!* That's not him! That's *not* him! Wait and see!"

Fox was examining his right hand, oblivious for a moment to Phelps and Roxanne approaching me in curiosity. Agent Ryan Phelps had never seen anything like this. "Where are-?" he started to ask.

"Shh," Roxanne said again. "It's okay. We're at Roland's place in Jersey City."

I stood up. Every one of me stood up.

Roxanne came over and looked at me. In unison, all of me looked over at her and smiled, grateful for her help.

She heaved a massive sigh of relief. "You did it, Roland," she whispered, eyeing all of us, and then she turned to the agents.

"Guys, I'd like to introduce Roland Bishop, Ethan Stiles, and Mohammed Atta. But... they're really all Roland Bishop."

We glanced at the clock on the wall. It was 4:03am
on September 11th, the day of the attacks.
The number *zero* flashed before my eyes.

0 Days To Go

September 11th, 2001 • Manhattan NY

They all eyed me curiously as I stood there. It was a good start.

I couldn't believe it actually worked. Oh boy, did I have a story to tell Penny.

"When you're finished gawking, we have to move out," Atta said, and their heads flipped over to me.

"Lord Almighty," Phelps breathed out, drawing closer to Atta. "You look just like him. Can you…do you…can you feel his memories, know his thoughts?"

"It doesn't quite work like that," Atta said. "I can speak Arabic, I have all of these memories from different timelines and different places. Like, I can see you, Roland, from inside The Frederick, as I crawled toward you."

"Weird," Roland replied. "That must be surreal."

"Wait-wait-wait," said Fox, still feeling his resurrected hand, "so all three of you are…*you*? How in the holy hell does that even make sense?"

"Nothing makes sense after you get struck by lightning," all three of me said in unison. Fox started in fright, backing away slightly. Phelps continued to eye Atta curiously. "Which one of you is in control?" he asked Atta.

"I am," said Roland. "I promise."

Phelps looked over at Roland, and a trace of a smile grew on his lips. "Boy, you guys weren't kidding when you said that this was something we'd have to *experience*. Why couldn't you just tell us back at the office?"

"You wouldn't have believed him," Roxanne said. "And you guys would have been frozen."

"Frozen?" asked Fox, squinting his eyes. She nodded. "What, like a meat locker?"

"You're a meathead, you know that?" she asked him. "No! Frozen in time. Stuck. In some kind of informed paralysis time loop thing. Roland, you say it."

Roland stifled back a laugh. "It's something I can't explain, guys. Once the knowledge of the exact date and time sets in, that's the truth. And when the truth hits you, it demands something of you. So you have to act on it. But the universe must not have been ready to let you act on it yet, so that's why you – and everyone else – gets stuck in time. Like a system crash. At least I think that's it."

"Incredible," breathed Phelps.

"So all of this went down after you got hit by lightning?" Fox asked.

Ethan nodded. "Ever since then I've received visions, and I've learned how to harness it and use it. I've been pinballing back and forth between dates, shuffling through this Inevitability Loop and trying my best to figure out what to do next. And where to be. Now I know where that is."

Phelps' eyebrows went up. "And where is that?"

"In four different places," said Roland. "We're going to stop some terrorists. And we don't have a lot of time, so let's get moving. I know precisely what to do."

Roland explained everything he had seen, everywhere he had been, all that he had witnessed, and all that he knew to be coming from the future, as the six of us sat down. The agents could not keep their eyes off Atta. Or Stiles. Or Roland. Any of us. They eyed us curiously, never sure who was about to speak or who was the figurehead. Ethan and Atta nodded along to everything Roland said.

By now we all knew what all the terrorists looked like, and we knew what flight they would be leaving on as well as the time. It would simply be a matter of being in the right place at the right time.

American Airlines 11 would depart from Boston's Logan Airport at 7:59am. Mohammed Atta would go there with Roxanne. Phelps was about to protest, but Roland explained that Atta would do the most damage to Atta *as Atta.*

United Airlines Flight 175 would depart Logan at 8:15am. Roxanne would handle Marwan al-Shehhi there.

American Airlines Flight 77 would depart Dulles at 8:20am. Roland looked over and nodded to Ethan. He would go there and confront Hani Hanjour with Fox.

And finally, United Airlines Flight 93 would depart from Newark at 8:42am. Roland would go there with Phelps, and they would confront Ziad Jarrah.

By the time Roland was finished, it was 6:22am.

They shook their heads wildly and sighed, widening their eyes to take it all in. It was, admittedly, a mind-job.

"So weird, Roland. How will you know which one of you is…you?" asked Roxanne.

"I'll know. And I can untether whenever I need to. I know it sounds weird, but I can feel myself in all of you," Roland said to the other two. They nodded right back.

"I can definitely. It's three streams of consciousness," Atta said. The agents muttered and swore.

"Man, you even have the accent down," Fox said.

"I don't 'have it down,' I *have* the accent," Atta clarified. "I *am* Atta…but it's just from a different timeline, and with Roland's consciousness at the helm." They shook their heads in incredulity.

Atta turned to Roxanne. "*Now* can I have a gun?"

She smiled. "Let's go. We're already late for Logan Airport, and that's two planes. We won't make it time."

"Yes we will. Trust me." Atta's eyes lit up blue.

Everyone had exchanged phone numbers. Roxanne and Atta were outside in her Bronco, once more parked at the curb. They had a date with Logan Airport. All three of me had grabbed jackets from the coat closet.

"Get there," Roxanne said. "Good luck, boys."

"See you on the other side," Atta said to them in his thick Egyptian accent. "You certainly are a handsome man, Roland," he added. Roxanne placed her hand in Atta's. They all shook their heads as a flash consumed Roxanne's Bronco and they disappeared from sight.

"Well, that's one for the books," Roland said. "Let's get a move on, Phelps. I say we try to catch these guys before they even get to their gate."

Phelps nodded and donned a fedora. "Here. You're gonna need this." He handed Roland a gun and a badge. "That was Agent Mulligan's. Use it and honor him."

Roland held it lovingly. "I will. I promise." Roland took Phelps' hand. Blue light consumed the two of them, and they vanished, somewhere along the Inevitability Loop toward Newark.

"Well, I guess it's you and me now," Ethan said to Fox. "Ready to do this?"

"*Ready?* No. Determined even though the three of you are absolute freakin' lightning-struck whackjobs? *Yes,*" Fox emphasized.

"I'll take that as a compliment," Ethan said, grinning. "There's only one thing left to do."

"Yeah? And what would that be?"

"We have to hold hands," Ethan said, grinning.

Fox grunted in disapproval and rolled his eyes, slapping his palm in Ethan's and squirming at the touch.

In three seconds, they disappeared as well.

Winston watched all of it curiously from the window.

It was a beautiful early-fall day that September 11th as I moved in three different directions, fanning out to my appointed destinations. The weather was gorgeous everywhere you looked, with not a trace of clouds.

A strong cold front had crossed the New York City metro area last night, apparently. Hurricane Erin was growing and massing out on the Atlantic Ocean last night. But the cold front had kept Erin out over the ocean, leaving the northeast in peace. It was crisp and clear and high pressure moved in, with winds up to twenty-five miles per hour. A perfect day for flying. *Or dying.*

We were all in uncharted waters and undiscovered country. We were rewriting history as we inched closer to our respective destinations, glancing off what was written, and writing our own pages as we went. Somewhere, Penny might be reading a book from 2020, watching the ink rearrange itself into different sentences.

It was election day in New York City. Voters were going to the polls for the mayoral primary, comptroller, public advocate, and more. That was the short-term, and the only thing people truly saw. No one had any idea about the long-term, and the sheer terror that was about to descend upon them if any of the three teams failed.

Simultaneously, all three of our teams emerged out of the fog together, stepped out of a churning spinning vortex that was growing in intensity.

Roxanne was behind Atta as they looked up at the Logan sign. Atta would be going for Gate B-32 to intercept the real Mohammed Atta. Roxanne would intercept al-Shehhi at Gate C-19.

My sight was taken to Ethan and Fox outside Dulles. They were heading for Gate D-26 and Hanjour.

Roland and Phelps appeared in my mind's eye arriving at Newark, heading for Gate 17 and Jarrah.

My mind swam as all three images flooded together, jockeying for attention. They overlapped, intersected, and played off one another.

One thing was certain: we couldn't call airport security or we would inform people of the plot and risk a time freeze once more. We couldn't involve anyone else, or we'd have to suck them all back through the vortex, and I just couldn't fit that many people in my little apartment. Winston would never approve of it.

The clock was ticking. As we drew near to each of our respective destinations, the flashes came. Stronger than they ever had before. I was bleeding in tandem out of all three of my right nostrils. Atta's left leg cramped up as he ran in the cold morning, and all three of us felt it.

"You okay?" Roxanne asked Atta.

"Fine," Atta said obstinately, though he needed to work out the charley horse in his calf. His nerves were on fire, and he hadn't had much water. "I can go on."

Roxanne and Atta made their way into the airport and prepared to split up.

"Your leg alright?" asked Phelps.

"Yeah, just needs massaging," said Roland. "It'll be fine. We're here. Flash your badge and let's get on our way to Gate 17." He wiped the blood from his nose.

The sun was rising in the east, and the crowds were growing, moving to their respective destinations.

"Dude, what's the problem? We don't have time to waste with a bum leg," complained Fox.

Ethan bent over and massaged the cramp out of his left leg as they slowed. Blood dripped from his nose onto the carpeted walkway. Fox was nervously looking around and scanning the boards for the respective flights and gates.

"I'm good," said Ethan. "I can go on now. Just a cramp." He sniffed and wiped at his nose.

"Fine. Let's move," Fox ordered.

Phelps went first through security, flashing his badge and whispering something to the security officer at the checkpoint.

Briefly Roland had a flash and a vision, and his head swam, stopping to grip the scanning counter. "Whoa," he said, dizzy, waiting. Finally he breathed again. "It's nothing. It's passed." But he couldn't shake the sensation of being instructed to remove his shoes as he went through security. He passed a hand over his eyes and dismissed it as perhaps an insignificant future vision.

Atta stopped in the middle of a run through the concourse, and Roxanne asked, "What is it?" He paused as if listening, and clutched his head briefly. "It has passed. It is nothing. Let us go," and he was off with the Detective once again. She flashed a badge at a security officer and was let through with Atta in tow.

At Dulles, Ethan stumbled and fell.

Fox was unsympathetic. "Man, I always get second string," he said. "Get up, dude, we gotta move. What's wrong *now*?"

"I don't know," said Ethan. "I just received a strange vision about…removing shoes? Blinded me for a moment. Something from the future, though I'm not sure where or when."

The Dulles airport was playing *Thank You* by Dido, and the music descended down from overhead speakers, filling all of our ears. I heard it in stereo: there and here.

Where my conscience was floating out there in the ether, I didn't know. The three of us were linked up somehow, and I could sense and feel everything that they could, as they could with each other.

"Can we go now?" Fox asked, annoyed.

"Yes, it's fine. We can go," Ethan replied.

Atta and Roxanne split up. "You got your phone, right?" Roxanne said.

Atta held up his little Kyocera smartphone. "You did not see, but I checked with Roland and Ethan before we left. Roland has the Nokia, Ethan has the Motorola V60. I have this." Atta smiled a thin-lipped smile at her, one eyelid slightly sagging.

"K, that's…that's great," she said a bit distrustfully. "Use it, Atta. I mean, Roland. Whoever. And be careful!"

"I will. You too," Atta said, and he felt his wrist, ensuring that his Winston collar was on snug.

Roxanne headed for Gate C-19 and al-Shehhi.

Atta raced on toward Gate B-32 and Atta.

"Here comes the gate," said Roland. "Right down concourse A." He began to feel nervous in the pit of his stomach. The gun bounced lightly inside his jacket, and he wasn't sure when, or *if*, he would have to use it. "Right down here, Phelps."

Phelps was to his right as Gate 17 loomed up.

Suddenly, Roland gasped and moved back, seeking to shelter from view. "What? What?" demanded Phelps.

"Possible sighting of Jarrah. Coming out of the restroom to your right."

Phelps retreated and held back. "Additional sightings. Roland, get over here!" They backed into the entrance of a gift shop while passengers ambled by. Phelps brought the rim of his hat downward.

An overhead announcement said something about a gate change. "Look. That's al-Nami, the little guy. You said you spotted him chasing Jarrah, right? That him?"

Roland peeked out beyond the entrance. Sure enough, there was al-Nami, sitting down talking to someone on a cellphone. They had to wait. If he was in any way communicating with the other terrorists, he could alert them to their position, and their cover could be blown.

They had to wait.

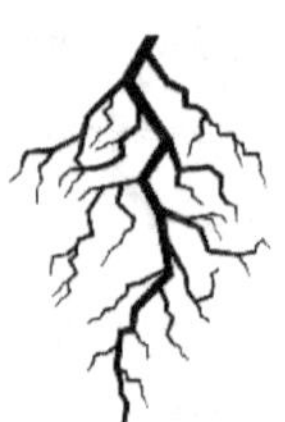

Atta continued down the concourse. Up ahead, he saw a man with a similar build, stocky shoulders and puffy, wiry black hair enter the men's room. Atta pulled his jacket up around himself and kept his eyes down.

The terrorist entered the men's room, and Atta pursued, though the white flashes persisted, and his nose began to bleed once more.

Images of people running. Of a gaping, burning hole in the side of one of the towers. Of people falling.

"For goodness' sake, Roland, wipe your nose, you're gonna attract attention," said Phelps. He handed him a handkerchief.

Roland took it from his hand and dabbed at his nose, wiping the blood trail that obeyed gravity and moved toward the floor. He looked around awkwardly as he, too, was beset by flashes of uncomfortable, blazing light stabbing through his brain. Images of a struggle in the sky. Of people screaming and a jetliner lurching violently midair. Of green grass below.

Byers had reached Gate D-26. al-Shehhi was not in sight, nor were any of his accomplices. She wondered. Had something changed, and they weren't here? It was already 7:15am. They would be boarding in a half-hour. Indeed, she thought, Atta's flight would be boarding in ten minutes.

In another area of the airport, Atta's mind continued to flash as he entered the restroom, wiping his nose.

Fox picked up his phone to dial Phelps. "Phelps, what's your 20? How's it going over there? Stiles here has a bit of a nosebleed and is going through those flashes, but nothing much yet. We think we might have seen one of the guys near the gate here at Dulles. Not sure."

"Standby. Positive ID on two of the targets at the gate. Do not engage any of them until you've ID'd all of them and none of them are on their phones!"

"Copy that," he said, and switched off. "Just wait here, Stiles. Yellow light."

But Stiles was not seeing yellow; he was stricken with white. Images of the Pentagon in flames. Of an entire section collapsed in an angular heap. Of bodies out on the grass. And everywhere you looked, smoke.

Phelps continued to watch and look inconspicuous. Someone bumped him on their way out of the gift shop. Oh, excuse me," said the voice. Phelps turned, and it was a sweet elderly woman with a younger lady in tow, holding a bag of purchased snacks, presumably for the flight. Phelps tipped his hat at her.

The agent took a quick breath to cleanse his stress palette, and moved his vision back over to the gate.

A Middle-Eastern man was right in front of him. Phelps jumped and recoiled. "Gah! Hi. Can I help you?"

It was Ziad Jarrah.

"Why are you watching us?" Jarrah said. Roland slid out of view. If this was the same Jarrah he had pursued a few nights earlier, he might recognize him, and the jig would be up.

At the same time, Roland's mind was awash with exchanging images. A ball of fire. A clear day. Rubble. A building standing tall. They flickered together, back and forth, like a Cable TV channel with interlacing frames, uncertain which to broadcast.

Phelps played dumb. "Watching you? I dunno what you mean."

Jarrah just stared at him, and then looked around for any signs of any accomplice. Jarrah had appeared seemingly out of nowhere, and must have caught both of them watching al-Nami.

"Sir, I'm looking for my wife," Phelps invented, trying to throw Jarrah a bone. "I thought she was sitting here but I can't seem to find her."

Jarrah continued to study him with deadened eyes. "I wish you luck in your search," he offered in a detached monotone.

"Thank you, much obliged," said Phelps.

Jarrah walked away from the two of them. At that moment, al-Nami emerged from the men's room in the distance with two other men. They all sat together. Phelps pulled his phone to his ear and pretended to be talking to his wife, waving his hands around as if he was frustrated with her.

Jarrah eyed him for a moment, then spoke quietly to his fellow jihadists. They glanced up at the departures board and the time. It was now 7:20, and they would be boarding in twenty minutes.

Roland's flashes returned to normal, and a smoking jetliner-shaped crater burst with a fireball from the ground.

At Logan, Atta entered the men's room, his head down. Two men were at the urinal. One finished up and started washing his hands. Feet hung down from the furthest stall. Atta waited until the terrorist was alone, hiding around the corner from the end of the stalls.

A young man came in and noticed Atta facing him. He turned uncomfortably, aiming his body away from Atta to shield his privates. Atta turned as well, pretended to pee into a urinal but quaking with hot flashes and trembling from visions.

Movement from the furthest urinal.

The young man continued to urinate. He needed to leave! Atta quieted his breathing and listened. More movement and toilet paper being dispensed.

Finally, the young man jiggled and zipped up his fly, turning away from the urinal with one final awkward glance at Atta. He did not stop to wash his hands.

Atta breathed out slowly. Flashes consumed him, and he was sweating profusely, but he held steady and willed himself not to collapse.

The stall door opened. Footsteps. The white flashes increased in heat and intensity.

Suddenly, Atta whirled around and faced his doppelganger. The terrorist's jaw dropped in utter surprise as he tried to shove Atta out of the way and burst out of the bathroom. But Atta had the strength of three men and lightning coursing through him. His eyes lit up blue. His hands began to smoke. The cat collar around his wrist burned with a righteous light.

In the unoccupied bathroom, Atta threw the terrorist into the stall wall, and the tile cracked. Atta cried out in pain as Atta went for him again, burying his hands into Atta's neck, choking him.

The terrorist flailed about in misery, attempting to punch and strike Atta, but Atta overpowered Atta. In a moment, the terrorist's neck was broken with a sickening crack. He slumped down to the ground, pulverized with a lightning grip that fried his nerves and severed his spinal column.

Atta dragged him back into the stall, locked it from the inside, took his shoulder bag, slid back out underneath, and left the men's room just as another male patron was entering. He slid the shoulder bag over himself.

Atta then returned to Gate B-32 as if nothing had happened. His associates were waiting for him.

Roxanne looked around cautiously. She was at D-26, but there were still no signs of al-Shehhi or the other men. She took a seat at the window, waiting and wondering if they had messed everything up.

In an instinct, she pulled out her phone and dialed Phelps.

Roland was recovering from the visions, but was still trembling. Phelps was keeping up the charade of the missing wife, holding his phone to his ear.

Roland could see the four United 93 terrorists sitting together, studying Phelps. One of them reached for his phone.

Suddenly, Phelps' own phone rang. He stopped his charade, frozen in horror. How could he be on his phone with his wife if his phone rang audibly? There was no way.

The jig was up.

All four terrorists started to move away, advancing down the hallway to beat a hasty retreat. As they passed Roland, his head exploded with vision after vision, interlaced and jockeying for power, each seeking to subdue the other and uncertain which would gain the upper hand. Screaming through all of them were blinding bursts and streaks of pallid white.

Phelps dropped his phone and whipped out his gun. "Freeze!" he cried, and the four of them broke into a run. He gave chase. Roland somehow struggled to his feet and sprinted after them. As he did so, his senses were renewed as the perpetrators drew further away. His vision became clearer. His focus was sharpened. He could see them up ahead. He did the only thing he could.

Phelps fell behind him as Roland became a freight train with momentum no one could impede. He cried out for Jarrah, and this time he had him in his sights with no escape. Roland careened into the air wildly and screamed a high-pitch wail that rent the very air. Everyone within hearing dropped to the ground and clutched their ears. The terrorists, on whom he focused his belch of cataclysmic sound, dropped solidly to the ground.

And that's the last time they saw the light of day.

An airplane flying out of the ground, uncrumpling. A horrifying ball of fire receding back into the earth, utterly extinguishing.

Roland stretched out his arms as bolts of sheer power jetted from his fingers.

A 747 pointed toward the ground yet flying backward into the air, leveling off.

Lightning was released from his digits as powerful and as hot as the sun. It connected with each of the jihadists and they flailed in agony. Other passengers fled wailing and screaming. Smoke rose from the bodies as they became charred and blackened with three hundred million volts of energy coursing through them.

A commercial jetliner full of living souls, flying backward but slowing, slowing, gradually coming to a stop as wispy strata settled upon it and it froze in midair, as if a videotape reel had been spun to a grinding halt.

Phelps cried out to Roland as continued arcs flew from his body and light streamed from his eyes. The random zips of energy connected with anything metal all around them, and innocent passersby were at risk of harm.

Slowly spinning forward again, a jetliner, holding its course and staying aloft, continued to fly toward San Franciso unimpeded, unmolested, and undestroyed.

The light faded. Roland panted through it, his hair streaming with sweat, and the visions faded. The flashes dulled and dissolved to peace.

Phelps put his hand out toward Roland's shoulder and cautiously touched him. "Hey. Hey, Roland. You okay?"

And then Roland grabbed Winston's collar and the vortex opened up behind them.

Fox repeatedly called Phelps with no response. "Dammit!" he hissed through his teeth. "I can see all of them! What do you-" he stopped. "Ethan? Stiles, where are you?"

Ethan Stiles was no longer with him. Fox looked about wildly. He was walking up to Gate D-26, trembling and tremoring with all sorts of hallucinations and real images, unsure how to discern the truth from the lie. And then a sudden peace took him, though racked with visions. He approached Hani Hanjour, who had another associate sitting next to him. He motioned back to Fox. "Hey, they're right here, come here," yelled Stiles joyfully.

Fox's eyes went wide. *What was the fool doing??* He hid all traces of his gun in his pocket and played it cool. "Hey, man, what's up?" he asked Stiles.

"Yeah, these are the guys I told you about!" Stiles replied. "This is Dave, and Jack. Hey, where are Mike and Will anyway?" he asked, looking around wildly.

"Sir, you are mistaken," said Hanjour, looking around nervously. "You have us confused with someone else. And are you alright? You appear to be ill."

Indeed, Stiles's legs buckled briefly and he composed himself and stood back up to full height. "No, I'm fine, thanks. You guys were the guys we hung out with that night at the tavern, right?"

"Sir. Please," insisted Hanjour, recoiling into himself and covering his face with his hands. "You do not know what you are talking about." His accomplice did the same. "Please go away." Other passengers around us began to move away, not wanting to be part of a scene.

"Oh, no problem, no problem," Stiles said, and he was trembling. Here were two of them, together. Here was their chance to draw out the other two. An overhead speaker announced Flight American 77 would now begin boarding first class and premium class passengers. *Perfect timing,* Stiles thought. *That oughtta bring them outta the woodwork.*

Stiles' legs buckled again, unsure what to think. Competing visions flashed into his mind of the Pentagon on fire, and then completely intact. Back and forth, as he swayed.

He decided to lay it out bare. "Listen, fellas," said Stiles. "I got this problem, see? There's this building in Virginia shaped like a star. You guys know which one I mean? It's really cool. We wanna go see it but we don't know how to get there, and we musta thrown back one too many, ya know what I mean?"

Fox was now following him. He started to laugh and play along. "Ha! Yeah, I know what you mean, buddy. You talkin' about the Pentagon?"

Hanjour seemed to flinch. "Sir, I really don't know what you are talking about. If you will excuse us, we must board now."

At that moment, the other two showed up, ready to board. "Is there a problem?" they asked Hanjour. He didn't respond to them; he flashed his eyes to Stiles and Fox. They looked over at them. "Do you have a problem, gentlemen?"

Stiles winced from a flash. "No, but you do," he said, nearly falling over. At that moment, Fox drew his weapon and trained it on Hanjour. The others backed away and started to flee.

Stiles exploded. The wobbly legs turned into stoic columns of strength as he grabbed one of the men and threw him into Hanjour. Hanjour fell under the weight of the first man, and the other two fled.

"Not so fast!" cried Fox, holding them at bay with his weapon. They froze.

"Hold it!" cried Stiles. "Don't move. Don't even think about it," he warned them, leaning forward and hissing a dangerous sound as bluish light burst forth from his mouth and eyes. Passengers got up and fled from the gate. The gate agent called security.

But Stiles wasn't done. Neither were the visions. The Pentagon couldn't decide whether or not it wanted to remain intact. It was still burning. There was only one thing left to do. He grabbed his cat collar and clutched it.

Straddle the line, Stiles mumbled. "Grab each other's hands. Do it, now!" he yelled to them.

Fires slowly dying.

Hanjour looked at him quizzically. They all did.

"Now! Fox, bring the other two over here. Hurry!" Fox escorted them over at gunpoint and made them hold the hand of their fellow jihadist.

A building being raised. A star being reformed intact.

Rapid footsteps could be heard running down the concourse. Airport security. They would fire upon Stiles without the slightest provocation once identified.

The terrorists were holding hands. Stiles moved closer to them. He grabbed the hand of the nearest one. "Immortality's over, fellas. No absolution and no large-breasted women in the afterlife for you," he hissed.

A jetliner-shaped missile stopped short of its target and pulled forcibly back up into the sky.

Fox recoiled as Stiles summoned a vortex of blinding color and fury, opening up behind all of them and taking all five of them into it. Roland untethered his consciousness from Stiles. Stiles' lifeless body fell in alongside theirs, suddenly bereft of a soul, and there was screaming in the wind.

The Pentagon, symbol of America's might, unharmed, as a passenger plane continued on through the sky toward LAX.

Detective Byers was waiting patiently. She hadn't heard from the other members of her team, and it was now 7:45am. Boarding would begin for Flight 175 any minute!

As if at the end of hope, there they were. All four of them, led by Marwan al-Shehhi himself. Her heartbeat quickened. She lifted her phone and prepared to call Phelps just as the overhead announcement signaled boarding would begin shortly. She stood, carefully eyeing them but being cautious not to draw attention to herself. She was, after all, a detective. The detective knew stealth.

Passengers began to line up for boarding. The gate opened leading out to the passenger boarding bridge. Roxanne dialed Phelps and lifted her phone to her ear. All she got was static. She dialed again. Static.

Roxanne tried Roland. Same thing. In desperation, she tried Mohammed. Static.

She sighed. She would have to take them by herself. There was no way she could let them get on that plane. No way. She held up her badge and trained her gun on al-

Shehhi. Fellow travelers squealed and moved away.
"Detective, NYPD, freeze!" she said.

Al-Shehhi turned and sneered. "NYPD? You're in Boston, miss!" he scoffed. The other terrorists stepped away from their leader, preparing for a quick getaway.

"I said *freeze*," she shouted at them, moving in closer. They complied. "Hands up!" she said.

The vortex opened up behind her quicker than she could breathe. Roland and Phelps were thrust out of it right behind her, knocking her off her balance. Lightnings arced all around them.

Shots were fired, though she didn't know from where. An undercover cop? A security guard? A sky marshal? Everyone scrambled for cover. Two terrorists made a run at her and she squeezed off a few rounds. They were down. The third held still with his hands upraised. "Shots fired, shots fired!" she screamed.

al-Shehhi ran for the ticket agent, and grabbed her from behind, choking her. Out of his pocket he pulled a box cutter: a simple and unsuspicious purchase from the local gift shop. He held it to her neck.

Roland and Agent Phelps stumbled up, weary. Roland was beset by tremendous pressure: the multiple hematomas were acting up as visions surged through him and assaulted his mind. Dimly through the fog he could see al-Shehhi holding the ticket agent hostage.

Roland cried out in pain as images of the South Tower alternated between intact or smoking; crackling with flame, or calm and noiseless.

"al-Shehhi, drop the knife!" the Detective yelled. As she did so, distracted and focused entirely on him, the other remaining terrorist lunged at her, ripping the gun from her hand. He threw a punch at her, but she was too fast. Her billowing hair twirled angrily in her wake as she whipped around, grabbed his punching arm and bent it backward at the elbow. She brought up her right knee and knocked the wind out of the jihadist, then clobbered him with a fist to the throat. He fell over, clutching himself and retching. Phelps ran to subdue him and hold him down. Other passengers assisted him who hadn't yet fled for cover.

al-Shehhi disappeared down the passenger boarding bridge with his hostage, into the bowels of the United Airlines plane itself. It was United Flight 175.

The Detective pursued them angrily, her gun drawn.

It was Atta now on the plane in first class. He was aboard American Airlines Flight 11 with his associates, speaking no word, and staring straight ahead, keeping up the ruse.

It was 7:50am.

They would depart in nine minutes.

al-Shehhi had locked himself in the cockpit of United Airlines Flight 175.

By that time, Newark Airport was on lockdown. I knew that Jarrah and his men were dead. I knew that Hani Hanjour was trapped in a phantom zone somewhere with his associates, thrown in by Ethan Stiles. I knew that Atta the terrorist was dead.

I knew that the *other* Atta – *me* – remained alive as did his fellow jihadists, but to what end, and for how long, I didn't know the answer. Nor did I know if they would somehow break free and resume their plans with at least these two planes. Time would tell. History was already being rewritten, but the clock was still ticking, and I still had visions of at least one tower collapsing.

Roland stumbled along into the passenger boarding bridge after Byers. He could hear violent collisions up ahead: she was trying to break in to the cockpit. The ticket agent lay dead at the plane's aperture. Her throat had been slit. Roland looked away in disgust.

The airplane's engines were warming up. Instrument panels were switched on and the plane itself was starting to back away from the terminal.

Oh no. al-Shehhi was going to complete his mission!

Roxanne must have surmised what was happening, because she came bursting back forth onto the passenger boarding bridge, and a sizeable gap was now opening between it and United 175. The plane was pulling away!

Roland stumbled forward and embraced Roxanne. "You okay?" he asked, panting.

"Yeah!" she yelled over the noise of the engines and the wind. "Did Phelps get the others?"

Roland nodded. Both of them looked out toward the plane, retreating into the distance and moving out of sight past the bridge. The nose cone disappeared.

"I've gotta go after that plane, Roxanne. I'm already weakened from splitting all of me, but I've gotta do something."

She looked at Roland stoically. "I'm going with you!"

They both looked down. It was going to be a jump, with a painful landing. They were at least fifteen feet up. Neither of them would be able to pursue after a fall like that.

"Pssst!" Roland looked over. "This way, dummy. We don't have to jump." She directed Roland to the exit door of the boarding bridge, and there was a nice stairwell waiting for them leading to the ground below. The two of them scurried down. Roland just caught sight of a United Airlines tailfin disappearing around the corner of the boarding bridge once more.

They ran. Roland was exhausted already from the confrontation with Jarrah, but somehow he found the strength to press on.

United 175 was retreating from them, hanging a right up ahead and taxiing for takeoff wherever it could do so. By now the tower must have demanded that they turn back, and they would have warned other planes to keep their distance.

Painful flashes tore through Roland. The South Tower was up. Then it was down. Then it was up. Bodies were falling from it and then rising back up into it like some freakish teeter-totter.

They continued to run toward 175. It looked like it was turning right again! That meant that they could cut it off at the pass. Roland was still exhausted, but they were almost there.

They crossed onto the tarmac directly in front of it. The engines were whining and increasing in pitch. Roland looked over at Roxanne. She backed away from him, breathing two words.

"Do it."

Roland looked away from her and let emotion swallow him whole. He was so spent; tired of this whole damned thing and all these terrorists. Roland stared down that plane as the engines started to roar to life. It sped wildly toward him.

Blue-light. Emanating everywhere.

Towers falling.

The plane roared at Roland. He felt hot. His feet lifted off the tarmac as the wind took him. His hands raised palms up. Energy swelled through him and lightning struck the ground all around him. He could almost see al-Shehhi's face contorted in amazement and dismay as this tiny human lifted up and threw himself against the nosecone, climbing up toward the window.

Massive ash clouds folding back, retreating as if into a vacuum. A building erecting itself. Tiny dots – humans – soaring back up from lifelessness on the pavement back into the sky, merging with reconstructed floors above.

Flashes of heat and thunder.

al-Shehhi backed away from Roland, reclining in his seat, his eyes wide with fear.

Roland lifted his hands and pointed his palms toward the terrorist, balancing on the nose cone.

A massive jolt of energy coursed through Roland! It enveloped the entire cockpit with blazing light. The aircraft's instrumentation malfunctioned as he heard a horrible cry from within. The plane had partially lifted off the ground but then came crashing back down to earth. Yet he held there, suspended on the nose cone.

The plane screeched and slid to a halt, dark black smoke billowing from the cockpit and sparks everywhere.

Through the smoke, Roxanne saw a tiny figure shoot across the tarmac toward Gate B-32.

Despite the mayhem, American Airlines Flight 11 had been cleared for takeoff. Atta was sitting in first class next to one of his associates, in seats 2A and 2B.

But I was losing him.

For whatever reason, the connection wasn't holding, and the timelines were getting distorted and out of sync. The connection flickered under the strain, and Atta's eyelids fluttered and spasmed as multiples timelines merged together and sought for mastery.

I was losing him. The connection would not hold for much longer, and if that happened, Atta was free to do whatever he wished, to whomever he wished. American 11 would continue on toward its final jihadist target.

I had to stop him.

Roxanne and Roland sprinted for a security desk. The detective flashed her badge. "I'm Detective Byers, NYPD, working in tandem with the FBI. You got terrorist operatives aboard American Airlines Flight 11 heading for LAX from Gate B-32. Five of them. They're readying for takeoff!"

The agent turned to her radio and began communicating with airport security central.

Roland clutched his head and moaned. He was still panting and could barely stand. "I'm losing him, Roxanne, I'm losing him." Roxanne whirled her head over to Roland in fright. "And I'm losing *me* in the process. I'm already weakened from losing Stiles and from that confrontation with ah-Shehhi. I can't hold on to him!"

She turned back to the security agent. The agent nodded. "We're on it. Okay, everyone stand back and wait here, we have a major security situation here. I'm going to have to ask all of you to step back and remove yourselves from the security line and wait. Foster…Harkins…with me!" She pointed at two other agents and rallied them to her. "Alright, let's go," she said.

"Come on," said Roxanne. "I'll help you. You're the only one who can truly stop him, Roland," she said, taking his face in her hands and staring into the well of his soul.

Roland breathed deeply, and his eyes fluttered.

Atta breathed deeply, and his eyes fluttered. Something was wrong with the connection, and he was losing himself. He turned to look back at his associates. There they all were.

Abdulaziz al-Omari.

Satam al-Suqami.

Waleed al-Shehri.

Wail al-Shehri.

The four other jihadists returned the gaze without a smile, nodding subtly to him. Atta turned back and stared straight ahead. His brain was suddenly pounding.

He looked down at the strange cat collar around his wrist, wondering how it had gotten there, and what it was for.

The plane began to move. It was 7:56am.

It was 7:56am. Roland, helped by Roxanne, made their way to B-32. They were close. Other security had already been dispatched out to the runway. Security vehicles raced out toward it.

They could see it, far away, moving slowly up the runway and in line for takeoff.

"We've gotta get out there," breathed Roxanne. "But how? We'll never make it in time."

Roland's head stopped thumping for a moment as remarkable clarity gripped him. He looked up with widened eyes at Roxanne. "I know what I have to do. I have to reset everything. I can do this."

He smiled at her, as a blue light emerged through his eyes in the most tranquil and peace-filled aura she had ever experienced.

With a ferocity that surprised her and made her recoil, he reached over and ripped off Winston's cat collar and flung it from him. Spasms took him, and arcs of energy blazed forth all around the two of them together.

And then, he was gone. Roland's lifeless body fell to the floor there by the gate window. Roxanne cried out and tried to steady him. He lay there crumpled at her feet, gone.

"No. No!" cried Roxanne, and she cradled his head in her hands, his nose streaming with blood. "Somebody get me a rag, a towel, anything!"

Atta's head stopped thumping.

The lead hijacker of American 11 shook his head and massaged his temples, looking around confusedly, gathering his bearings.

Suddenly, the plane slowed, and then came to a full stop. The Captain came over the speaker. "Uh, folks, we've got a security situation at the airport. I'm going to have to ask you to remain seated and patient for a moment. We should be back underway shortly."

Atta leaned forward and gasped, wholly seized by a primal force that inhabited him from head to toe.

I looked down. The cat collar was intact around my wrist. I could see, plainly, the 'RB' logo on it.

I'm Roland Bishop inside Mohammed Atta, and I know who I am.

White blazes barraged my innards and racked my body with an epileptic reverberation. The jihadists noticed it. They jumped up in dismay. One of them started advancing toward me.

"Sir, please, I'm going to have to ask you to get back in your seat," said a flight attendant with the name badge *Betty Ong.*

"I don't know, I don't know," cried Roxanne. She was on the phone with Phelps. "It's like he just died. *Can I please get a paramedic here?!*" she shouted.

"Just hold on, Byers. Hold on. They're coming," said Phelps through the phone.

"Hold on, Roland. Hold on. They're coming," she whispered to his expressionless face.

But the blood still streamed from his nose.

"Sorry again for the delay, folks. We've been asked to disembark the plane. I'm going to have to ask every one of you to be patient, follow the instructions of airport security and do as you're told. I realize this is a hiccup in your travel plans but hopefully we'll be back underway shortly." The captain switched off.

Nearly every passenger either groaned or cursed. But not the four jihadists. I could tell that they were silently stewing, knowing that this unanticipated delay would cost them dearly and perhaps even sabotage their plans. Their brothers were underway, or were going to be. With each passing moment their risk of discovery grew.

My body, Mohammed Atta's body, was not itself. Inside this Egyptian body, there was an Italian-Portuguese American burgeoning within, controlling all his limbs and all his thoughts. I stood, and filtered up and out of the plane like the rest of them, pointed at by men with guns. My Egyptian nose was bleeding heavily. I removed my black button-up shirt to staunch the bleeding, holding it to my nose.

A small security force was gathered outside, brandishing weapons. I slowly looked back at my fellow jihadists, tilting my eyebrows up and directing them to remain calm. My head swam, awash with competing visions. The North Tower crumbled, and then it stood. Its antenna mast descended dangerously toward the earth, and then rose back up. Over and over again, like a childish game of give and take.

I read the jihadists' thoughts. In their minds, they would have to flee. Their intuition told them that they had been discovered, and all was lost. They would never now make it to the World Trade Center.

We all filtered down the aircraft boarding stairs onto the tarmac below. A lineup of planes formed behind us. More security personnel were pulling up with men and women brandishing weapons.

Two of the jihadists were talking quietly to each other.

"Hands on your heads please!" cried the security force. "Single file!"

Suddenly, one of the jihadists, passing by a security officer, thrust his body into her and knocked her to her feet. He seized her automatic rifle. The other jihadist took a woman hostage and held a box cutter to her throat, blocking his compatriot behind him so that neither would be shot.

"Let us go, we demand it! Or you will have the blood of this woman on your hands! I swear it!" he shouted.

The security personnel fanned out and pointed their rifles at them, screaming for them to put down the gun and the knife. The female hostage started to cry and plead with her hostage-taker, begging for her life.

In a flurry, the remaining two jihadists repeated the actions of the first two, each seizing a passenger and holding a box cutter to their throat. They backed away and stood close to their jihadist counterparts.

I watched them. And then, I calmly started to walk over to them, and our eyes met. "Brothers," I said, holding my hands up. "Please. This is not the way. Listen to me."

"Sir, hold it!" cried a security officer, training his weapon on me. I was free of the others and an easy shot. My nose had ceased bleeding.

"Brothers, please," I pled. *Allahu Akbar,*" I said calmly, continuing to stride toward them as time seemed to slow. I smiled gently. "God is great."

And then I did it. It let it all unfold, churning up every primal force within me, every urge, every complaint and lust, every fierceness and ferocity, every sadness and regret.

My eyes began to blow with a bluish frenzy, steam pouring out of them. I opened my mouth to reveal white-hot bluish light blazing forth. The jihadists froze in horror. "Allahu Akbar!" I cried once more, but the voice was different, laden with multiple dissonant clashes of notes together into an alien cry.

The four terrorist compatriots clustered together as I approached, banding together out of fear at this seeming betrayal from Allah.

"Sir, I will fire on you if you do not freeze!" yelled a voice. And without another word, in a single, blinding moment, the security officer shot at me.

The bullets did not connect.

I disintegrated before their very eyes in a dazzling explosion, and the bullets went wide. Mercifully, they did not connect with anyone else. And somewhere, a body in a bathroom stall began to glow.

All three of me were now released into the ether, becoming formless and, thus, unconstrained. Limitless. The circuit was now complete. Mohammed Atta's dead body appeared from the restroom and then dropped to the ground, pulverized by bullets. The glow faded.

I had transformed into lightning itself. I veered and swooped through multiple dimensions, returning to the tarmac at Logan Airport, the four focuses of my wrath before me, and three hundred million volts at my disposal.

A deafening roar engulfed the entire passenger crowd, swarming their eyes and making them cover their ears. The hostages were freed and bolted. The howling wind swirled amongst them, contracting, diminishing in size as it formed a diameter around the four jihadists. One shot wildly into the air, but the hurricane force winds jerked his rifle into spastic directions and he lost control.

Bodily they were lifted together and thrown about like spineless rag dolls, smashed together. The compressing lightning storm sent shockwaves and three hundred million volts of energy into each of them. Flesh seared and melted in the heat. Unearthly cries of agony – the sounds of two-thousand nine-hundred and ninety-six reclaimed victims' protests – screamed through them.

Their bodies were pulverized. Ghastly skeletons dripping with entrails burned entirely in the flashes, disintegrating and sprinkling to the ground as the storm subsided.

The wind abated, and the passengers, terrified and fearing the end of the world, were lying prostrate on the ground, covering their heads.

The security guards had been blown backward, their weapons dislodged from their hands.

The pilots stared down from their cockpit window, horrified and entranced.

The calm returned, and the sun still shined.

The five terrorists were nowhere to be found.

And neither was I. I had straddled the line to the end.

"Please, somebody, please," Roxanne cried into the air. "Isn't there a medic in this whole damned airport?" She slammed her fist into the ground, looking endearingly down upon me.

My eyes fluttered open. My lungs began to expand. I felt a sizzling pop jump through my hand into Roxanne's, and she recoiled. Electrical current coursed from me through her, as I reinhabited this human shell. But my eyes felt distant. My pupils dilated briefly into tiny dots. I could feel it. I could feel *everything.*

Roxanne slapped my cheek lightly.

"Roland! Roland? Are you okay? Talk to me!"

"Ow," I mumbled, my pupils expanding once more.

"You did it, Roland, you really did it!"

"Did I do it?" I mumbled. "Well, you said 'do it,' so I did it."

She laughed nervously in relief. "Do you always do what you're told?"

I smiled at her, taking in her beauty, hovering above me. "No. Only when ordered by hot detectives."

And suddenly, peace engulfed both of us, and we were stricken with a lungs-expanding moment. Visions were given to both of us as having borne witness to the other side of time, out there in the vortex.

Planes flew unimpeded through the sky.

Bodies never fell.

Flames never licked the sides of buildings.

Cancers never inflicted rescue workers.

Firefighters, policemen, and port authority workers lived on.

A grassy field in Shanksville, Pennsylvania remained completely intact.

Buildings never toppled.

Ash clouds never engulfed Manhattan.

The world never wailed and mourned.

Passengers never lost their lives.

Planes were never used as missiles.

Terrorism had failed terribly.

Flags fluttered in the breeze, but not filled with any more patriotism than they had been before: in continued vigilance…not in unified mourning.

As in separate gifts of vision, we were taken into the air and saw beautiful vignettes of American 11. United 175. American 77. United 93.

All were coming in for a landing.

It was the purest and most beautiful thing I ever saw.

Next to Roxanne, that is.

She smiled at me, lovingly, and then bent down and kissed me, as I ran my hands through her hair.

"You did it, Roland. You exceeded my expectations and have kept your sunny disposition," she said to me.

"I sure did, Penny. But I have you to thank for keeping me on the straight and narrow along the way. Oh! And this," I said, holding up my wrist so she could see Winston's collar.

"Well, you were daft enough to keep it on *and* to take it off. Not many could manage that properly," she said, sipping her steaming tea. There was that look again, eyeing me over the rim of her drink. "It would appear that the lightning never left your body."

I shook my head. "No, apparently it didn't. Not until the very end."

"And Winston's cat collar kept you grounded through it all." Penny just stared at me, deep in thought. "What will you do now?" she finally asked me.

I thought for a moment. "Well, Jenette is already gone. Renita has someone new, and prospects with Roxanne are looking pretty sunny." I offered a sly smile.

"I daresay you've earned that. You deserve someone nice, Roland. You truly do."

I nodded in thanks. "So do you."

"Indeed I do! Honey, would you come in here please?" There were noises behind her. "Honey, this is my client, Roland Bishop. A very fine chap, though American through and through."

I laughed and stood. Mr. Eggers didn't have a trace of violence in his body, and the smooth and cheery crinkles around his eyes spelled a story of warmth and pure love for his wife.

"So nice to meet you, Mr. Bishop," he said, shaking my hand. "Penny tells me a lot about you," he said.

I narrowed my eyes. "She does?"

"No. Just pulling your leg, my boy. Patient-client privilege and all that." He winked at me.

Penny looked at him endearingly, and grabbed his hand. Her blouse shimmered at the connection, and there was not a trace of a burn to be found on her arm.

"Well, I'm off. Got to trim the lawn with the scissors and put out the garbage, you know."

"Uh, they have mowers for that," I offered.

He just winked again and waved me off, bobbing out of the front room, through the front door and down the steps to his yardwork.

She shook her head playfully and sighed. "I do deserve someone nice, don't I?" she said, and she beamed. "I really do."

"Yes, you sure do," -here I paused and looked at her under my eyebrows, holding up my bottled water in cheers- "*Lady Divinitus*. I'm glad for you. I'm glad for all of us."

She held up her tea and returned the cheers. "Here's to cranking up the willingness dial."

"To cranking up the willingness dial," I agreed.

Penny paused, eyeing me curiously. "I have only one question for you, Roland," she said, leaning toward me. "Just who was this Ethan Stiles person?"

I smiled at her. "I don't know *exactly* who he was. But he was in the park with me that day when I got struck. He must have gotten struck as well. I remember seeing him sitting on a bench as I walked toward the grass. He's been in a missing persons bulletin since then; I saw it with my own eyes. I don't know who he was other than someone who also had a part to play in all of this."

"Hmm. Well, God rest his soul. It sounded like he played his part," she concluded.

I nodded. "We all did," I said, agreeing. "All of us. We helped prevent 9/11. We all helped reset everything."

Penny and I eyed each other warmly as we sat there. It was a good reset, indeed.

THE END

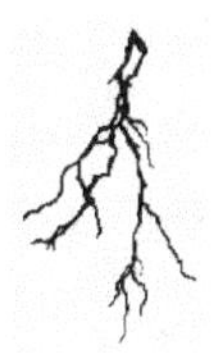

Afterword

The "Dissonance" sci-fi series was *so* hard to break away from. For a whole year of my life, it was where I lived, and I didn't want to live anywhere else. With every fiber of my being and the fire of a thousand suns, I love that story, I love the characters, I love the settings, and I'm inordinately proud of how much work I put into it, fleshing out those stories in so short a time, being caught up in a whirlwind of creation from 2023 to 2024. I miss it.

But this book was something that kept calling me, and I was remiss to continue putting it off. I hated belaboring it and drawing it out, putting it back up on the shelf like a castaway in favor of returning to *Dissonance*. It simply couldn't compete. But, all things considered, I knew where I was supposed to be the moment I completed the alien invasion hexalogy.

Right back here, with Roland Bishop. I mean Ethan Stiles.

This is a story that has haunted me, and one that I really needed to tell. 9/11 looms like a specter over the lives of so many, and it still holds sway today. The phantoms of the past don't really give us breathing room, and I wanted to revisit it in a revisionist sort of way, writing historical fiction, which is a genre that I hadn't really dabbled in much before. All I knew was that somehow, in some way, I wanted to write the wrongs done to so many, and to give a reprieve. I wanted to wrest control out of the hands of the hijackers and keep those beautiful buildings towering high into the sky. I wanted people looking out their windows; not jumping from them. I wanted them to remain; not crash into the dust. I wanted the 343 firefighters and all the other heroes to live on.

When 9/11 happened, I was undergoing some personal trials that required some heavy introspection. I wasn't myself. I needed to really strip all else away and focus on who I was, and what I needed to be healthy. As such, I unfortunately missed the power and potency of the human spirit defying all odds to survive. I missed the heroism of the firefighters, the port authority workers, the NYPD, the priests and volunteers, the rescuers, the unidentified heroes, the valiant United 93 passengers and crew, the rescue dogs, the food and beverage servers, the caretakers and babysitters, the parents, the children… every single person who was involved in consoling and being consoled, rescuing and being rescued: all of them were part of the human spirit that I missed on 9/11 since I was so self-absorbed. The full gravity of what happened that day didn't hit me until 2005, at which point I wrote some poetry and music that reflected on the weight of the day, and how America was forever changed. I desperately wished to have been there, to have played a part in saving lives, to have done *something*. All of us wish we could have done *something*. Hettie Jones said of that day, "We are breathing the dead, taking them into our lungs as living we had taken them into our arms." I wished I had been there to take them into my arms and take them into my lungs. To be with them and to have shown them that they were loved before they were lost.

That's what historical fiction is: rewriting the past. Oh, if we could only do it in reality, and undo the damage and trauma caused by that single day. For now, I'm content to have offered a bit of escapism from the harsh realities of the present and the past by diving headlong into a version of history that didn't contain such an atrocity.

Ethan Stiles, er, Roland Bishop allowed me to do that.

I thank you, my dear reader and friend, for partaking of this story with me, of living it out and being willing to explore the dangerous and sacred ground of September 2001 with me, humbly, together. It's an odyssey that I hope will impact many in a healthier way than the real-life event did.

And to all the Roland Bishops and Ethan Stileses out there who desperately tried to undo it before me on the actual day-of, I salute you and honor you. I will always remember, and never forget that all gave some, and some gave all.

With love,

Aaron Ryan

About The Author

Aaron Ryan lives in Washington with his wife and two sons, along with Macy the dog, Winston the cat, and Merry & Pippin, the finches.

He is the author of the bestselling alien invasion "Dissonance" 6-book hexalogy at dissonancetheseries.com, several business books on voiceovers penned under a former stage name, the self-help business guides "The

Superhero Anomaly" and "How to Successfully Self-Publish & Promote Your Independent Book" as well as a previous fictional novel, "The Omega Room." He has won the 'Readers Favorite' award for all six books in the "Dissonance" series.

When he was in second grade, he was tasked with writing a creative assignment: a fictional book. And thus, "The Electric Boy" was born: a simple novella full of intrigue, fantasy, and 7-year-old wits that electrified Aaron's desire to write. From that point forward, Aaron evolved into a creative soul that desired to create.

He enjoys the arts, media, music, performing, poetry, and being a daddy. In his lifetime he has been an author, voiceover artist, wedding videographer, stage performer, musician, producer, rock/pop artist, executive assistant, service manager, paperboy, CSR, poet, tech support, worship leader, and more. The diversity of his life experiences gives him a unique approach to business, life, ministry, faith, and entertainment.

Aaron's favorite author by far is J.R.R. Tolkien, but he also enjoys Suzanne Collins, James S.A. Corey, Marie Lu, Madeleine L'Engle, C.S. Lewis, Tom Clancy, John Grisham, Michael Crichton, Stephen King and Dave Barry.

Aaron has always had a passion for storytelling. For Aaron's books, visit authoraaronryan.com or getthesebooks.com.

If you liked Aaron's book or the "Dissonance" saga, please visit the Amazon and Goodreads pages for this book and leave a positive review. Once it shows up, please email the screenshot of it to me@authoraaronryan.com for a discount on your next book purchase from him! Thank you so much. Reviews really do help a ton!

Visit Aaron's website and sign up at the Blog:

Subscribe to Author Aaron Ryan

Follow Aaron and connect on Social Media:

Connect with Aaron

Feel free to check out the following links for further information on Aaron:

Subscribe to Aaron's blog for free giveaways, news and new releases at https://authoraaronryan.com/blog

Join the Author Aaron Ryan Facebook community at https://facebook.com/groups/authoraaronryan

Subscribe to Aaron's YouTube channel at https://youtube.com/@authoraaronryan

Visit Aaron's social media links to connect with him at https://dot.cards/authoraaronryan

Visit https://dissonancetheseries.com for information on the entire epic "Dissonance" saga, or Aaron's website at https://authoraaronryan.com

Also by the Author

As Aaron Ryan:

The Slide

The Ring of Truth

Dissonance Volume I: Reality

Dissonance Volume II: Reckoning

Dissonance Volume III: Renegade

Dissonance Volume IV: Relentless

Dissonance Volume Zero: Revelation

Dissonance Volume Up: Rising

The Complete Dissonance Sci-Fi Alien Invasion Saga

How to Successfully Self-Publish & Promote Your Independent Book: A Self-Publishing & Business Marketing Guide For The Independent Author

The Superhero Anomaly

Reflections: A compilation of journals and poetry by Aaron Ryan

The Omega Room (abandoned in the early 90's)

Autobiography (no longer available)

Glimmerings – works of poetry

As his former stage name, Josh Alexander:

Voiceovers: A Super Business, A Super Life

Voiceovers: A Super Fun Pursuit

Voiceovers: A Super Responsibility

Running a Successful Voiceover Business

How do I get started in Voiceovers?

Five T's to Triumph: The Secrets to Getting Cast in Voiceovers